STINGRAY

THE RUSSIANS ARE LISTENING

Alan C. Thomas 8/28/1 6

ALAN C. THOMAS, HMCM/USN, RET.

PublishAmerica
Baltimore

http://www.alancthomasbooks.com

Hardcover 9781627722414
Softcover 9781424115143
eBook 9781627720342
PUBLISHED BY PUBLISHAMERICA, LLLP
www.publishamerica.com
Baltimore

Printed in the United States of America

This book is dedicated to the men and women, who know too much to write the whole truth and nothing but the truth. These fellow human beings write historical fiction to tell readers about their real life secret histories. Others go quietly to their graves with their secret memories, because they believe that the telling of those memories would threaten the lives of the loved ones they leave behind.

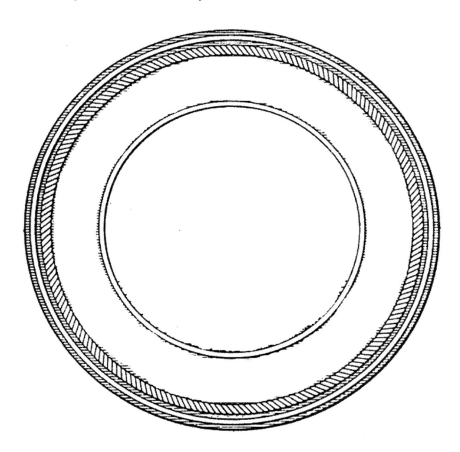

PROLOGUE

A QUESTION OF DUTY

For Rob Thomas, it felt like a lifetime ago when he served in the U.S. Navy, as a 22 year old Hospital Corpsman on a failed rescue mission to free two POWs, during the Vietnam War. This is his story within the story told in FLASHBACK Vietnam: COVER-UP PTSD. As was the case with the failed mission of the Marine squad to rescue two Prisoners of War (POWs), our leaders failed to rescue more than 4,800 POW from prison camps in Quang Tri, Laos, and Cambodia/ Kampuchea.

In 1980, Rob's life became entwined in the midst of another clandestine operation with one key difference. That operation did not fail. It was alleged that the Russian KGB codenamed their operation "Stingray" or "Operation Stingray." "Stingray" made it possible for the former Soviet Union and more specifically the Russian Navy to know in real time the coordinates of our "Fast Attack" Class and "Boomer" Class submarine fleet. Many of us know that our submarine fleet is America's last line of defense, because in the event of a nuclear attack, our submarines will launch retaliatory strikes. Our last line of defense has been compromised by spies, such as the notorious John Anthony Walker, Jr. working for Russian Intelligence at U.S. Naval bases and shipyards in the 1980's.

Rob's involvement with "Stingray" began with his acceptance of a position in The Office of Environmental Health, also known as Code 100X, at Mare Island Shipyard in Vallejo, California. As shown in Rob Thomas' <u>FLASHBACK</u> story, it is difficult to keep a secret from the public eye. The task of hiding "something big" more often than not requires the sacrifice of those who know too much. That task is not always given to an "Asset" to carryout, because an act of violence is noticeable in the worst way. It is best when feasible to discreetly discredit those, who know too much. The discrediting must be devastating to the "Target" so much so, that if the discrediting is completely effective, the perpetrators drive their "Target" to suicide. The discrediting can be in the form of ridiculing the targeted person in the presence of respected colleagues and/or discrediting the targeted individual's performance. Also, if the targeted person has a mental health issue, it may cause their boss to require that the person be evaluated by a Psychiatrist. Desirably, the Psychiatrist will convince the patient to take psychotropic drugs that cause the patient to experience tremors and/or lethargy, which makes it impossible for the patient to keep a job. Rob's "friends" and the Operatives for John A. Walker, Jr. and the Russian KGB knew that Rob would oppose their plan to attach coordinate transmitting devices inside the hulls of the U.S. Submarine Fleet. It was now time for them to begin Rob's discrediting and drug regimen in earnest.

If the discrediting did not bring about the desired result then they were willing to eliminate "The Problem." While an "Asset" could be assigned to carry out the apparent accidental death of Rob Thomas; discrediting and medicating Rob would be easily done, because Rob did suffer with a mental condition. It would later be defined by Psychologists, as Post Traumatic Stress Disorder (PTSD). Rob acquired his PTSD from his combat experiences, during the Vietnam War. Two of Rob's co-worker friends and Operatives for "Operation Stingray" were given the job of simply giving Rob the time and space to figuratively hang himself. They would only need to motivate Rob to act out in a way that would make him appear to be mentally unstable. That would require Charles Slater, Rob's boss, to order a psychiatric evaluation. Hopefully Rob would be diagnosed by a Psychiatrist to be a mentally ill.

The outcome of Rob's visit to the Psychiatrist was viewed by the Operatives, as a success. The diagnosis of Rob's condition was that he suffered from Manic Depressive Disorder with Paranoid Features. Rob's American traitor friends knew that Rob's new "nut case" label would be yet another tool to rebuff any effort that Rob would make to reveal Operation Stingray to anyone who would listen. Rob's diagnosis coupled with his self-inflicted guilt stemming from his belief that he had failed his comrades in arms, during Operation Sunrise was enough psychological baggage to keep Rob from being considered a credible witness to their treasonous plan.

The Operatives were glad to hear Rob tell them about blaming himself for the death of twelve Marines and a Vietnamese woman in the village where American POWs were held near Quang Tri, Vietnam in 1970. Rob believed that he failed to save the members of his squad and the mortally wounded woman. The Operatives knew that it would be an easy task to get Rob to set his own trap and do something in an act of desperation that would make him appear to be unstable to the degree that his own family would doubt him. Many people know that once the "Incredible" label sticks to a discredited person, they no longer pose a threat to their adversary. Friends, colleagues, and family accept the discrediting, as justified, because it came directly from Rob's boss, who they perceived to be a figure of authority. Rob's opponents were in positions of power and free to carry out their game plan without further interference from him. The little known clandestine operation could go forward with the objective of neutralizing America's last line of defense. In the case of "Operation Stingray," Rob Thomas and other unknown proponents working for our nation played into the hands of the perpetrators against America.

Thanks to the success of "Operation Stingray" the Russians maintain the ability to reduce the last Superpower to a state of anarchy and defenselessness, making the American people ripe for a takeover from within.

Operation Stingray remains unacknowledged by the United States Department of the Defense.

There is an unwritten policy: WHEN IN DOUBT: DENY, DENY, DENY.

Table of Contents

CHAPTER I

THE FALL OF '70 - BEGIN AGAIN

FREE AT LAST ... I'M FREE AT LAST ... those were the words that echoed in my head after processing out of the United States Navy on October 2, 1970. I hitched a ride from Philadelphia to my parent's home in Laurel, Maryland with a fellow former Navy Corpsman, Jim Paulowski or "Ski" for short. We all preferred to use only our last name, which was one of those unwritten rules of military life, which states, "Do not know too much about the man next to you, because if he "gets it" then, it will hurt less and the unit can continue to move forward without him." Needless to say, this is not a perfect concept, because people get hurt, feel loss, feel pain and anger and even rage. Every emotion can be triggered with the loss of a friend, buddy, or comrade-in-arms. At the moment of sudden loss, in the heat of battle, it is best to "swallow your sorrow" or "bite your tongue" and move forward. Those of us, who have had the experience, know that the hurt, loss, pain, anger, and even rage may be waiting to resurface at another time. These feelings may resurface when you are alone in your barracks, apartment, or even mansion sometime in the future. Maybe you will be drinking or using some other drug to numb your sadness. But trauma begets post trauma and that has a name today. It is known as Post Traumatic Stress Disorder or PTSD.

Knowing my own more impersonal horrific combat experiences where I generally knew a fallen comrade only by their last name, it makes no sense to me for our military leaders to burden today's soldiers with the outrageous concept of having a "Battle Buddy." The idea is simply a bad idea and it will only result in Post Traumatic Stress Disorder, which will be far worse for the current generation of soldiers. An impersonal death is easier to deal with than a personal one, so why burden our fighting men and women with making their combat experience personal. I SIMPLY DO NOT UNDERSTAND!! All of this is important information for the reader but I should get back to telling my tale.

Ski offered me a ride home, as Laurel, Maryland was not out of the way from his route home to Charlotte, North Carolina. I threw my Sea bag, which contained everything I owned, into the back of his Cherry Red El Camino and sat down in the passenger side bucket seat. Ski was driving and I waved my "Dixie cup" Cover out my side window, as we drove away from our last and final duty station. Ski knew his way around "Philly," so I just sat there in my "Whites" and prepared to enjoy the ride. We approached a traffic light at a four way intersection within a mile of the hospital, when the light turned red. Forty years later, I can still hear my favorite song "Tighter, Tighter" by the rock group Alive N Kickin, filling the interior of Ski's car, as we pulled up to a traffic light. Out of my left peripheral vision came a streak of motion. It was an older blue and white Ford Galaxy sedan, which continued through the intersection and slammed into the left door of an early 60's rust bucket pickup truck. The truck skidded sideways into a concrete curb and rolled upside down onto a muddy patch of grass on the side of the road. Ski and I jumped out of his vehicle and, as we will always be Hospital Corpsmen at heart, instinctively raced toward the accident. When we arrived at the scene, the driver of the Ford had managed to exit his vehicle and started to run away. Two other witnesses exited their vehicles and tackled the runner to the ground. The driver and passenger of the pickup were unable to get out but rather hung by their seatbelts, as gasoline poured down the side mounted fill pipe and into the passenger compartment. Gasoline vapors filled the air and the two trapped men were yelling for someone to get them out. I could hear the sounds of police and fire engine sirens heading our way, so I knew that they would arrive momentarily. The possibility of igniting the gasoline vapors was my biggest concern. Ski said, "Man this whole thing is going to make me sick," as he turned to walk away. I put my hand on his shoulder in an attempt to comfort him but he did not seem to notice. Ski was not a coward but he was a reluctant hero, who served with the Marines at the battle of Khe Sanh in 1969. Ski was a damaged man, who attempted but failed to extract two Marines from a burning tank.

Suddenly Ski shouted the words "GOD DAMN SLOPE." At that moment, my eyes focused on a man walking toward Ski and me from the opposite intersection, who had a lit cigarette in his hand. I instinctively put up my left hand and began shaking it back and forth at arm's length yelling "STOOOOP!" The man looked puzzled, as he stopped walking; then, yelled back "WHY?" I pointed to the flowing gasoline and told him to put out the damn cigarette, which he did reluctantly. By this time, the gasoline had soaked the young man in the passenger seat of the truck. He shouted hysterically "NOOOOOoooo" having seen the man smoking the cigarette approaching him. The driver sitting next to him appeared to be attempting to calm his passenger, as they helplessly hung by their seatbelts. Both vehicles began to emit smoke from the engine compartments. At that moment, a firefighter stood next to me and ordered everyone to stand back. Thinking back about that moment, I realize how fortunate it was that the firefighters arrived on the scene. They thoroughly drenched both vehicles with their water hoses. Ski and I had both lived through the hell of firefights in Vietnam but our failures to save the lives of Marines, who had been injured in combat, caused me to wonder about my ability or the ability of anyone to save a fellow human being from dying.

Anyway, we were no longer needed, so Ski and I got back in his car and waited for the policeman directing traffic to motion us around the accident and continue on our way home. The rest of the trip was uneventful, so we made good time. Ski pulled up in front of an apartment building at the intersection where I was to meet my father. My dad had told me to wait there for him to pick me up on his way home from work. I got out of the car and grabbed my Sea bag from the back compartment. Setting the bag on the ground, I leaned into the passenger side open window and thanked Ski for the ride. I said, "It sure feels fucking good to be home. Ski said, "Hey Thomas, keep in touch" but we both knew that that was not likely to happen, as we both wanted to erase the whole Vietnam War experience from our minds. Today, people thank you for your service but back then it was different. People glanced at me, as I stood next to the high rise apartment building in my Navy White Uniform. Many cars, trucks, and an occasional pedestrian passed me, as they moved through the intersection or walked in and out of that building. No one waved or said anything to me. I silently and nervously awaited the arrival of my dad.

Dad, who was a "Detail Man" for a large pharmaceutical manufacturing company, drove up in his new company car. I waved and smiled and he smiled back. Dad said, "Son, toss your bag in the back seat and get in." That said, I got in and buckled up for the two mile ride to my parent's home and my home for the foreseeable future. I tried to start a conversation with him when suddenly he turned the steering wheel abruptly to the right causing the car to leave the road. We skidded onto the dirt and gravel shoulder, as he applied the brakes and finally came to a stop, as a cloud of red clay dust passed over us. Dad was obviously very upset, and he pointed his finger at me saying "I can't take you home to your mother with that mouth." I did not understand what he was referring to, so I asked him what he meant. He said, "Drop the F word." I was shocked to hear his comment, as the words fuck, fucked, or fucking were part of everyday conversation between shipmates. On a typical day aboard ship, a conversation included statements such as, "What the fuck are you doing,' or 'you really fucked up' or 'pass the fucking salt and pepper.'" Dad informed me that he never used the F word while he was in the service, which I doubt to this day. I questioned him about his repeated use of the words God Damn It or God Damn, when he was angry. He said, "God knows that I don't really mean it, because it is simply an expression that I learned in the Marine Corps. Also, I know that because of where I learned to say those words, God will forgive me."

Anyway, we agreed that I would not use the F word in my mother's presence and I said, "Yes sir," as we pulled into the driveway. Dad told me to go hang that uniform up in your closet, take a week off, and then that I needed to start looking for a job. I said, "Yes sir," as I opened the car door and met my mother, with a smile on her face. Mom reached up and I reached down to meet face to face and give each other a warm hug and kiss on the cheek. I WAS HOME AT LAST!! That first week at home passed quickly and it was time to get a job. I started my search with the newspaper Classified Section or "Want Ads," as advertised job openings were referred to and looked for Medical Lab Technician positions. I earned the Military Occupation Specialty code (MOS) of Medical Laboratory Assistant. Jobs were plentiful then, and I found an ad for a Medical Technologist at Prince George's Medical Center. It was located on old Route 1, just before it crosses into the District of Columbia (D.C.). Dad told me that I should wear a coat and tie to each interview or "Cold call" to apply for an advertised job. It was Monday morning and Mom, Dad, Prince, our 11 year old Siamese cat, and I got out of bed early.

Upon my arrival at the Medical Center, I immediately noticed a car without wheels parked in the upper lot. It appeared to be resting on four cinder blocks placed under each axle, which kept it from setting on the asphalt. As I had only seen a car without wheels at a junkyard, I asked the Alliance Security Guard, just inside the front entrance about the car on blocks. He suggested that apparently the driver had parked it overnight in the lot and chuckled.

He said, "At least the thieves were kind enough to leave their cinder blocks behind."

I said, "Probably not kind but rather in need of exiting the scene in a hurry, hey." The guard just laughed out loud. I asked him about the location of the laboratory, which he directed me to. Like most hospital labs, it was located in the basement next to the Morgue. I took the elevator to the Basement Level and followed the signs to the lab and walked into the reception area. An elderly lady sat behind the reception desk.

I nervously approached her and I said, "I have an appointment with a Mr. George Schmidt at 1 PM. She immediately responded that he was probably in his office, so she dialed his phone number and we waited for him to answer. After six rings, she hung up the phone and paged him on their intercom. Shortly thereafter, a short, gray haired, balding man, wearing thick black rimmed eyeglasses arrived at the front desk and immediately looked at me. I held out my hand and introduced myself to him and asked him if he was George Schmidt, before I noticed the George Schmidt name tag pinned on his white lab coat.

George responded to my question with a smile and said, "Yes, you must be Rob Thomas?"

I acknowledged, "YES, I am," using the most assured sound I could muster. He ushered me through a door leading into a large room behind the reception area and then into a small dark office next door. As he walked in, he turned on a small desk lamp.

George said, "please sit," and directed me to a Chippendale style high-back chair in the corner of the room. I noticed that George did not have any papers with him and I did not see my application. He began to speak, "So I understand that you were in the Navy."

I replied, "Yes, I was honorably discharged on October 2nd of this year." George looked pleased and commented that he too served in the Navy, during the Korean conflict. I immediately noted that he did not say Korean War. The issue of war versus conflict, versus police action was weighing heavily on my mind because my application to join the American Legion had been refused. I was told in a letter from the Commander of the American Legion that serving in Vietnam did not qualify me to join the Legion, because I had not served in a war but only a police action. I did not make my feelings known to George.

George said, "You're hired." We shook hands on it and he told me that my time card would be at the time clock next to the elevators on the Basement Level. I was to meet my supervisor Virginia Randolph at 11 PM that night at the laboratory front desk. I was surprised that the interview and hiring process was so simple. Prior to joining the Navy I was hired as a cashier for E.J. Korvettes Department Store in Glen Burnie, Maryland, but only after making a passing score on their written exam. Anyway, I was assigned to work in the lab on the graveyard shift, midnight to 8 AM. Once again, I found myself working in a medical laboratory but this lab was located in the bowels of the hospital and adjacent to the Morgue. At that point in my life working in a medical lab had been limited to medical labs in Naval Hospitals and on a Navy ship. In the case of Naval Hospitals, the lab was always located on a floor or wing away from the Morgue but this was not the case in civilian hospitals. This Morgue could be accessed only through locked double doors at the end of the common corridor. On several occasions, an unusually tall fellow, whose eyes seemed to be sunk in deep, dark colored sockets would pass me in that long corridor as I made my way to collect blood and urine samples, ordered by doctors. This tall fellow wore a white knee length coat, and always seemed to be pushing a hospital gurney bearing what appeared to be a human body completely covered with a white sheet. Each time we passed, I would make an effort to glance and nod at him in a friendly way, expecting that he would acknowledge me. After several meetings in the corridor, I realized that this tall fellow with the sunken eyes was not going to acknowledge my attempts to greet him. In fact, he would always pass silently while looking straight ahead toward the double doors leading to the Morgue. Eventually, I mentioned my encounters with the unusual fellow to Virginia. She immediately said, "Who Lurch?" As I had watched the Addams Family television series in the '60s, I laughed out loud.

Certainly the fellow she referred to resembled the T.V. character Lurch. Not long after our discussion, I noticed that "Lurch" had been replaced by a new fellow, who actually acknowledged my greeting and even greeted me.

It was at that time that I learned about what had become of the Center's Lurch. Apparently, during the preceding week, a young woman 18 years of age had been transported to the Emergency Room by ambulance only to be pronounced dead by the physician on duty, who made every effort to save her. Reportedly, her body was perfect and unblemished. She had an exceptionally beautiful body and blond hair, which careened around her bare shoulders and fully developed breasts. Upon her death, the attending nurse called the Morgue for a Morgue Attendant to transport the young lady from the emergency room to the Morgue, where her body would be kept refrigerated until arrangements could be made by her family to pick-up her body. Shortly after the attending Registered Nurse left her message on the Morgue answering machine, Lurch arrived in the Emergency Room to transport the newly deceased to the Morgue. After their departure from the ER, the attending nurse realized that the personal effects of the young lady had been left behind. As was standard practice, she called for a Security Officer to pick-up the plastic bag of personal effects. The officer would hand deliver the items and the Morgue Attendant who would sign the Chain of Custody form documenting receipt of the items. It was rumored that Security Officer Tew opened the locked double doors and entered the Morgue. He waited at the Reception Desk but no one was there to receive his package. Officer Tew rang the bell on the counter top in front of the desk to summon the Morgue Attendant. After several minutes passed without a reply, Tew used his pass key to open the inner door next to the counter and walked back toward the closed Autopsy Room door. He announced himself, as he opened it. Much to his surprise, Officer Tew found "Lurch" positioned on the gurney in a state of undress.

Tew reportedly stated in his report, "I found the male Attendant atop of the deceased young woman, as I stood there holding the bagged personal effects. The Attendant named Mark Sweat had apparently used some K Y Jelly from the tube found on the floor next to the gurney to facilitate his penetration of the deceased woman's vagina with his fully erect penis and continued his assault until subdued by Security. Mr. Sweat demonstrated no indication that he was aware of our presence in the room. Three additional Security Officers arrived at the scene of debauchery and immediately removed the kicking and screaming Mr. Sweat from the gurney and pinned him to the floor with the combined weight of their bodies until he was cuffed and shackled. I stabilized the deceased women from falling to the floor, during the tussle with Mr. Sweat."

I found it interesting that the televised Lurch of Addams Family fame, while frightening to look at, always appeared without emotion. Later the newspapers reported the story, as <u>A Case of Assault by a Necrophile</u>.

I worked for Ms. Randolph, who was 40 years old at that time, which made her much older than my 23 years, at least in my mind. Virginia was a member of the coveted American Society of Clinical Pathologists (ASCP) and a certified Medical Technologist; while I was neither. In the wee hours of the morning, we often chatted about our families.

I proudly said, "My grandfather Thomas served in the Army, during WWI.

Virginia replied, "Well my distant grandfather graduated from the Naval Academy in 1847." I did not grasp the significance of her comment until I realized that we were a generation apart from each other, which seemed hard to believe. She explained, "My great grandmother had my granddaddy just after her 40th birthday. That was in the year 1820; then, my granddaddy married his second wife when he was nearly 70 and she gave birth to my dad in 1900. His wife was only 18 years old when they married and began having babies shortly after their marriage and for the next fifteen years. I was born in 1930, being the last child to be born into the immediate family of Randolph's."

Given her explanation of the long periods of time between births, it was not implausible to me but caused me to let myself slip back into a feeling of wonderment and awe about talking with someone, who was so closely connected to the founding generation of our nation. I guess you could say that I have been a student of American History, since my childhood, when my parents gave me a copy of the Golden Book of the American Revolution on Christmas morning. That book became one of my prized possessions and as I read it, I would often fantasize about what it was like to live in Maryland, during the American Revolution. Of course, my fantasy was just that, a fantasy rather than reality. Only after my horrific experiences, as a combat Medic with the Marines in Vietnam did I understand the reality of war and the damage that implements of war do to the human body, during military engagements on a battlefield. I was in awe of her knowing that she was a fourth generation away from someone, who probably lived in Virginia with George Washington and a member of the Randolph family, who founded the State of Virginia.

Shortly thereafter, I left my employment at the hospital having found daytime employment at USA Plasma, Inc. (PI) in Washington, D.C. There I met Judy Ruffen, who worked as an RN at PI. My new supervisor was a very rotund man named Stanton Kowalski who had reached the age of 54. Stan, as he told me to call him, was the General Manager at PI. He hired me to fill the advertised position of Assistant Manager. Stan wanted me to become familiar with all of the operations of a plasma phoresis business. He assigned me to my first job as Laboratory Technician responsible for the various tasks necessary to separate blood plasma from red blood cells. The process began with the collection of a pint of blood from a donor, who was paid $20.00. Before, the donor's blood could be accepted by the Center, the donor would have blood drawn to be analyzed and found to be free of infectious agents and drugs. Desirably, donors could be found to donate every two weeks thereby providing a steady supply of blood for resale to pharmaceutical companies, hospitals, and medical schools.

I was employed at PI for about a week when my libido kicked in and I became attracted to Judy. One afternoon I found myself seated at a table in the restaurant located across the street from PI. As I began to eat a sandwich, Judy walked into the restaurant and proceeded to the counter. Judy was a gorgeous 28 year old woman, who I found to be very sexy. As she waited for her order, she glanced my way and I waved. Judy smiled back and then she picked up her order to go and walked over to where I sat.

I said, "Hello, my name is Rob," as I extended my hand toward her, which she shook gently.

She said, "Hi, I noticed you yesterday; while you and Stan walked through the Drawing Room."

I said, "Yes I noticed you too."

I could feel the electricity between us and she was obviously interested in me, so I asked her if she would go out with me that coming Saturday.

Judy said, "YES" with considerable emotion and a big smile on her face.

I said, "GREAT ... Can I have your phone number, so we can talk later."

She took a pen from her white nurse's uniform pocket and wrote a number on the napkin that I had set next to me. Judy was separated and lived in a two bedroom apartment in the Fairfax Gardens complex on the other side of the tracks from the beautiful townhouses in Old Alexandria, Virginia. She had a seven year old daughter named Marty, who lived with her. I continued to live with my folks in Laurel, Maryland. We dated every weekend and after several failed attempts to get into her pants, I succeeded. That happening led to me staying with Judy and Marty every Friday, Saturday, and Sunday night. On one memorable weekend, I arrived on Saturday morning and knocked on the front door. A man with coal black hair and mustache, who appeared to be about my age but taller opened the door with a look of both surprise and puzzlement on his face. My heart pounded in my chest, as I introduced myself to Judy's estranged husband Bo. Bo was a strong man, who drove a bread truck for a living. He seemed relaxed with my presence, as he sat on the couch with his legs crossed reading the morning newspaper. I sat in a chair opposite to him, and I tried to relax. Marty ran into the room with us and Judy followed closely behind.

I said, "Hey there Marty and Judy," as they both kissed me on the cheek and Marty joined her father on the couch. Bo hugged his daughter and they sat together, as Bo continued to read. Judy walked into the kitchen and I could hear her pouring herself a cup of coffee, which smelled wonderful.

I said, "Say Judy, I'd like a cup please."

Bo said, "I'd like a cup too," which broke the ice and everybody was more comfortable with each other. Before long, I was telling Bo a joke, which caused him to laugh out loud. I joined Judy in the kitchen where we worked together to get breakfast on the table. I looked up from the pancakes that I set on the small Kitchen table and met Bo eye to eye, as he stood in the doorway. He had a smile on his face, as he leaned on the door frame.

Bo said, "I think that everything is going to be just fine."

Judy said, "I am happy to hear you say that Bo."

Bo said, "I knew that you would find someone new and that is really okay!"

I was at a loss for words and continued to set the table for the four of us.

Bo continued, "Janet and I are happy that you two are together. She told me to tell you that, as I left the house this morning." Judy told me earlier that Bo was living with his old friend, Jim's former spouse Janet. Bo often drove his deceased friend's black Ford van, where Jim chose to shoot himself in the head. We sat down at the table and enjoyed breakfast together. After breakfast, Bo told us that he had other things to do in town so he opened the door to leave. He commented that he would like for us to visit the farmhouse where he and Janet were living. Judy stood with Marty and I in the living room, as Bo closed the door. About a month passed and on a Sunday morning, Judy suggested that we take a drive to the farmhouse in the countryside. The drive went without event but upon our arrival at the house, I immediately noticed a faded black van parked in the weeds next to the dirt driveway.

Judy whispered, "Don't say anything about the van," as she, Marty, and I got out of the car. The house was very old and poorly maintained. Very little of the last coat of white paint remained on the outside. I guessed to myself that it was built in the 1800's. Judy walked ahead of us and onto the sagging wooden porch. Marty and I stood behind Judy, as she knocked on the door. Shortly thereafter, the door opened and Judy greeted Janet. Janet was a woman in her late twenties. She was about 6 feet tall, having dark brunette hair, and a flawless complexion. Judy introduced me to Janet, as Marty bumped around us and ran into the house calling out to her father. Once inside, I found the interior to be lit only by sunlight entering through the windows. Considerable dust hung in the air that was made obvious by the Tindal effect of the sunlight.

Janet said, "Rob, did you know that my late husband and I purchased this farm only one week before he died?"

I said, "No, I was not aware of that. I am very sorry to learn of your loss."

Janet said, "Thank you Rob. Did you know that my husband Jim had enough money to pay for this house and the one-hundred acres of land that it sets on? He was a good man to me and our three children."

I said, "Well, that was a good thing. How did Jim make his fortune?"

Janet said, "Both Jim and Bo were members of The Rockets! Have you heard of them?"

I said, "No, Judy did not mention it to me."

Janet said, "Jim played lead guitar and Bo sang and played backup bass. The group nearly made it big with their first album all but in the can when their drummer Bill Price got arrested and later convicted for possession with intent to distribute heroin. Anyway, you know what they say about guilt by association."

I said, "Wow, now that is a sad story. So did that break up the band?"

Janet said, "Yes, without a drummer to replace Bill, who is in prison today, the band could not perform, so they had to default on their contract with The Fountain Club. Six months later, Jim is dead." At that moment, Bo walked into the room and handed me a beer. He glanced at Judy and Janet with a knowing look in his eye.

Bo said, "I know you girls would prefer something else to drink, so Janet would you fix it?"

Janet said, "Yes darling and stepped toward Bo giving him a kiss on his cheek. Why don't you show Rob around the property while I make us lunch."

I gave Judy a kiss on her lips; then, I followed Bo out the front door and into the sunlight of a beautiful fall afternoon.

Bo took a long breath of fresh air and said, "God it feels good out here! So how did you and Judy meet?" I told him the story mentioning that the PI was my second job after leaving the Navy. He asked me about what I did in the Navy. I told him about my service in Vietnam but left out the gory details about Quang Tri.

He commented, "My lottery number is 304, so considering that the war is winding down, I doubt that I have anything to worry about. You know, it is a real kick in the ass that Jim blew his brains out when his lottery number was 315!"

I said, "Judy told me. I am sorry to hear about your friend's death."

Bo said with tears in his eyes, "I know that Janet and I are to blame. Jim was devastated when he came home one night from a second job. It was after 3 AM, when he quietly entered their bedroom and saw Janet and me asleep in their bed. I still can't believe that we had fallen asleep after sex but we did." I was speechless. Bo's confession about his guilt did not fit with Judy's story about how Bo would drive Jim's van like it was his own. Later, I learned about another side of Bo. One Friday afternoon, he drove his bread truck to Marty's elementary school to give her a ride home. Judy and I arrived at their apartment to find the truck parked out front. Judy used her key to open the apartment door. We walked in to find Bo and Marty on the couch. Judy looked quizzically at Bo, who looked very uncomfortable to me. He quickly got up from the couch and excused himself, as he left the apartment. Marty was watching T.V., as Judy and I followed Bo to his truck. Bo got behind the wheel, started it up, and put it in reverse to back out.

Bo leaned out the door and said, "You know there is one good thing about driving a bread truck, you never have to look for a restroom to take a piss, ha ha." I didn't get the joke but Judy explained that he would fill up a loaf of bread when he felt the urge. The following Monday, Judy and I arrived at work early and met Stan at the Reception Desk.

Judy said, "Good morning Stan, as she walked back to and entered the Women's restroom. I nodded to Stan and stated "good morning" but Stan stopped me.

Stan said, "Rob, I want to do some training with you today. I have noticed that when business is booming, you have a hard time keeping up in the lab." Stan's statement was true. The process of receiving the pint size bags of warm blood through the turnstile, logging in the bags, and balancing the bags in a centrifuge to separate the red and white cells from the plasma was not an easy task. The final processing step called for the technician to remove the bags from the centrifuge and hang each in a spring loaded plasma expressor device that would squeeze the installed bag, so the plasma at the top of the bag would pass through plastic tubing into a separate bag for shipment. The remaining bagged cells could be sold separately. There were several critical steps for the technician to perform. After hanging a bag of blood in the clamp device; a Hemostat would be used to temporarily clamp off the plasma delivery plastic tubing. The technician would fold the tubing immediately after the Hemostat and crimp an aluminum clip in place. This action would permanently stop the flow of plasma and allow the removal of the Hemostat and bag from the device without the loss of the cells.

I said, "Okay, I will look forward to working with you today."

Stan said, "Good, I will join you after your lunch break around 1 PM." I walked back to the Men's Room to put on my white lab coat. Judy and I had lunch at the diner across the street and I returned early, so I would not be late for Stan's arrival. Just after 1 PM Stan opened the lab door and entered the room.

Stan said, "I want you to do as Naomi trained you to do and I will observe."

I said, "Great" and proceeded with my work. The afternoon donors began to arrive in the Drawing Room, so it was not long before Judy passed the full bags of warm blood through the turnstile to me. I was a bit nervous and my hands were noticeably shaking, as I handled the bags. Also, I had difficulty balancing the bags in the centrifuge, which caused Stan to step between me and the centrifuge.

Stan said, "Rob, let me show you how this is done." As there was no space for me to stand between Stan and the workbench, I stood back to watch. Stan talked his way through each processing step, as he looked frequently at me. After each step Stan would say, "Do you see how this is done? Do you think you could do it this way? I will finish this run; then I want you to try again, okay?"

I answered, "Got it, in response to each question."

I admit that Stan was an impressive sight, as he kept up with the flow of bags coming through the turnstile. He was really far more experienced with the process than I and it showed. Unfortunately, for Stan and me, he was about to show me his level of incompetence. Stan completed the processing of a run of bags.

Stan looked pleased and said, "Rob, now that is how it's done;" then, he suggested that even he could do better. Stan set three more plasma expressor devices on the workbench. The next batch of warm bags of blood began to arrive.

Stan said, Rob, "I want you to write down what you see me do, so you will have notes to follow when you are ready to do what I am going to do now." Stan consecutively loaded the four expressor devices with the bags of blood. He consecutively released the four hand press locks and started the process of transferring the plasma into the respective receptacle bags. Everything went perfectly until something happened. Something awful and unimaginable happened that neither of us could understand at that moment. As the flow of plasma finished from the bag closest to him, Stan cut the tubing behind instead of in front of the clip that he had installed on it. Of course, the bag of blood was under pressure at that moment, which caused the blood to exit the tubing and jettison like a geyser splattering against the ceiling in the room.

Stan yelled out loud, "HHHEEELLLPPP!!!!," as he attempted to correct for his mistake. Not knowing quite what to do, I stood back from the blood cells raining on Stan, the workbench, the centrifuges, the walls, and floor. When Stan managed to release the pressure from the spewing bag the contents of the other three loaded bags had been transferred but not lost. Stan was covered in blood and his eyeglasses dripped blood. Judy and another nurse ran into the lab looking horrified at the sight of Stan. I offered Stan the handkerchief from my pocket, which he accepted and immediately began to wipe off his glasses with it. Stan exited the room with Judy and the other nurse close behind. Custodial Services for the building cleaned up the mess and a half dozen ceiling tiles were replaced. Shortly, after the event, Stan called me into his office.

Stan said, "Rob, I want you to meet my new Operations Manager, Linda Evans." Needless to say, I was puzzled about Stan's need for another junior manager; however, the following Monday morning things became clearer for me. Stan walked into the Lab and told me that he had a special job for me to do.

Stan said, "Linda will fill in for you here." I followed Stan to the hallway elevator, which we entered. Stan pressed the number 7 and the door closed. Stan did not speak but I noticed a slight smile on his face. The elevator stopped, the door opened, and we stepped out into what appeared to be a storage room. I followed Stan to a short stack of cardboard boxes like the boxes I had used to ship the bagged blood products and cool packs the previous week.

Stan said, "Rob I need you to put together twenty boxes with dividers." Stan demonstrated how to do the task, and then he left without saying another word. I completed the job and returned to the lab just in time for closing. Tuesday morning arrived and I reported to work, as usual. I noticed that Judy had not arrived yet, as I headed for the Men's Room. I changed into my lab coat and left the room. Stan was waiting in the corridor.

Stan said, "Rob, come with me please." I followed him into his office, where we sat. "I am going to have to let you go without cause. Regretfully, I over hired and the owners cannot afford to employ Linda and you." He handed me a check for the amount of $250.36, which he mentioned to be my last pay check, which included an additional $100.00 severance. "I wish you luck with your job search and certainly I will be happy to write a letter of recommendation for you." I will never be able to prove it but I suspect that my witnessing his level of incompetence was a factor in his decision. Stan had to be deeply embarrassed, so I knew what I would do rather than have continuing eye contact with someone, who happened to witness my level of incompetence.

During my second year of post Navy employment, I worked as a Medical Lab Technician for Chuck Vance, Supervisor at an Outpatient Clinic in Takoma Park, Maryland. About a year into that job without a notable event, Chuck called me into his office.

Chuck said, "Rob, you have performed your work here conscientiously but you and I know that you're not going anywhere in our career field without credentials and that means completion of at least an Associate Degree." I heard Chuck, loud and clear, to be saying that I would never advance beyond being a lab grunt or lab rat status, as some would call uncertified lab technicians.

Chuck continued with "If I were 25 years old with the opportunity to get Uncle Sam to pay for my college education, well I would go for it." I was relieved that he didn't fire me and I thanked him for his advice, as I turned and opened his office door. When I returned home from work, I talked with my parents about continuing to live at home, work part time to pay for my rent, and go back to school on the G.I. Bill. They agreed, so in January of 1972, I applied to Prince George's Community College for admission to Spring Semester classes. In March of that year the Veterans Administration notified me that I would begin to receive money for tuition and books in time to begin classes the following April. The next Monday morning, I handed Chuck my two week notice and informed him that I would start back to college in two weeks. As Chuck was the person, who put the college idea in my head, he smiled his characteristic broad smile and gave me a firm hand shake, wishing me the best.

Chuck added, "Rob, be sure to look me up after you finish your degree, as I certainly will be happy to give you a recommendation. Of course, if there is an opening for a certified Med Tech at that time, I am sure you will meet the requirements for the position." I never looked back after completing requirements for an Associate Degree, as I would meet my future wife, Mary Small in the fall of '72 and my future career goals changed forever. Little did I know at that moment, that the skills I learned, as a Navy Clinical Lab Technician as well as in the private sector would be a good foundation to rely on when money was tight.

CHAPTER II

THE FALL OF '73 – THE THOMAS'

A lot happened in the next three years. First came my introduction to Mary by her brother Tom, who I met in an Applied Mathematics class at the Community College. Tom told me that he typically hitchhiked to and from classes, so I offered to give him a ride back home. This went on for about three weeks when he mentioned that his sister Mary had returned home from upstate New York, where she had been living with their Aunt and Uncle after graduation from High School. Mary and I hit it off well from the start. We liked the same places, the same movies, all of the same stuff. We shared everything and got married in December of 1974 just before moving to the University of Georgia Married Housing complex. Mary got a clerical job at the University and I struggled with the math and science courses that I had postponed, during my Freshman and Sophomore years at the Community College. I transferred to the university with the intent of getting a Bachelor of Science degree in Environmental Health.

College was truly a new way of life for me. It was the first day of classes at the beginning of Winter Quarter at the University of Georgia in Athens. That Monday morning I reluctantly left my bed with Mary, as she lay quietly asleep under many layers of covers. Our apartment was cold but not because the University did not provide adequate heating equipment. Rather, it was the result of keeping the temperature in our apartment hovering around 60, during the winter months to lower our electric bill. I cautiously slipped out from under the covers and searched with my bare feet for the slippers that I had positioned on my side of the bed so my foot search in the morning would not require much effort. I slowly found my way in the darkened room to my side of the double dresser and my underwear. At that early stage of our marriage, Mary and I slept in the nude. Nudity was not something that Mary took to naturally and later in our marriage I would learn why but in an effort to please me, she would slip out of her nightgown before getting between the sheets with me. This was a dream come true for me at the age of 24 as my erection was typically fully extended for her to play with, although I must admit initially with her very cold hands. In Mary's case, her hands clasped around my erect penis seemed to do little to arouse her interest in sex. Mary had been routinely raped by her father beginning at the age of 10, so the damage of those nightmarish encounters with her father left her with little desire to have sex with me or any other male. Only on two occasions do I remember Mary expressing pleasure during our bedroom romps. I still cherish the thought of those times today. Each passing year with my first wife found us arguing more about having sex rather than actually doing it. Certainly, I wanted to continue our romps in the bedroom but Mary gradually withdrew from my sexual advances toward her. More times than not, we got into bed, kissed good night and she found the edge of her side of our bed. I would lie there next to her, as I starred at the ceiling and listened to the sounds of the night, which usually included our cat, Princess, jumping on to the bed and settling between us for the night. I would gently put my hand on Princess' back and she would begin to purr. Before long, I would drift off to sleep and begin again the reliving of my horrific experiences in Vietnam as a Navy Hospital Corpsman in the field with the Marines. Usually, I did not awaken from a fitful sleep, as my brain replayed my memories of the shooting and dying of Marines and Vietnamese villagers. Instead, I would be shaken awake by Mary, as I had disturbed her sleep by either rapid movements and/or shouting words that always included the words no no followed by noooOOO!

Unfortunately, our lack of a good night's sleep continued throughout the time that Mary and I lived together. It certainly did not help Mary deal with her Post Traumatic Stress Disorder, which probably remains buried in the recesses of her mind. As I understand it, Mary has not sought therapy for her PTSD, as she, in some kind of a mind funk, continues to feel shame for the childhood rapes committed by her father. As long as she continues to blame herself for her father's unforgiveable actions against her, she will continue to relive in dreams that horrific trauma in her past. Looking back on that time, I understand how my own PTSD contributed to the deterioration of my relationship with Mary, which was born in love and lust for the gorgeous twenty-one year old woman, who married me.

Anyway, in short order, I was dressed and ready to meet the even colder outside air, as I made my way from our second floor dwelling. The University bus transportation around campus was free, so I rarely drove to classes. On a typical weekday I would walk quickly down the building outside stairs and up the 25 stairs of a stone walled staircase; then, two city blocks to the Bus Stop. One Monday morning in January I met classmate, Jim Fowlen on the bus, who would be my lab partner in microbiology for the next two years and more importantly, he became my lifelong best friend. I came to call him Birdman. Just after boarding the bus, I noticed him sitting in the back of the bus holding a thermos bottle. Later, I learned that Birdman did not drink coffee, so that bottle always contained hot tea. He lived in an old Victorian house where he shared a small apartment not far from the Married Housing complex with four of his old high school buddies. Birdman told me that he considered himself to be an "unreconstructed confederate." I said, "OK Birdman; then I guess you fit the mold of every Thomas family member from the south, whom I have had the unfortunate opportunity to meet, ha ha." He laughed too, so I knew that he had a good sense of humor like me.

We rode the bus to the first stop on campus and from there it was on foot until the end of the day. Anyway, all of that movement on foot certainly helped to keep my body warm after I left Mary in our cold apartment. Cold, because it cost more than we could afford to heat the place and emotionally cold, because Mary was losing interest in having sex with me. Mary planned to study to become a Registered Nurse after I got my degree. Some people would say that my pursuit of an Environmental Health degree rated pretty low when compared to degrees that required four years of mathematics or engineering classes but the completion of 40 quarter hours in math and science course work was enough for me. I didn't have to take most of the typical engineering classes, but instead a lot more statistics, chemistry, microbiology labs, and health program administration. I know a lot of people thought that it was a strange thing to major in and it did lack the prestige of studying to be a Mechanical Engineer or Physicist, but in my opinion my studies at the university were comparable to the studies of any major.

In later years, as the Manager, Environmental Health Programs, engineers routinely called upon me to measure the amount of a given air contaminant and calculate employee exposure levels, before they could recommend the ventilation equipment needed to reduce the amount of a given air contaminant. Ensuring that America's products were made in safe workplaces meant that our society was the best in the world. Many years earlier, I had read about it in Life magazine. I read about how the Japanese transformed their reputation for manufacturing junky products into a reputation for manufacturing the high quality electronic products that we have come to know. The Japanese made products in safe and healthful workplaces where the government enforced even more stringent standards than in the U.S. The highly structured way that the Japanese workers produced things in their robotic plants grabbed my interest like nothing ever had. The more I thought about how the only dependable things were stamped Made in Japan, the more committed I became to making a positive difference in American manufacturing plants, which in the 1970s had taken a "Back seat" to their Japanese counterparts.

Wilbur Tyrone Thomas or Uncle Ty, as he liked me to call him was my role model, during my childhood and adolescence years. Ty was cut from a different mold than Birdman and me, as he was a child of the great economic depression in the 1930's. My Uncle Ty was forced to grow up fast, as he and my father were children of a former World War soldier, who had been physically and mentally damaged, during the fighting in France. All too often, my Grandpa Thomas used alcohol to self-medicate himself, which usually resulted in raging physical abuse on his wife and children.

Ty said, "We were just boys of 8 and 10 years old but it was up to me and your father to protect our mother from our dad's attacks on her, usually with his large hands balled into fists. One day, Bug and I pointed loaded shotguns at our father and threatened to kill him, as he lunged at us in a drunken rage. Fortunately, our old man collapsed before he reached us. He laid in the yard until morning and insisted that he did not remember why he awoke in the grass." I remember Ty's vivid stories of fighting the Japanese, during World War II. Some of his stories about his early experiences with the military were very funny and sometimes shocking to me.

Ty said, "With 'Bug,' short for my brother's nickname June Bug, serving in the Marines in the South Pacific, I did everything I knew to do to join the Marine Corps. I remember I was at the military draft Induction Center and told that the Marines get to pick 11 out of every 150 men to be drafted into military service. I walked over to the Marine Sergeant and told him that I wanted to join the Corps. He looked at me like I was crazy and told me that he already picked 11 men today. You will need to come back in 10 days. I pleaded with him to let me take the place of one of those men. Again, he looked at me like I was nuts but told me to walk with him to the holding room. We walked into the room where 11 men sat in chairs lined up against a wall. The Sergeant looked at the men and asked them if anyone would like to swap their drafting into the Marine Corps with this man for the Army draft? If interested, then stand up. Ten of the eleven men immediately stood up." Ty told me that he believed that he was the only man, who completed basic training in civilian clothes, because the clothing manufacturing plants could not keep up with the demand for military uniforms. He was told to keep wearing the clothes that he wore the day of his induction until two weeks before graduation from basic training at Camp Pendleton in southern California.

Ty said, "I washed that shirt, pants, underwear, and socks by hand in a bucket of soapy water; then, I would dump the soapy water and fill the bucket with just water and rinse everything in it. After that, I tied up the "clean clothes," on a clothesline behind the barracks, using Clothes Stops, which were ten inch cotton cords with metal clips on each end." Later, I found out, first hand, about Clothes Stops, which I was required to use in Navy Boot Camp. I was told that the Navy designed the Clothes Stops, because a clothes pin would not hold clothes on a shipboard clothesline.

He said, "My hand washed clothes did not smell bad to me but I knew that if I stood'em up in corner I probably could jump from my bed into'em;" then, he would let out a loud laugh, as he put his hands on his waist and cocked his head, as far back, as it would go. Whenever Ty told that story, I would bend over laughing hysterically.

Ty said, "Japanese soldiers repeatedly tried to gain access to Marine positions in the combat zone trenches by yelling the words, hey Joe, I come in now. I yelled back, hey, nobody named Joe in here." According to Ty, he and other Marines, who conversed in the dark with those Japanese soldiers would fire five bullets in the air and wait for the Japanese soldier to rush into the trench with his bayonet fixed on the muzzle of his rifle. The Japanese did not know that the Marines were issued new semi-automatic Garand M-1 rifles equipped with 8 bullet magazines earlier. Until that time, Marines had been issued the old bolt action Springfield rifle equipped with a 5 bullet capacity holding chamber. The Japs would rush the Marine's position and receive the 3 remaining bullets in the M-1 magazine.

During the Russell Island campaign, Japanese soldiers were known to attempt to get a Marine to get out of his foxhole and walk to the sound of a Jap, who sang our national anthem. Marines were told to ask the unseen singer to sing the second stanza of the anthem. If the singer started to sing, they were told to shoot and take cover, because the national anthem is only one stanza long.

In the Pacific Ty served under Marine General Halim "Mad Dog" Smith. Halim, whom the enlisted men called "Howling Smith" took orders from General MacArthur. During the fighting on the islands, the Generals stayed aboard ship, as Ty and his fellow Marine "Grunts" met and killed but rarely captured the enemy Japanese soldiers. He hopped 17 islands with General MacArthur, which included the bloody retaking of New Guinea.

Ty said, "I was too stupid to do anything different."

The career field of Industrial Hygiene was wide open in the late 70's. The federal agencies, particularly the Occupational Health and Safety Administration (OSHA) under the Department of Labor and the industrial military complex, were jumping on the hiring bandwagon with the Defense Department right behind. Job opportunities in the federal government, during the Jimmy Carter presidency were far better than today although the government continues to hire more people than the private sector. My Bachelor of Science in Environmental Health degree from the University of Georgia would make my job search relatively easy. Even today, I still feel good about my contribution to the betterment of our country although I am haunted by my father's thought about my working for Uncle Sam and particularly working for OSHA. At that time, Dad was a small business owner and manufacturer, who operated his business out of the basement of his home. Although his business was small, he was required to adhere to all federal and state regulations just like General Motors. Dad had more than one run in with government inspectors from the Food and Drug Administration or FDA, as they would arrive unannounced at the home basement office door. He would hand polish the silver tips of an instrument used to remove cataracts that he invented and patented. Dad would sit at a workbench for hours, using a microscope to finish the silver tips of his DU-AL Cryoextractor. He told me that he could not find anyone else, who would do that work to the high standard of quality that he demanded of himself. One day, there was a knock on the basement door. Dad took off his magnifying glasses and stepped away from his work to answer. He opened the door to find a man dressed in a white dress shirt and tie. The man introduced himself to be an Inspector for the FDA. He showed his credentials to Dad, as he asked to come in. As I mentioned earlier in my story, Dad was a very personable man, so he invited the man into his office/manufacturing facility/home. The Inspector named John informed my Dad about the FDA regulations pertaining to medical devices and then, he proceeded to walk around the basement with Dad walking behind. John the Inspector made many notes on various government forms that he had attached to a clipboard, which he carried with him. When finished with his inspection, John informed Dad that he was in violation of FDA regulations pertaining to signage in the workplace. Dad was shocked to learn about the problem found by John. Anyway, Dad received a letter from the FDA about three weeks after John's departure. The letter stated that he was in violation of several statutes and given ten days to comply or face stiff fines and possibly ordered by a judge to close down his business. Dad complied by hanging signs above the locations mentioned in the letter. Medical product handling locations were noted in the FDA letter. On one sign, Dad printed the words "Storage Area," on another cardboard sign he printed the words "Product Finishing Area," and on another sign Dad printed the word "Office." I don't think that my father ever got over that visit from the government. Dad said, "You work for Satan son."

For Mary and me things were really good outside our bedroom. We knew that Registered Nurses, and Quality Control Engineers were routinely sought by employers. I was to find out about the Industrial Hygiene profession from a classmate, who sat in our Dairy Science class. I asked George about what he was reading. He handed the pamphlet to me. On the cover page were the words Industrial Hygienist, which I had not heard or read about before that moment. More specifically, at the bottom of the back page, the words Occupational Safety and Health Administration, U.S. Department of Labor and an address. According to the pamphlet, Industrial Hygienists were in demand by the government. I picked up a copy of the application for federal jobs, during my visit to the

Post Office in town. Anyone, who has filled out the SF-171, knows that it is a formidable task to complete. I learned that the federal jobs were posted in the UGA Library, so not long after completing the application. I found a posting that stated that the Occupational Safety and Health Administration is accepting applications for an Industrial Hygienist, GS-5 position in Jacksonville, Florida. Mary and I agreed that I should apply for the job. Since neither of us was particularly deep rooted, it made sense to look for an area in the country that needed our newly acquired skills. The job offer came to me about a month after graduation, from USDOL/OSHA in the Jacksonville, Florida Field Office. That suited us well, since it was a short hop from Georgia where our immediate families and most of our college friends lived at that time. I was happy, because since it was a government job, all of my military service counted as seniority; therefore, I got started at the higher GS-7 pay grade. Mary found another clerical job just three blocks from our new house in Jacksonville, which allowed her to come home for lunch.

Like I said, things were going real well. We made new friends at work and in the neighborhood. We were becoming the stereotypical middle-class couple. We bought a new car for Mary but the old one was fine for me, as I typically drove a new car that I picked-up for the coming week of inspections from the GSA Motor Pool downtown. Everything seemed ideal. But then someone entered our married life and changed our relationship forever. Her name was Shirley and she was a lesbian, who befriended Mary and introduced her to that lifestyle. I do not know if Shirley was sexually abused by her father or another male in her family. I do know that the child abuse that Mary experienced with her father made it difficult for her to let herself enjoy the sex act with any male.

During our more than six years of marriage, Mary and I experienced more than our share of ups and downs. Unfortunately, I do not refer to the bedroom but rather to the spirit. Mary and I were both raised in families that were dysfunctional in different ways. One significant difference between my family and Mary's was the fact that she lived her first 16 years, as a sexually abused child and adolescent.

My sister Lindy and I were never abused sexually by our parents but in place of that horror, I routinely lived in fear of my father, whose anger would explode into rage in the middle of a heated argument with my mother or another adult. I never knew what to expect from him emotionally, therefore I did whatever I could to avoid my father or simply do whatever he asked of me. My sister Lindy chose to argue with Dad. After Lindy would feel the pain of our father's belt, she would typically scream the words "YOU CAN'T HURT ME DADDY," which seemed to encourage our father's anger to go into a rage. In that state of mind, after her beating, I was always amazed that our father had not beaten my sister to the point of unconsciousness or even to death. Dad's anger was misplaced anger rooted in this abused childhood. Dad had become a child abuser.

Dad said, "My father used the his wide leather belt more than once on my bare back, butt, and legs after tying my hands together around one of the floor supports in our basement. Your Grandpa Thomas told me that his father, my great grandfather would whip him and his brother with the buckle of his leather belt." Upon experiencing the belt and learning of the father's and grandfather's whippings, I decided that if God gave me children, I would not whip them!

Sometimes I find myself reminiscing about my life and how I came to hold the values that I hold today. On a typical Sunday afternoon during the year 1958, following worship as a family at the local Episcopal Church, we would return to our modest home with milk and on occasion donuts from the local High's Dairy convenience store. Lindy, our mother, father, and I would sit down at the Dining Room table to enjoy those heavenly donuts with milk or coffee. Lindy and I always chose milk. During those early teenage years, a pot of coffee was prepared in an electric Percolator. It required about 20 minutes to brew a full pot from the ground coffee beans. Dad preferred the Bokar blend of coffee beans from the local A&P Grocery Store. At that time, coffee beans were packaged in a coated paper wrap with the top of the bag folded and secured shut with a paper wrapped wire. The whole bean package was opened after purchase at the register and the beans were ground there to the customer's specified size from course to fine ground. In 1958, A&P operated grocery stores which offered customers 8 o'clock Coffee, Red Circle Coffee, Bokar Coffee, or Condor Coffee. The Eight o'clock blend of coffee was the least expensive. I remember those Sunday brunches vividly in my mind's eye, as I watch my role model dad sip and savor his cup of Bokar coffee.

Dad said, "Bokar flavor is far superior to the Eight o'clock coffee, because of the Columbian coffee beans." As time passed, the old A&P Company was acquired by another larger company. The new company management chose not to sell the Eight o'clock blend of coffee, and the Bokar blend was likewise sold to yet another company and my father's favorite coffee became the product of a newly formed Eight o'clock Coffee Company, which continues to market that product as 100% Columbian Bean Coffee. I found it ironic that the originally cheaper Eight o'clock coffee became the standard brand for the company with the same name. Today, if available, I will purchase the 100% Columbian bean product rather than the Eight o'clock blend, because that's what my role model Dad taught me. Maybe the Columbian grown coffee bean is not superior to the Arabica bean used in the Eight o'clock blend but for me, Dad was right and I will go to the grave believing it. Such is the bond between father and son. Oh well, I know that my World War II U.S. Marine father continues to influence my thinking even after his death in 2007.

For Mary, her sexually abusing father, continued to influence her thinking although I do not know if his influence over her included her preference in coffee. She was definitely damaged physically and psychologically by him.

The day of our wedding was seasonably cold. It was a Saturday. As fortune would have it, I caught a cold sometime during the previous seven days, so on my wedding day I was popping decongestants and Tylenol as I put on my tuxedo two hours before the ceremony. I remember standing in front of my bedroom mirror in my parent's home feeling all of the misery that goes with a cold. My image in the mirror verified my physical condition, which was not good; therefore,

I knew that my runny nose and low grade fever spelled disaster for our 'Wedding Night.'

On that December day, I did not know that my bride was a victim of rape and incest, so Mary's decision to have her father, Ernest Small give her away at the Altar made traditional sense to me. Knowing that awful truth would have easily justified my killing him, however it was not my nature to kill another human being even at the Landing Zone (LZ) in Quang Tri, Vietnam. Nearly four years before the day of my wedding to Mary, I had been forced to kill three North Vietnamese Army soldiers or be killed by them, so I am fairly certain that I would not be the person to take Mr. Small's life. Today, Ernie Small is a very frail 86 year old man, who survived alcoholism and the death of his co-dependent spouse, so I guess that God is not done with him yet.

Because I was so dedicated to my job, I mean really dedicated to the principles behind what I was doing, I went about it with zeal, much more so than my coworkers. I suppose they were jealous because it started to cause some nasty conflicts around the office. I started to avoid them and they returned the favor. But strange things began happening.

I remember one time I was out evaluating a program at this subcontractor and found that they had really done nothing to comply with new regulations. They had disregarded all of the guidelines we had set up. It was a Thursday. I can't remember the name of the place and I don't suppose it really matters. I didn't think I would ever forget that place. But anyway, they weren't happy to see me. I explained that in order to be a subcontractor they had to comply and show that they were committed and that they were implementing a safety and health protection program for their employees according to federal regulations. All they really had to do was show me that they were beginning to look at things in a different way. But instead they got real defensive and started calling me and the program a lot of names, real abusive stuff. But I was just doing my job and I was right. I left and went back to the office to file my report. It's not like it was such a big deal. All I wanted them to do was to demonstrate a sincere interest in working safely. I was there to help.

When I arrived there for my second day on the jobsite, the foreman was waiting for me. It seemed that the company CEO called my boss, Dick Graber, to complain to him that I didn't know what I was doing. Reportedly, the man said that I got abusive with his foreman and even threatened him when he wouldn't grease my palm, so to speak. It was the most preposterous thing I had ever heard. I knew my job but apparently my arguments didn't hold any weight with Dick, because upon my return to the office he called me into his office and told me to close the door behind me. Dick started rambling on about how this wasn't the first complaint on me and how he was sick and tired of all this crap even though he surely knew that I hadn't done anything wrong. I was doing my job. I guess it all had to come out sooner or later.

It seems to always come down to that, some small minded person doesn't want me to do a good job for their own ulterior motives. When you dedicate yourself to something and give it every bit of your attention and ability, these small people, who think that they have power over someone else keep throwing hurdles in your way. I watch foreigners come in and take over our failing businesses and I think that if we Americans just gave it our all; then, we would succeed rather than be ashamed to be citizens of the greatest society the world has even known.

My small minded Supervisor grounded me after the incident. Instead of going out in the field and doing my job, I was forced to stay in the office and update the thirteen government manuals set on my bookcase. It seemed that Dick had a good thing going. The thought that he was taking money from businessmen in town crossed my mind. If he did have a good thing going; then, he certainly didn't need me rocking the figurative boat. If all I had to look at all day were boring government directives and errata sheets, it was sure to drive me out of there. I had played right into their hands.

I made a vow to myself that I was not going to let Dick's attitudes chase me away. I stuck with it and even took on the task of calibrating the personal air sampling pumps, noise dosimeters, and Sound Level Meters and even sorting the mail for the other safety and health compliance officers. Whatever Dick wanted from me, he got it. It was driving Dick crazy that I appeared to find my new responsibilities okay. Problem was it was really driving me crazy too. Mary didn't seem to understand or didn't want to understand. We were settling into the community and her message was don't upset the apple cart.

Since we had moved to Florida, Mary and I had been frequenting this little lounge located in a downtown hotel. I've never been a drinker but I liked this place. It was tastefully decorated and just dark enough. Everything about it was pleasantly understated. Mary and I would meet there after work on Fridays. We would have a drink and decide where to eat that night. We went out to eat every Friday, nothing real fancy most of the time, just a chance to get out of the house. I always got there about forty-five minutes before her, so I would nurse a beer and watch the other people. I could hear parts of some of the conversations and it seemed like everybody in Jacksonville sat in a bar having a drink and unwinding on Friday night. I would see guys who looked like stock brokers drinking martinis and trying to pick up girls that also looked like stock brokers. I would see girls that looked like hookers trying to pick up old guys who looked like they were loaded. I don't know what I looked like but no one ever paid attention to me. That is, until Mary walked in.

When she came in, people looked. Heads would turn, conversations would stop, and the guys would check her out. She was striking in appearance, as much by the way she carried herself as by how pretty she was. She was a girl who needed no makeup, although she did use some. Her complexion was smooth and golden. She didn't wear her office clothes home but rather she always changed into a loose fitting blouse and very tight blue jeans or slacks, so she would always be dressed in a less than formal stylish outfit. She was really good at only wearing outfits that flattered her figure. Mary and her sister called themselves "The Butt Sisters," to each other, as both women were endowed with beautifully pear shaped rear ends.

Everyone would watch her walk over to me. She would give me a teasing kiss and order a drink. She liked those fancy frozen things with a piece of fruit sticking out. After finishing our drinks, we would decide to stay there for dinner or go somewhere else to eat. She liked to try different things and we figured that after a week of work it was only right to let someone else do the dishes.

On the Friday after a month of busy work in the office, I didn't feel much like going out. I didn't even care if I ate dinner. I just wanted to go home. Mary walked in looking exceptionally happy that night. She had just gotten a big raise and was anxious to go out on the town and celebrate. She wasn't happy to see my reaction, in fact, she looked really upset. I didn't want to spoil her fun but I wasn't in the mood for fun. I suggested that she call some of her friends if she wanted to go out but that I was going home. She used the pay phone next to the ladies room, as I stood next to her. I heard her say, Shirley! I went home.

I didn't hear her come in that night, but things weren't the same in the morning. I don't think she ever forgave me for that night. It wasn't as if I had done anything wrong. I needed to deal with my own problems and going out on the town was not the way to do it. I couldn't make her understand what I was going through. She was just so wrapped up in having a good time on Friday nights.

The next few weeks went along the same way. I met Mary at the same place. We had our drink together, she would call Shirley and head out and I would head home. Soon Shirley and other female friends were meeting her in the lounge too. I had to listen to them cackle for a half hour until they were ready to leave. I was the only guy sitting at the table when Mary got there. I started to notice that her attention was immediately directed to the women at the table. She would turn to me to let me know that they were going out. I knew that. The house would be quiet for a long time after I got there.

After a half dozen Fridays like that, I remember that I had an urge to drink another beer after she left. I ordered up another frosty mug and just as I took a sip, a voice from somewhere in the lounge caught my ear and stopped me cold.

I knew that voice and when I turned to scan the area I saw him, my old friend Mike Nobel.

He was seated in a booth with two girls who looked like fashion models.

I thought, "Same old Mike." We had been friends years ago in the Navy, stationed in California. In fact, I once shared his apartment for a few weeks until I moved into a place of my own. Back then we called him Mr. California, because he was more at home on the beach than on a ship. And he always had an admiring group of sun-tanned beauties. He never did much work, because he had to conserve his energy for the evenings. I kind of envied him sometimes but mostly I was so tired when I got off duty that I just crashed off to sleep. I think one of the main reasons that I moved into my own place was that I needed the rest. He had offered his spare room to me. Some things never change. Here he was again in all his regal splendor, dressed in a custom tailored suit, looking like a magazine cover. In the Navy, he was the only person I ever saw that really looked good in an enlisted man's uniform. He had them tailored. We used to joke that with his name he ought to be an officer. Maybe it would have gotten him more girls. But we were both just Navy Corpsmen, passing out drugs and changing sheets. He got out just before I did and the last I heard he had some government job out in California. You wouldn't get him away from there. So what was he doing here? I grasped my mug and walked over. I was in no mood for a conversation, so I opted to avoid eye contact and more quietly walk past his booth. As fate would have it, I would not be successful at my attempt to disappear and before I was out of his sight, he raised his eyes to look directly into mine and smiled.

Mike said, "Rob, you old dog, you. I never thought I'd be seeing you again. I thought I got rid of you once and for all;" then he laughed out loud in the way that I remembered.

I said, "Mike, I thought you said that you never left California and something about you couldn't bear to lose sight of the Pacific."

Mike began to tell me about how he was in Florida for a week long seminar.

He told me all about how the job he took after the Navy had turned out really good. He had been promoted about a dozen times and was making tons of money. He consulted with industry and he was employed with the Defense Department, which made it possible for him to work with the Navy on his own terms. I wasn't really sure what he meant by that, but I was enjoying hearing him go on and on about himself, which he did so well.

The evening was really flying by and before I realized it, I was telling him about myself. Not near as exciting, though I mentioned that I was married and also had a government job and I knew he could sense that I was not happy with it. He asked me if I liked the IH profession. When he found that I also did indoor air quality consulting he told me that there was a real need for people with our background where he worked.

He said, "I know a lot of people and I could pull some strings."

I said, "No thanks" and he said "here's my number."

I thought, "Good old Mike. If I wanted a change, he would take care of it."

I left after my sixth beer and the whole way home I kept thinking about a change and a chance to really do what I was trained to do. A chance to start over again. I knew I would have to talk it over with Mary in the morning but then it would not work, because tomorrow morning would be one of those mornings after she had been out late. She would want to sleep in. I dared not discuss issues that influenced our future together after a night out with the girls. I kept putting off talking to her day after day, for one reason or another. A week later, I called Mike.

I really didn't think he would come through but two days later he called back to tell me he had arranged an interview for me with his boss, Charles Slater, who consulted with Bectech Corporation. Mike's plan called for Mr. Slater and me to meet with his counterparts at Bectech. At the meeting, it would be determined if I would be offered a consulting opportunity in conjunction with joining Charles and Mike at Mare Island Shipyard, as an Industrial Hygienist.

He said, "They are even going to pay your expenses out and back." All I had to do was take the time off of work and the rest would be no problem. I decided to tell Mary at the lounge that Friday. She probably wouldn't understand but I knew what I was doing. I got excited just thinking about the possibilities. I waited an hour past her usual arrival time and asked the bartender if he had seen her. After these past months, he certainly knew us. He was no help but suggested I check at the front desk of the hotel. People sometimes leave messages there, he said. Sure enough, there was a note for me from Mary saying that she had met her friends right from work and would see me in the morning. I went home and packed. I spent the weekend in that same hotel and took a cab to the airport Monday morning. I hoped she didn't lose any sleep when she read the note I left on the table.

San Francisco was overcast when I arrived and considerably cooler than I had anticipated. I pulled my jacket tight around my chest as I hailed taxi. Two hours later I was seated in the Reception area of the offices of Bectech Corporation awaiting the arrival of Charles Slater, Executive Director of Environmental Quality (EQ) for our Nuclear Submarine Fleet. As I sat there, one of the double solid oak doors opened and a tall African/American man in his mid 50's walked into the room. I knew from Mike's description that I was looking at Charles James Slater. His skin complexion was black and his eyes were olive green. He wore many gold colored rings on both hands and a very fine gold chain with a small cross pendant hung from it. I immediately stood up and extended my hand, as I introduced myself to him. At the meeting, I learned that Charles Slater was one of the most highly regarded people by the Executives at Bectech. In addition to EQ, Chuck Slater was the Department of the Navy consultant to Bectech concerning the design and installation of all stealth compliant equipment, which included on board heating, ventilation, and air conditioning systems. Slater had a TOP SECRET clearance for access to Naval operations at Mare Island and Long Beach, California shipyards. His immediate reports were comprised entirely of civilian Industrial Health and Safety professionals like Mike and I. We were there to monitor worker safety and health, as they installed and administered the quality checks on the most sophisticated electronic equipment going into the stealth Boats, as the Navy refers to her submarine fleet. He was a man, who truly held power and had a lot of clout.

CHAPTER III

THE WINTER OF '80 – CALIFORNIA OR BUST

I flew back to Florida the next morning. Mary was working, so I didn't expect her to welcome me home. When I called her at the hospital, her supervisor told me she had called in sick that day. I felt like I was in the middle of a bad dream. It was like everybody was trying to make my life miserable. I was ridiculed at work and now my wife had conveniently disappeared. As I looked around our house, at our stuff, I became more excited about moving to California and starting the new job and a new life. I had made the right decision. I had another day left on my vacation, so I sat at home writing my letter of resignation and transfer to Mare Island Shipyard.

There was nothing left in my desk that would warrant a trip back to that office, but I wanted to hand the letter to my boss. I figured my co-workers would probably fight over my coffee mug and pencils. I needed the next week and a half to pack and plan for our move. I figured that I would move out ahead of Mary, start the job, and search out suitable housing for us if she decided to join me in California. I figured that if our marriage held together, we would put the Florida house up for sale and with the profit from it we could buy something small in the Vallejo area. Even though we hadn't been there that long, property values had shot through the roof during the previous years. I figured we would clear a nice chunk of change. It was all pretty simple actually. I even started sorting through our stuff to find those special articles to take with me. You know, the silly stuff, the stuff that reminds you of home. I don't have any of that stuff now.

It was weird to go to the lounge on a Wednesday, different bartender and different crowd. I leaned on the bar and felt good. I hadn't felt good on a Friday night in here for a long time. There probably were only two or three other people in the whole place and they were wrapped up in their own lives. I felt like I had the entire place to myself. If I called for a drink, the bartender would come running. If I wanted to scream, nobody would think it peculiar because no one would hear. Sometimes now I want to scream, but I don't remember how.

The time flew by real fast. I didn't keep track of how many beers I drank but when I looked at my watch it was after ten. The place was crowded now but I didn't care. I needed to talk to Mary.

I realized how much I had drank when I slipped in behind the wheel of my car. For a moment, the whole street rocked back and forth. I took a few deep breaths and got myself back in control. As I drove, I thought about how I was going to tell Mary about the job and moving. She understood the problems I had on the old job trying to do the right things. I think she kind of felt the same way, too, sometimes. And we had said from the beginning that we would look in areas that offered jobs in my field first. She could get a job as a nurse anywhere. I had thought it out really well. Logic and rational thinking were always strong points with me. When I pulled into the driveway her car was in its usual spot.

Mary was sitting in the Living Room, curled up in a chair, staring at a window even though the drapes were pulled closed. She didn't acknowledge my entrance; just the silent treatment for rushing off so suddenly. I asked her where she had been that day and she replied "same place as yesterday." I asked her again and she remained silent. I told her that we had to talk. I told her that I had taken a new job in California and I was going to be moving in about a week. I tried to explain how I had worked out all the details. I showed her how simple I had made it. I was starting to feel really excited about telling her the great news. At that moment I wanted to drag her into the bedroom. I got as far as touching her breast.

Her body went rigid and she looked at me for the first time, since I had gotten home. The look in her eyes was pure evil to me. I knew that it was now her turn to talk. She made it clear that she didn't quite follow my logic. It wasn't her that was dissatisfied. It wasn't her that wanted to move. She had a lot of friends here. She was just a few hours from her family. No, in fact it was totally out of the question. She was not going anywhere.

Suddenly I realized that deep down I didn't want to move without her. Even though things had been real shaky between us, I knew that I still loved her. I wanted her with me when we made these kinds of changes. I had to convince her that I was doing the right thing. If she would just listen to me she would see. But she would not listen. She stopped me to say that if I wanted to go, then just go. She was staying in Florida with her friends. I couldn't believe that she would desert me like that. I always did what was right for Mary. Obviously I was going to be making the trip alone.

I asked her again where she had been and she refused to answer. It wasn't until a few months later that I found out and then only by accident. It seems she had a "friend" to take my place lined up before I even decided to move. Mary hurt me badly by not going to California with me and then screwing some guy behind my back. That night in Florida I slept in the spare room. I don't wish she were dead anymore but I'll never forgive her. She had driven a stake through my heart. I decided to leave as soon as I could.

It wasn't hard to pack since I planned to leave just about everything to Mary. Besides my clothes, I took just my things, the stuff that had meant something to me before Mary, an autographed baseball, old photos, stuff like that. It didn't really amount to very much so I determined I could drive my car out to California, instead of renting a truck. I really hadn't thought about how I would have gotten around without a car in California anyway. I never liked buses and things like that. I have never liked being forced into that kind of close contact. Everything fit nicely into the car. Most things went into the trunk with the remaining items on the back seat. I rigged up a cover that cleverly kept them out of the view of anybody that might walk by. I was going to be in a lot of strange places and you never know who you might run into.

Mary hadn't talked to me since that night. She left for work each day and I kept rounding up the stuff to take. Having gotten my packing done a few days earlier than anticipated, I decided to leave and take more time crossing the country. I had never done it by car before. I had to try to talk to Mary once more, not to persuade her to go, but to know that we are parting on decent terms. I couldn't just throwaway our life together. I got her to sit down one night and listen. I told her again why I was leaving and that I loved her and that I really wished she were coming along. She didn't say a word. She barely looked at me. I think she felt bad. The next morning I left.

I had planned the trip out pretty well. I knew where I wanted to be by the end of each day and I even allowed for stops for any attractions I might come across. I had read about the roadside attractions in a magazine once. Most were just rip offs but all were entertaining. It seems that if you had the money and the time, they were worth seeing. I mean it's not every day that you can see a seven foot tall jackrabbit or a five legged buffalo. At least that is what I remembered the magazine saying so I built in some extra time just in case.

I did decide to stay mainly on the highways, though. I wanted to see the country but I also wanted to make time. I had my road atlas marked in orange, so that I could follow the route at a glance. West along the panhandle of Florida; then, around the Gulf to Houston. Then I would head north to Kansas, cross the Rockies in Colorado, and then straight to California. I expected to see a vivid cross section of the country. The more I thought about it, the more I started to forget about leaving things behind. I decided that there would be no behind on this trip, just ahead. Here was my chance to start fresh and prove myself. If Mary wouldn't come, I wouldn't let that stop me.

It was bright and sunny when I drove away. I thought that was a fitting start. Mary hadn't left for work but she was indifferent to me putting the last items in the car. I thought that I saw her looking out of the window when I backed out of the driveway, but it might have just been the glare.

I knew that leaving like that was going to change a lot of people's attitudes about me. The neighbors kind of knew we were having problems. We hadn't tried to disguise them much. Most of our friends would probably side with Mary since I had never bothered to tell them my side of the story. My mother dreaded the mere thought of divorce. She thought that counseling was the answer. She would say "look at your father." My father, of course, would agree with her. Mary's parents never really accepted me anyway. But I was leaving all of these attitudes behind. And since I had refused to let behind get in the way, I was ready to roll.

The trip across country could have been a great vacation for us. We had talked about taking a long vacation like that once. Just being free and wild and drinking in the landscape. We once talked about taking our tent and sleeping bags and lying out under the stars at night. But it was just talk and we never got around to anything other than trips to visit relatives.

The trip really didn't go quite as I planned. I had a flat tire in Louisiana when I picked up a piece of glass passing an accident scene. My spare tire was flat also. It took five hours to get it fixed since all available service people were at the accident scene. I picked up a case of minor food poisoning from this little diner where I ate while waiting. I was forced to spend the night in a motel there. Trying to make up time through the Midwest, I burned up an alternator and had to be towed 41 miles to a service station. By the time they were done with me I was $500 poorer but the proud owner of a new battery and a rebuilt alternator. They also replaced a few belts while I was there. Again I was forced to spend the night before I had reached my next intended stopping point. I tried hard that night to remind myself that I was going to enjoy this trip and really see America. But, I was starting to think about Florida.

The next morning was crystal clear and I knew that in just a day or two the mountains would begin to loom up ahead. Again the excitement started to swell inside me and I pressed onward. The Rockies were everything that I had imagined they would be. I was in awe as the highway climbed and wound through the passes. My second flat tire came in one of those passes and I cursed myself for not having the spare fixed after the first flat. But I had figured that the odds were in my favor for the rest of the trip. A Colorado Highway Patrol car pulled behind my vehicle. The Patrol car lights were lit up like a Christmas tree. Looking back through my rear view mirror, I could see a man wearing a uniform, who appeared to have a corded microphone in his right hand. I decided to wait for him to walk up to my driver side window. Sometime, during the 1970's policemen started using their vehicle mounted loud speaker to inform the driver of a stopped vehicle and to remain seated. I understand that in the early days of cops pulling over cars, it was standard practice for the driver of the stopped vehicle to walk back to the police car. At some point in time, all of that changed following the death of several policemen, who could not respond quick enough to gun wielding criminals because they remained seated behind the wheel of their patrol cars too long. Momentarily, I watched the officer exit his vehicle and cautiously walk toward me. For a moment I thought about the scene in one of those Dirty Harry movies, since the officer wore those reflective sunglasses under the brim of a tan colored cowboy hat. As he approached my side window, I rolled it down with the manual crank handle. The officer said, "Do you need assistance with fixing that flat?" I said, "YES SIR," which seemed to please him, and I could sense that he had relaxed to a certain degree. He gave my car the once over; then, he said, "you were in the Marine Corps?" He gestured toward the Anchor & Globe sticker, I had attached to the corner of my rear window. No sir, I served as a Navy Corpsman with the Marines in Vietnam. He smiled back at me saying "That's even better," which surprised me, as it had only been thirteen years since Hippies threw rocks out of second floor windows, as my uniformed buddies and I walked across a street in Old Town, Chicago. I thought to myself, that things were changing in America for the better when it comes to respecting the military but then this man was a policeman and I had not known of cops abusing servicemen. The unnamed officer said that he would call in for a tow, then, walked back to his vehicle, which he started and drove away before I could respond. I sat in the car for six hours until the tow truck arrived. I got out and met the driver at the back of the rig. He remarked that there were three others calls ahead of me. It got real cold in the mountains once the sun went down, so I welcomed the opportunity to sit in the passenger seat of a warm truck. It was late morning of the following day, before I finally got going again. I was beat. I stopped again at a town near Bakersfield, where I spent the next eight hours in a mom and pop motel, which looked a lot like the motel in the flick "Psycho" but in my case, I got some good sleep, a hot shower without the interruption of a knife wielding maniac. The "mom" prepared a wonderful home cooked meal. I was already behind schedule so I decided to spend a few extra hours at a local strip bar, before heading west. The sunset was beautiful and for a moment I wished I was stopping right there. But, looking at all of that beauty only made me feel lonely.

The rest of the trip was without incident. The weather stayed pleasant and the car ran fine. I arrived in Oakland on the eighth day after leaving Mary. That was longer than I had anticipated but looking back now, I guess it was worth it. Since that time I have never had time to really see the country. In fact, these last few months have run together until they are just a blur. I couldn't tell you what towns I've been in or passed through. It seems that all I've been doing is running and looking over my shoulder. It has taken me until now to realize that it is over. It doesn't bother me anymore to tell the story.

CHAPTER IV

CHARLES J. SLATER

Traffic was heavy but moved along at a steady but slow pace on the Interstate. I will never forget the courteous motorists, who joined me on that highway. Before arriving in Vallejo, my big city driving experience had been limited to the east coast, therefore I was surprised to watch other drivers make an opening between two cars so another vehicle could smoothly merge from an on ramp. I do not have very many good memories of my stay in California but that surely was one. It was a long ride across town to Mike's sister's house, Suzanne, where Mike and I were to meet. She lived in a small bungalow that I could only describe as lush. Since Bectech Headquarters were north of the city, it seemed that most of their white collar employees lived in this somewhat ritzy section of the bay area. They all had their reasons. Some had gone to college there and some, like Mike Nobel's sister Suzanne, just found it a great place for parties, socializing, and just looking good.

Mike arranged for me to start work at Mare Island the following week, so that I could become more familiar with the San Francisco Bay area. He said he wanted me coming to work fresh and ready to go and not preoccupied with the problems of settling into an apartment in Vallejo later that week. Every day I was feeling more and more like this move was right and things were starting to fall in place.

Suzanne's house was small but uncluttered with furniture. She had cleared out a room in the back for me and fitted it with a single bed, a dresser, and a small writing desk. Mike had arranged for me to stay with her temporarily. I found out later that the room was selected in the back of the house because it would be quieter there. I told her that I had been working in the Industrial Hygiene arena for OSHA in Florida, which had become a hassle for me. Then I told her that I had met Mike and how he had set up the interview for the job out here.

She told me that her friend Bev had accepted Mike's offer to work with him at the shipyard. Bev had come down from a consulting job in Oregon about a year earlier to talk with Mike when the civilian inspection program was getting started.

I was pretty much on my own. I was learning my way around, how to get to work, how to get to stores, opening a bank account, and looking for an apartment. Mike had suggested that I stay with him, but I felt that in all fairness I had to look for my own place. I figured that with their lifestyle, I would need a place of my own before too long. When the weekend hit, I found that my suspicions were right. From right after work on Friday until about Sunday afternoon there was a constant stream of bodies flowing through Suzanne's home. Aided by drugs and the alcohol they seemed to drift from room to room. If I tried to rest, every few minutes someone was peeking in, and then apologizing. My only choice was to join the party. I drank a few beers and tried to talk to Mike. I decided to go back to my bedroom but when I opened the door, I found that two lovebirds had found my vacant bed and didn't care to be disturbed. I sat on the back porch.

Before long I was joined by another refugee. This time it looked like the kind of girl Mike collected. She was tall and beautiful. She introduced herself as Rose and she was in fact, Mike's girlfriend. She was a model and had been doing TV commercials while trying to land an acting job. She was drinking a soft drink. Mike joined us after about a half hour. He said he needed some fresh air. He apologized for the intensity of the party and assured me that every weekend was not this loud. At this point I didn't really care, I just wanted some sleep. And things did quiet down in a few hours. Mike and Rose slipped away to another bedroom and the other bodies were lying about the living room and dining room like corpses. Bev was nowhere to be seen. I grabbed a soda and went back to my room for the second time.

Like me, my friend, Mike Nobel was formerly employed by the U.S. Department of Labor/Occupational Safety and Health Administration (USDOL/OSHA). He and I were former and fellow Industrial Hygienist/Compliance Safety and Health Officers (IH/CSHOs) with the agency. By Monday morning I had decided not to take Mike up on his offer to move in with him. I was not due to report for work until Wednesday morning so I got up before everyone else and left a note for Mike and Suzanne. I drove directly to the Rental Office to sign a lease for a condo I had seen several days before. As I entered the building, a young, attractive woman with long blonde hair greeted me with a smile that showed her perfect front teeth. I admit that I was taken with her good looks but remained composed and formally introduced myself. I told her that I was here to sign the lease for the condo that I had seen and to pick up a key.

She said, "My name is Pam" and proceeded to a filing cabinet and retrieved a folder, which she placed on the table where I sat. Everything looked in order, so I initialed and signed about 5 pages of paper that comprised the agreement. Pam and I shook hands and she handed me two keys to B-306. I thanked her and I headed to the condo. As I walked back to my car to gather my bags, I thought about how fast my life seemed to be moving. Mike and I had little in common, with the one exception of our mutual friend, Roxanne Flynn, who introduced us. Like Mike and I, Roxanne was an Industrial Hygienist/Compliance Safety and Health Officer or IH/CSHO with OSHA however, she followed her own path to accept a position with the California Occupational Safety and Health Administration, which was known to most people in our profession as CAL OSHA. Prior to leaving Florida, I telephoned Roxanne to tell her that I was looking to make a career change so apparently, she told Mike that I was looking for a new job. She knew before I knew that Mike was looking to hire an Industrial Hygienist, who would work for him in the newly created Office of Occupational Safety and Health or Code 100X at Mare Island Shipyard in Vallejo, California.

It was still early in the day, so I headed over to the shipyard to begin the process of reporting in. The United States Marine stationed at the Main Gate stood, as some would say, straight as an arrow and seemingly motionless. I inched toward the Marine's Post in my somewhat faded blue 1974 Ford Maverick in line with other vehicles assembled there. With my Department of the Navy orders in hand, I slowly made my way to the Gate and the awaiting Marine. It was unseasonably warm that day but the Marine showed no sign of discomfort. He presented himself in a highly starched long sleeve tan shirt, tie, polished brass accoutrements, dark brown trousers and white gloves. A white dress hat with polished black brim was perfectly positioned atop his head. The Marine's shoes were polished to a mirror shine. Certainly, my appearance paled in comparison. As I arrived at the Gate, I offered my official travel orders for the Marine's inspection. With my papers in his hands, the Marine performed an about face maneuver and stepped into the Gatehouse. I thought to myself that the Marine's performance was somewhat unnecessary however our country was under attack by a mob of Iranian students and other radicals. They had recently seized the United States Embassy in Tehran. At that moment, these radicals held hostage Marines and Civil Servants assigned to that embassy. The Marine returned to my car and handed the envelope back to me saying "Building 698" and motioned for me to move forward with his left hand. As I had not previously visited Mare Island Shipyard, the location of Building 698 was not known to me. The cell phone had not been invented yet, so I looked for a pay phone booth. I noticed a bank of phone booths on my right, as I entered the yard, so I pulled my vehicle up to that location. I got out without turning the engine off, and pulled open the folding aluminum door of the booth. I searched my pockets for the thirty-five cents that I needed to place a call to my old friend and new boss Mike Nobel. I deposited the coins in the slot and waited for a dial tone, then punched in the number, using the keypad.

Mike answered the phone with a very informal, "Hello." I thought to myself, what a change from my greeting at the gate. I replied with the same informal, "Hello" but added "Mike, I'm at the Main Gate."

Mike said, "Rob, glad you made it."

I said, "Yes, me too....so how do I get to the office?"

Mike said, "Well, just make sure you follow the yellow line painted on Boomer Street, as that will keep you heading in the right direction. Once you pass Building 696, you will be one block away from the Office of Environmental Health located in Building 698. Pull in to any of the parking spaces next to the building. Come in through the front double doors and walk down the hall on your left, just after you enter the building. Our offices are located within Room 101. Look for 101 painted in black letters on the door. Mary Hubbard or Bev, as she likes to be called arrived from Oregon last week and she selected the desk on the right, as you enter the room. Bev said that she is anxious to meet you. Vicki Gilliam's desk is on the left side and Butch Rydel's desk is next to mine in the back of the room. Of course, Charles Slater or Chuck to his staff has his own office in the back left corner and his Secretary, Monica Sandia occupies a desk located just outside of his office."

Mike said, "Chuck told me last week, that in the near future, the office will be identified by a new sign, which will read: OCCUPATIONAL SAFETY AND HEALTH (Code 106). It will be hung from the wall above the entrance door to our offices."

I said, "GREAT, see you in a few" and hung up the phone. I turned away from the phone booths and looked for the painted yellow line that Mike referred to. Sure enough, I could see the line, so I got back into my car and followed the yellow line to Building 698. The roadway surface was a patch work of asphalt over cracked concrete, which made for a bumpy ride. Many of the old concrete slabs had buckled, so the surface was uneven. Asphalt had been used to fill in the gaps between each slab but that too was old and no longer smooth.

The land occupied by Mare Island Shipyard was the first United States Navy shipyard established on the Pacific Coast. It is located on an island on the Napa River and south of the San Pablo Bay in Solano

County California. The shipyard is approximately 25 miles northeast of San Francisco. The Napa River's Mare Island Strait separates the peninsula shipyard on Mare Island from the City of Vallejo. From its' beginning, MIS made a name for itself as the premier U.S. West Coast submarine port.

Just as Mike said, I found Building 698 at the end of the long row of buildings built along the roadway that I had traveled. I parked my car in the lot and headed inside. I easily found the hallway on my left, which led to Room 101. I stopped at the door for just a moment to take everything in, then I opened it and as I walked into the room, I immediately noticed the words Mary B. Hubbard, CIH cut into a dark wooden name plate on the desk to my right. My old friend, Mike Nobel sat at his desk but upon my appearance he got up from his chair and greeted me with a warm embrace and hand shake. Mike mentioned that everyone else was at lunch, so he suggested that we join them at the shipyard dining hall located near our office. Mike was very knowledgeable about history and as we walked, Mike told me about how the Navy had purchased the original 956 acres of MIS in 1853 and commenced shipbuilding operations on September 16, 1854 under the command of then Commander David Farragut. Tears welled up in Mike's eyes, as we stood by a memorial dedicated to Admiral Farragut. The granite base bore a large cast bronze plate, which Mike read out loud, saying "Admiral Farragut gained fame during the U.S. Civil War Battle of Mobile Bay, when he gave the order, "Damn the torpedoes, full speed ahead!"

MIS served as a major Pacific Ocean repair station. Ordnance manufacturing and storage were two further key missions at MIS beginning in the late 1880's and continued service in that capacity until it was closed by the Navy in 1996.

Mike and I continued our stroll to the Dining Hall with a cool breeze on our backs. It was truly a beautiful day. We entered the building through an old wooden screen door, which was painted grey. I noted that the paint was old and flaking. Obviously it was lead based paint, which immediately caused an alarm to go off in my head. At that point in history, OSHA literature identified lead, as a heavy metal that if inhaled or swallowed would poison the body. The Consumer Product Safety Commission banned the sale of lead-based paint by paint store operators; however, the ban did not apply to ships and shipyards. Anyway, as we entered the hall the spring on the door slammed the door shut behind us creating a small cloud of dust in the air. I thought to myself that this was not good! Tables for four filled the hall. Most of the tables were in use, as the lunch hour was underway. I followed Mike to a table where two women and a man were seated. Mike waved to the group and the three seated people immediately stood up from their chairs, which I thought was a bit odd but apparently they were my new colleagues and Mike was our boss. We all stood there, as Mike introduced me to the group. Mike looked at the group and said, "Bev meet Rob ... Rob meet Bev, Vicki meet Rob ... Rob meet Vicki, and last but not least Butch meet Rob." We all shook hands and they sat down. Mike and I sat at the table next to theirs. Shortly, Bev, Vicki, and Butch got up, as a loud mechanical whistle could be heard outside. Vicki said, "I don't think that I will ever get used to that thing!"

On Tuesday morning I arrived in the office along with Mike and he gave me another quick rundown on all of the people I would be working with. He had Bev show me around.

She said, "Let's meet with Charles Slater." I had not shared with her that it would be my second meeting with Slater but the first time in his office. His office was enclosed in glass, which I found unusual. Bev walked passed his glass door, as it was propped open and I followed her in. Charles was standing at the window and appeared to be intently watching something outside, as we entered the room.

Bev said, "Chuck, Rob arrived yesterday afternoon from Jacksonville, Florida. I am giving him the tour, so naturally, you are first stop."

I said, "May I call you Chuck," as I extended my hand to shake his. This time, he seemed to look through me rather than at me.

Charles said, "Please, everyone calls me Chuck," and then winked with his right olive green eye. He suggested that we sit, as he pointed to the two grey colored metal chairs in front of his grey colored metal desk and swivel style grey colored metal chair.

Charles said, "My furniture is Navy issue and he let out a chuckle," then, we all sat. He gave me a brief history of what was going on at the shipyard. It included the custom installation of equipment and how the government had organized our civilian group to watch over things from a safety and health standpoint. Bev had already told me most of that but I listened intently, because I was glad to be sitting there and I was ready to go to work.

Chuck said, "Any questions?"

I said, "Not at this moment, Chuck, but I am sure I will have questions." Bev thanked Chuck for his time, I smiled and Chuck smiled back at me and then we left the room. Later on, Mike introduced me to all of the other people, who occupied our office. Besides me and Bev, there were four other technicians. Everybody seemed to resemble either Bev or Mike in personality. That seemed okay, though, because it looked like everybody got along real well. Bev gave me a hard-hat and we started our tour of the yard. She started off by showing me the huge boat docking area. Then she showed me where the equipment was tested pre-installation. This was where most of her studies had been concentrated. She didn't possess a high enough clearance to have access to some areas so, like me, she was limited in her assignments. It felt good to walk with Bev. She was pretty and her long streaked blonde hair flowed behind her. As we walked passed a group of gawking yard workers, each one took an obvious long look at her. Just as we were about to enter another building on her tour, I suddenly found myself asking her to dinner that night.

Surprisingly, Bev said, "Yes, but at my house." The rest of the day went very smoothly. I learned a lot and reviewed it in my mind on the ride home with Mike. Mike told me that if I felt comfortable enough I could start in working with a technician the next day. Maybe it sounds silly but that made my day. These people were giving me my chance right off the bat. They were respecting me for my knowledge and experience. Even though this feeling was shattered later, I can still remember how good I felt that night.

Mike gave me directions to get to Bev's house. Giving directions was not one of her strong points. He told me that her house was in the Vallejo Hills and was 'impressive.' Apparently she came from a wealthy family who didn't want their only daughter to have to worry about money. I would characterize her house as a mini-mansion among mansions. She lived there alone.

She answered my knock almost immediately, as if she had been watching from the window. She was dressed in a casual skirt and a knit pink colored blouse. On her feet were beach style sandals.

Bev said, "My normal outside-of-work clothes," as it was obvious that I was taking it all in. The house smelled good, a combination of food smells and incense. I drank a beer and leaned on the kitchen counter while she finished preparing supper. We talked mostly about work. She seemed reluctant to talk about her past. I had picked up on a few things that first day but being with her not only gave me much pleasure, it raised many questions. She was more complex than she was willing to let on. I was becoming intrigued with finding out all about her. Although I don't really remember it now, I know that the dinner was very good. Afterwards I opened a bottle of choice Beaujolais while she chose some music from a collection that made me envious. We talked well into the night about anything and everything and only occasionally could I get her off track and into a more personal mode. I was naturally attracted to her femininity, so I hoped she would open up to me. Being a man, I also yearned for her to give me a glimpse of her panties----or perhaps, no panties. My own mind began to race in two directions at once. At one moment I wanted to make love to her so bad that my muscles ached and my heart raced. In the next moment I had the eerie feeling that something was not right in that house. I couldn't place it exactly but it made me want to run out of the door and race home. I finally figured that it was just some strange paranoia probably brought on by the wine and the lateness of the hour. It had been my first day at a new job in a new city with new people. I needed to ease up a bit.

My first week went very smoothly and in fact the weeks after that went well, also. I had always been able to learn things quickly and apply them equally so. I had a chance here to prove what I could do. There wasn't a sense of competition like I had had in Florida, which made the transition process go much smoother. I spent a lot of evenings immersed in manuals and procedures. I wanted to know everything. And as I was spending so much time on work I began to push Mary out of my mind, or at least well into the background. That made it easier to spend time with Bev.

Because I had learned so quickly, I was working on my own in a relatively short time. I had spent at least one day with each of the other technicians and I had watched each one closely to pick up shortcuts and tips. Everybody worked a little differently and I intended to pull what I needed from each one to be the best. The time that I spent on the job with Bev was always a bit strange. She went about her job very diligently but there was still that strange feeling that had hit me that night at her house. I was still starting to like her quite a bit not just in a sexual way. In fact it started to bother me how the other men in the work areas would look at her. If she had been flirting, it would have been different. But she was usually quiet, going through the day as if no one else was around. Outside the shipyard she opened up a bit, but just a bit.

But like I was saying, I learned very quickly. I was getting to know a lot of the yard workers, too. I wasn't out there to cause disruption but to ensure safety and a healthy workplace and they understood that. They knew what the program was about and that made the job a whole lot easier. I had decided early on in my career to really work with people.

The thought of a security or safety incident upset me. But I wasn't worried here. Things were different. Maybe Mike was right, California is the place to be.

I was not a single man but I did feel like a burden had been lifted from my shoulders by being on my own again. I realized how much I enjoyed the peace and quiet and the privacy. I used to sit alone on my porch that overlooked Vallejo Drive and just watch the cars go by or the occasional person walking up and down the street. I could spend evenings reviewing my studies from that day or I could find ways that made me better in my job. I did find that I started to head out on my own and showed up at fewer and fewer of Mike's parties. I thought that he was beginning to take it personal, because he became colder toward me. We stopped talking and our relationship became exclusively professional now that I was living in my place. It wasn't that I didn't like him as a friend I just didn't care for his lifestyle. It wasn't my lifestyle. One night Bev told me that I should hang back before one of his parties got underway and sit and chat with him. She said that I did owe him something for setting up this whole California move. I knew she was right. The suggested chat time never happened. Mike's parties were every Saturday after 9 o'clock, and I arrived at his condo unannounced at about 8:30 pm. He was surprised but glad to see me and that made me feel good. Looking around I realized that I didn't know anyone in this crowd. Either I had picked the wrong night or he had changed his social circle since last I was in attendance.

The room was filled with working class types, dressed in blue jeans, smoking Marlboros, and drinking beers. These were not the snobby group that usually showed up. I actually felt comfortable around them that night. At two in the morning I was still having a good time. I had begun to think that I needed to be alone with Bev to enjoy myself but I was wrong.

CHAPTER V

JACK DEMPSEY

Late in the evening of that party I realized something unusual.
These working class guys were actually workers from the shipyard
and service men out of uniform. They were really loosening up and
talking pretty freely about work. I suppose I didn't take much notice
of it at the time because it seemed like everybody there was from the
yard, so what could it hurt. These were the same people you worked
with all day, so a bit of idle chatter, even if it was classified, was
pretty harmless. That's the way we all felt. They talked about things
that I didn't even know about. It seemed that most of the talk centered
about gripes and grumbling. They complained about this person and
that person. I listened to hear my name but it never came up. They
complained about equipment and procedures and ships and working
conditions. In spite of it all, I had a really good time and I told Mike
so.

Mike seemed preoccupied as he was letting the departing guests
out the front door. On Monday he still seemed troubled and deep in
thought. He wasn't very approachable. I kept my distance and did my
job. I figured it was just some upper management problem that had
him perplexed but his changed attitude persisted. I began watching
him closer and taking note of his sudden peculiar ways. I talked to
Bev about it and she said I should just stay clear of his business.

She said, "Mike was not afraid to ask for help or assistance if he
got into a tough spot. That was how he had built such a strong team

at work. Everybody worked together and shared in a team victory."
I considered Mike a good friend so I tried hard to mind my own
business but my curiosity kept me from completely succeeding. It
came to mind about what happened to the curious cat. During my
first week on the job, I asked Mike to be my sponsor for admission to
the American Industrial Hygiene Association or AIHA, as most IH's
referred to the organization.

Mike said, "Rob, I will be happy to sponsor you for full membership
in the AIHA. I will write a cover letter to go with the AIHA Membership
Application, which Butch and I will sign for you. Both Mike and
Butch were full members of the prestigious association.

DEPARTMENT OF THE NAVY
MARE ISLAND SHIPYARD
VALLEJO, California 94592

IN REPLY REFER TO
100X
19 February 1980

Chairman
Membership Committee
American Industrial Hygiene Assoc.
475 Wolf Ledges Parkway
Akron, Ohio 4431-1087

Dear Sir:

I wish to recommend that the association accept Mr. Robert Chandler
Thomas with full membership status upon review of his application. Mr.
Thomas worked in the industrial hygiene profession at the U.S. Dept.
of Labor/OSHA since April 9, 1977 until February 2, 1980. On February
3, 1980 Mr. Thomas began work as an Industrial Hygienist at the Mare
Island Shipyard, Vallejo, California.

Mr. Thomas was highly recommended to me by his supervisors at
USDOL/ OSHA, and I am sure that he will continue to be a valuable
employee/I.H. throughout his tenure with the USN and USDOD.

Sincerely,

M. Nobel, Supervisor
Industrial Hygienist

At about this time I was beginning to go out alone several evenings each week. Sometimes I would check out a movie or maybe try some new restaurant that I had been passing on trips to and from work. I also started stopping for a beer now and then at this neat little lounge a few miles from the yard. It reminded me of that place back in Florida but was much smaller. It had that comfortable kind of interior and the bartender knew your name and your brand after the first order. Even sitting alone at the bar, I felt good there. I felt like I could really escape all of my troubles there. I was beginning to experience life in the bay area without Bev or Mary, so the timing was perfect. I didn't want a divorce and I didn't want to stop seeing Bev. I was just trying to build a stronger life for myself. I was feeling uncomfortable having gone from Mary to Bev so quickly, although I had to admit that I was enjoying myself.

But like I said, I really liked that place and sometimes I would run into some of the workers from the shipyard. Like me, they had discovered that little haven. Sometimes they would wave or nod to acknowledge my presence. At other times they would come over and talk. I had built a good relationship with the workers because I was fair and thorough. I didn't play games but I wasn't a hard ass either.

One night I ran into a guy named Bob who was a civilian foreman at the yard. Like most of the others that I met there, I knew him well enough to call him by his first name. He was an electronics wiz, who had floated around different government agencies primarily as a trouble shooter. He worked at the yard for a long time, ever since the Navy had started fitting out the first Polaris Class boats. What he didn't like was being a foreman. He was a hands-on kind of guy and sincerely did not like supervising people. Being a family man he had taken the promotion along with the increase in pay. He was just trying to cope with the situation. He wasn't doing very well. Some of his workers were Navy enlisted men. He believed that the Navy men didn't like him because he was in charge but had never served in the military. They would give him a questioning look whenever he exercised his authority, especially when he was aboard the subs.

Bob said, "I went home every night feeling like they hadn't done their best, in an effort to make me look inferior to my superiors. I couldn't go back and do their job over again, because their work passed my quality control checks. I just had to cope with it."

The boats had a special radio on board that was used in case of an emergency such as war. At such a critical time, all normal frequencies would be shut down. Each submarine had a top secret frequency that could only be used for critical communications between the boat and squadron command. It was over this frequency that instructions were dispatched and status reports were filed. If the top secret frequency were hacked into by an enemy, then the location of a boat would be known to them. If an enemy has the capability to target the location of the boat then, that enemy would probably have the capability to destroy it at sea.

The radios came in from a contractor in the Midwest with the frequency already installed. The identification of the frequency was known only to the people with top secret clearances. The radios were transported to the yard under the most exceptional security conditions. The only possible matching of codes to unit was through deciphering several layers of code to reveal unit serial numbers. That was not an easy task. Once, when I was in the Navy, we spent eight weeks trying to break a code that wasn't nearly as sophisticated. And besides that, the information was closely guarded at headquarters. The whole situation bothered Bob and we talked for a couple of hours that night. In fact we didn't stop until the bartender announced last call.

He said he felt that too many people were allowed to casually pass through his area. Considering the highly classified nature of the work, I had to agree with him. His repeated requests for more security had been denied. He talked about seeing people snooping around the units before they were installed. He mentioned Bev. He said that he suspected that she might have exchanged favors for access to paperwork. He was very discreet. He might have known that Bev and I were seeing each other. He said that he even saw signs of tampering. That, too, was shrugged off but he was sure something was going on. However, he was powerless to pursue it any further because his area of responsibility was limited and he couldn't afford to stir things up too much. After all, he had a family to support. I don't think he was asking me to do something about it or anything like that. I just think he needed to talk to someone and I was there and I knew a little about the stuff he was concerned about. I think he felt better when he left to go home. Naturally, it started me thinking again.

I have always done a lot of observing where ever I've gone. Jobs, trips, etc., I always look around. I suppose it was no different there. I had been watching the people around me since the first time I interviewed. I watched to see what the accepted practices were and to learn the best ways to perform the job. And I suppose I had seen some strange things going on but was never able to put things in the right perspective. Maybe I was just a bit naive at times. I knew that everyone wasn't as dedicated as I was and that didn't really bother me. I just concerned myself with doing the best job I could, but after hearing Bob talk, it made me take a second look around. Maybe some of the strange behavior could be explained. If Bob was right, that is.

Right away I thought of Mike. He had been acting weird lately for no apparent reason and being a manager; he was in a position to manipulate people to gain access to things that were unauthorized. But I'm getting ahead of myself here. I didn't immediately start accusing people but I started watching them closer. Bob's comments about Bev bothered me a little and it was true that I didn't really know much about her. In fact, I didn't know much about anyone in California. Needless to say, I decided to find out.

That's when I met Jack Dempsey in that same watering hole on a quiet Thursday evening. I was sitting at the bar when I noticed a well-dressed man about three stools down. He was drinking a Coke. I had been sitting there close to an hour without talking to anyone except Seth, the bartender. I hadn't been aware of anyone else in the place. He glanced in my direction as I was looking towards him and I responded with a cordial greeting. He nodded and raised his glass slightly. I thought that it was a strange gesture and I guess he saw it in my face. He smiled and introduced himself, holding up his fists as he finished talking. I didn't get the connection at first and he seemed a bit disappointed. Then it clicked, Jack Dempsey was a boxer. He showed me his card. He was a freelance investigative journalist based in the Midwest and had been bumming around California accumulating friends and looking for stories. He said he almost won the Pulitzer Prize one year for a piece about a murder in Iowa. He was a likable type of guy and kind of fun and very interesting to talk to. I asked him why he was accumulating friends and he said it was for contacts and sources of information. Suddenly I realized that I might be able to use him as a contact for information. The timing was uncanny.

It became obvious that before long I would have to start telling him about me. That worried me a bit because I knew that he knew the right questions to ask. As he talked I began formulating how much I would be willing to divulge. The conversation did, in fact, turn around and I kept it pretty general. I had moved from Florida to take a job. I didn't disclose any personal information or circumstances about back east or anything else and I hadn't said anything about the job I had now. But then he asked me straight out what I did. I back pedaled a bit but kept it vague using the classified information defense. He smiled as if he knew that with enough prodding he could get the whole story. He probably would have. On his card he wrote the phone number of where he was staying, a nice hotel downtown. Why was he sitting in a bar at this end of town? He said to give him a call if I had any good stories. I kind of believed him.

When I got home that night my mind was really racing. That guy was both the answer to my prayers and my worst nightmare. He could help me find out the background information that I wanted through his contacts. But to get him to help I would have to let him in on all of my suspicions, and observations that had caused me so much concern. I decided I needed to leave it alone for a while longer and just continue with my observations. The fact that my job allowed me to move around freely gave me plenty of opportunities.

At first, I remember watching Mike the most. He really looked like something was bothering him. He was having occasional closed door meetings in the conference room with men that I had never seen before. They didn't look happy either. But they did look official. They reminded me of those movies about gangsters. Whatever business they were discussing, it was not pleasant. At least once a day I would see him leaving the office and head for the warehouses or shop areas. This was perfectly normal behavior for someone in his position. But I tailed him anyway. I was looking for clues in a puzzle where I had no pieces. He usually tracked down a foreman or a worker, conversed with then briefly, and returned to the office. He seldom made more than one stop.

Once he went into Bob's area and he and a young electronics technician spent a few minutes looking over a radio unit. Bob wasn't around at the time. Since I was undercover, I didn't get close enough to hear what was going on. But I had seen enough detective shows on TV to know that I was picking up a pattern in Mike's behavior. He was spending a lot of time in areas where he wouldn't normally go. And rather than talk to the supervisor in these areas, he often went directly to the worker. If he went back to an area for a second time, he went to the same person as he did the first time.

Over the next few weeks I watched him closely. I was able to float around from area to area unnoticed and I could still get my work done on time. I knew my job well and since the rest of the office had cooled down around me, I didn't suspect anyone of following me. I started to watch Bev occasionally, if she was in the same area as well as some of the other technicians that were particularly chummy with Mike. If I was going to suppose that Mike was involved in something, then the odds were good that there were more people involved with him. I began to realize how big this thing was. And I really wasn't even sure what it was.

CHAPTER VI

MIKE'S PARTIES

I had been keeping records of Mike's movements, complete with date, time, where, who with, and for how long. Even if I missed a few trips while I was completing my own work, I was developing quite a file. I would sit home at night and try to evaluate it. I looked for patterns in time but there were none. He seemed to be making his rounds randomly. I knew that he went to the same person in each area each time. So I started looking at who he talked to. I knew most by name although I didn't see them much outside of the yard. Then the first clue hit me. Originally I had been introduced to nearly all of them at one or another of Mike's parties. They were all part of Mike's crowd. I needed to know what they were talking about. Then I thought about Bev again. I hadn't kept any records on her. I suppose, because I liked her I was trying not to think that she could be involved.

I decided maybe I needed Jack Dempsey to help steer me in the right direction. I figured that if I had a chance to check him out a bit before unloading the story, I would be able to decide whether I could trust him enough to take in a partner. He arrived at the condo with a six pack of beer and his leather briefcase. He listened intently as I gave him a brief description of the scenario. Then he stopped me and asked what was really going on. I really thought I was covering it over pretty well but he saw right through me. If I wanted his help, I was going to have to tell him the whole story. I started by telling him how I first got suspicious and how I figured that Mike was playing an important part. I showed him the notes that I had taken while following Mike around. I talked about his parties and I mentioned Bev. I told him that Bev was coming over that weekend and that I had to find a way of getting information from her without causing her to suspect anything.

Jack agreed that this was a tricky plan and suggested that I play it cool, just make it a friendly dinner and see if anything in her conversation was strange or in some way linked. He kept saying not to force it. Don't try to pull things out of her. He said she would see through that in a second. Jack seemed to know what he was talking about. I realized that I trusted him. I gave him a list of the names of everyone at the yard that I had seen fraternizing with Mike. He was going to run them through some database that he had access to see if there was any background stuff that we should know about. He was excited about it. I was excited to have someone who believed me. He kept telling me to take it slow. And he said to cover my back. Later I realized that he understood the delicate nature of espionage. At the time I didn't have the word for it.

He called me Saturday morning with the results of his check. He had a few interesting items. It seems that Mike had three arrests for breaking and entering years earlier. He got off on all three for lack of evidence. Two other guys, both shop workers, had served on the same ship in the navy as Mike. The rest of the list had come up clean, including Bev. He cautioned me that people can change names and identities when circumstances required it. He told me to be cool. He was starting to scare me.

Bev came over that night and we had a terrific evening. It reminded me of those evenings when I had first come to California. I was a little bit afraid that I would come across kind of strange since I was armed with new information and new suspicions. But since she was clean on the list I suppose I loosened up a bit around her. There was nothing in her conversation or her tone of voice that caused me to doubt her loyalty. We talked until midnight and spent the rest of the night together in my bed. She left shortly after breakfast. Jack called Sunday night so we could strategize. He wanted me to keep watching

Mike but to keep one eye open for anyone that might be wondering what I was up to. He specifically cautioned me about Bev. Don't let your guard down. Monday, I was back on the watch and things were much the same as they were the previous weeks. Mike made his rounds and chatted with his buddies, always within a few feet of the electronics equipment. I knew there had to be a connection. Midway through the week I was able to get closer and pick up a bit of the conversation. They mentioned breaking a code and something about a receiver. I couldn't get the whole message since I was trying to stay undetected and, after all, I was new at this stuff. I wasn't able to get close very often. Most of the shops were large and very open. It was only because they were so stacked up with equipment and supplies that I got as close as I did. But the more I tried to get closer, the more I feared getting caught. And the more I followed Mike, the less work I was getting done.

I guess I really wasn't surprised when Mike called me into his office. His attitude from the past weeks hadn't improved and I could tell right away that he was unhappy with me. He asked what the hell was wrong with me lately, incomplete work, incorrect checks, all around shoddy performance. He said he knew I was better than that. I knew I was better than that. I didn't have any excuses for him. I just said that I had a lot on my mind lately and that things would improve immediately. He didn't smile but he seemed content with my answer. I knew I had to get myself back on track real fast. But I remember something peculiar about when I walked out of his office. The other technicians in the area all looked at me. That's when I figured that everybody in the office was involved. I couldn't watch anybody if everybody was watching me. I better cool things down and concentrate on what they meant by codes and receivers. I had followed Mike enough that I knew his routes and his contacts.

About this time there was a big surge to production. All of the technicians were offered opportunities to work overtime so that all units would be free of waiting inspections when the first shift arrived in the morning. Our testing normally took a while. At four o'clock, the servicemen went home and we had the place to ourselves. Each of us had our own set of instructions. Our lab was working over but only about half of the technicians stayed. I needed the money but more than that, here was a chance to move around among the equipment virtually unnoticed. For the first week my assignments were in areas that Mike did not frequent. It was pretty routine stuff and I could take a little wider look around on my way to the men's room or the cafeteria. Mike and Bev did not take the overtime so I didn't worry about running into them. And since my movements were limited to going from one place to another, both authorized, there was no reason for anyone to suspect me.

I spent that first week getting a feel for whom was working and where they seemed to be sending us. I didn't trust anyone so I had to make sure the coast was clear before I started investigating.

The second week I was ready to start. I could finish most of what they gave me to do in just a few hours. Then one night I decided to retrace Mike's route checking out each of his stops. The first stop was the radar test range. When radar sets came in they were put through a rigorous simulation exercise before being installed into the sub. It used to be a secure area but just a few months earlier it had been declassified.

A lot of people thought it was a mistake, perhaps some sort of clerical error or something. But then the word came down from headquarters that the order was correct. On a shipyard that meant that was the end of the conversation. The area was completely deserted that night.

I walked around cautiously looking at the equipment scattered over most of the floor space. It wasn't a very large area. At a workbench along the back wall Mike would talk to a burly mechanic named Gus. I had never been able to get close enough to hear but they often pointed as they spoke. Trying to remember exactly in what direction they had pointed, I reenacted their conversation and turning to my right, I saw a bin of electronic components, diodes and resistors and stuff. There were actually two bins. The first looked like a trash bin. Most of the parts in it looked damaged, or at least discarded. The second bin was behind the first and partly covered. It contained similar parts but these looked brand new. I know that this doesn't seem suspicious and I guess I wasn't sure at the time what I was even looking at. The next day I had a chance to work in that area and a workman told me that he couldn't understand why he had to replace perfectly good parts with these new ones that kept coming in. It wasn't that he was concerned about wasting money or anything, but he just didn't like the extra work. He didn't like working with little, tiny parts. That made me think about something else. I figured that maybe Mike was taking kickbacks from some supplier and since he had the authority to order part replacements for quality purposes, it became an easy task. Seeing his lifestyle with the parties and everything, I could almost understand why he would do such a thing, almost. What he was doing was wrong. I made notes of everything I had seen and quietly slipped back to my work area. I finished the last of my tasks and went home. I wasn't ready to call Jack yet.

It really bothered me when I thought about what Mike was doing, I wrestled with the fact that he was my friend, the guy who got me the job out here and gave me a chance to change my life. I owed him a lot but yet I couldn't accept his behavior. I tossed most of the night.

I was real tired the next morning but I had to work to get the overtime so I could explore Mike's next stop.

That night I was able to get into the receiver shop. That was the place that I had been able to hear some of the conversation. They had talked about codes and receivers. There were receivers in the shop, of course, and I knew that this was a real critical element even though I had never worked there. I also knew that there were top secret frequencies used on them. But I wasn't sure what they had meant by codes. Since the whole area was deserted and I had been working in a room right next to it, I didn't worry as much about being caught. I wandered around the equipment looking for some clues when I came across a unit that had a broken seal. Each unit is sealed at the manufacturer and an adhesive label is placed over the seam. In order to open the unit up, you have to break the seal and that required a lot of paper work and security checks to explain why. It was something you just didn't do. It was strange but still no connection to anything as yet. In fact these types of strange things were becoming amazingly common the more I looked around. I was suddenly startled when I heard the voices behind me.

I ducked behind a pallet of empty packing crates and hoped the beating of my heart wouldn't give me away. It was Mike with a technician named Judd Perth. He was the guy that I had overheard talking to Mike that day. Without any noise I could hear them well this time. They talked about the receivers and how they had come up with a way to get inside them and then reseal them, so no one would ever know. They seemed real satisfied. They laughed a bit and repeated that no one would ever know.

"Know what?" I thought.

CHAPTER VII

BORIS & SASKIA

The more I thought about "know what?" the more I thought about all the spy movies I had seen. First I tried to put this scenario into the scenario of the movies, but there were no similarities. Obviously they were doing something that was not right and probably illegal. I knew I had to find out more about the transmitter/receivers. Once I noticed a receiver location list on Mike's desk, so I knew that some of the basic data was available in our office. During my orientation, Bev had pulled out a number of folders and had shown me how all of the electronic equipment that could interfere with our noise dosimeters, microwave meters, and other IH instruments. The communication devices, although considered a classified piece of electronics, were described in the information she showed me.

The next day at work I looked for the folders that Bev had pulled out, but there was no trace of their existence. Not only were the folders gone, but there was not even a place in the file cabinets to store them. I needed a good reason to ask Bev for them, just to find out where the drawings were stored. Once I knew their location, I knew I could dig them out after hours.

I remembered a particular drawing outlining the navigational hardware describing how each unit was connected. Since I had been collecting sound level meter readings in various compartments on the boats Bev would have no reason to suspect anything if I asked for that drawing. I caught up with her right after lunch. She was cordial. I explained that I was a bit confused about the layout of the compartments and asked her if she still had that great drawing she had shown me when I had just started. I thought for a moment that she was going to take me right to it. But then she paused and apologized saying she really didn't know what I was talking about. I described it again and she just shrugged her shoulders and smiled. She winked at me as she turned and walked away. Either she was softening up to me or she knew exactly what I was up to. That night, Mike left the door to his office unlocked.

I was beginning to get afraid at this point, because it was obvious to me that something big was going on, and that the people that I worked with everyday were involved in it. No matter how good I worked at what I was doing, I knew that they were sneaking around and up to no good. I couldn't help but fear that they might be on to me. I was doing a lot of looking over my shoulder. Jack had told me to cover my back. Although I got home from work pretty late, I called Jack to fill him in on what I had come up with. He felt it was still pretty sketchy but that there was a certain degree of suspicion. He came over and reviewed the various documents I had accumulated. They were assorted work orders, drawings, and memos that by themselves probably meant nothing. But I was convinced that together they would begin to open up some doors. I had carefully photocopied each sheet and marked on them where and when I had gotten them. I had gotten them all on my late night raids while working overtime. Jack did not seem impressed. Again I tried to explain how they fit together. He still didn't get it. I suggested that he take the entire folder (it was about 85 pages) back to his hotel room and read them thoroughly. We could talk about them later. He left and I tried to get a few hours' sleep before I had to go back to work. Like most of my coworkers, I was beginning to burn out with the long hours. I really liked the extra money but 12-15 hour workdays, five days a week, and just finishing up the sixth straight week, I was dragging. I wasn't disappointed when Mike announced that the overtime was to be discontinued the next week.

Also, it didn't bother me when Bev approached me and suggested that we try again. No need to move fast, just a nice peaceful dinner among friends. In a way, that was what I needed to hear. Mary was just about completely gone from my mind, and I realized more and more that I wanted and needed companionship. We made a date for Saturday.

She said, "Meet me at my house at 7."

I said, "Wonderful, I won't be late!"

That was Friday morning and that night I only worked until five, so I stopped at the lounge and drank a beer at the bar. It tasted good. The place was crowded and there were a few faces that I recognized but I stayed by myself at the bar. When someone finally sat next to me it was Steve Bocco, one of the technicians from my office. I hadn't worked with him, but I knew he had been there a year or so longer than me. He didn't look happy, and I figured that he had come over to talk. Either I was in a good listening mood or else I thought maybe I could squeeze some information out of him. He talked for more than an hour. He was upset, because he had been reprimanded that afternoon by Mike and was accused of stealing classified documents.

Steve said, "I was shocked and confused by Mike's allegation, because it was not true. During the course of our heated conversation, I convinced him that I had no idea about what he said. Suddenly, Mike told me that he did not plan to go forward with a formal charge against me."

According to Steve, Mike said, "I will not involve Naval Intelligence at this time. Just know that you are under my microscope." Steve went on to say that he had been working for Mike for nearly two years and hadn't been involved in any kind of foul play.

Steve said, "I am keeping my nose clean. It is a good paying job and I am planning to get married in a few months and bring my bride Cindy up from L.A. to live. I wouldn't do anything to risk losing my job." I was stunned by his words but I just listened to him talk. He told me that when Mike was yelling at him, he really thought that he was going to be fired. He continued to repeat that he really had no idea what Mike was talking about.

During our entire conversation Steve kept looking at his watch. He only drank a sip or two from a long neck bottle but it was obvious that he had finished several before coming over to me. I had the feeling that he was on the edge of being drunk. At that moment, he stood up and nodded goodbye. Then he left in a hurry and I followed shortly thereafter. I hadn't planned on staying that long, but Steve's story seemed to fit somehow into the whole scheme of things. I couldn't stop thinking about Steve's words, as I continued my drive to Bev's.

Before my meeting with Steve, I was feeling real good because I had a date with Bev that night. I picked up a bottle of wine, Beaujolais, since I knew it was her favorite. I was just cruising along enjoying watching the sun slowly set in the west. At that time I didn't notice the car, a white sedan, parked across the street from Bev's place. Later, I would see that car again at both Bev's and Mike's place. It became clear that someone was watching me.

When I arrived at Bev's house I was ready for a good evening. She looked great and her house dangled those wonderful food smells in front of my nose. Her house always smelled that way when she cooked and when she wasn't cooking; it had the fragrance of herbs. It was very comforting. She opened the wine right away and we sipped it over mild conversation. We didn't talk about work or about our past problems. We talked for about an hour or so and then and we opened a second bottle of wine from her rack and I helped her with the finishing touches of dinner. We ate on the patio under a clear, starry sky. It was so romantic that it was almost painful. The wine was starting to affect me by dinner's end and all the signals I was getting from her indicated that she was feeling about the same way. I slid my arm around her waist while we cleared the dishes and she didn't resist.

She whispered in my ear, "later."

The music was soft and we sat for another hour sipping more wine and chatting. She made a comment about Steve having been reprimanded and shook her head as if she couldn't understand why anyone would do such a thing. I didn't answer her, partially because I was afraid of giving myself away, but mainly because I was too drunk to respond. The strongest thought I had at that moment was what it would taste like to run my lips all over her body. I put down my glass and kissed her on the neck. She moaned softly and sunk back into the sofa. I ran my hands and then my lips all over her body. We made love on the sofa and then retreated to her bedroom where we laid together all night. We made love again as the sun was rising. We didn't talk too much at breakfast but she brought up the Steve issue again and said that Naval Intelligence would probably be watching us pretty close. I figured that this was a subtle warning and I certainly wasn't suspecting her anymore.

I returned home sometime around noon and just kicked back and relaxed the rest of the day. It wasn't until he called me that evening that I thought about Jack. He had read through all of the papers I had given him and although he did not see a clear connection to anyone yet, he was sure there was something going on.

Jack said, "I had a phone call from an anonymous caller yesterday, who said that a KGB Agent by the name of Boris Evonovich was working in the city." Jack asked the caller if she knew why he was here but the caller hung up. He did some snooping around about this Mr. Evonovich and learned that he worked with a subordinate female agent named Saskia. Reportedly, Saskia did his dirty work. Jack was told by his source, who did not want to be named, that if Boris Evonovich felt the need to eliminate someone, then Saskia would be given the job. Also, Saskia would always bring an amputated "pinky" finger from her victim, as required by Boris, simply because he liked trophies. Given my own experiences in this life nothing was beyond belief.

I said, "Now that is interesting. I wonder if this Boris has been involved in bugging the boats at the yard."

Jack said, "Don't know but I will keep my eyes and ears open." He was always thinking of things as a story. We talked for about an hour and once off the phone I felt tired, drained actually. I kicked off my shoes and went to bed.

At work that Monday, Steve had been reinstated and even though they never gave any explanation, I knew they were just looking for a scapegoat, someone to pin something on to bring in the Naval Intelligence guys. I was now certain that they were suspicious of me. Things were happening too fast to be coincidence. I kept telling myself that they didn't know who but were trying to flush the culprit out. I would have to lay low. I played it perfectly straight for the next few days. When I got home that Thursday, I had no sooner taken off my jacket when there was a loud knocking at my door. On the other side were two large guys flashing badges in my face and inviting themselves in. They were from the Naval Intelligence Office and they started firing questions at me about Jack Dempsey. I told them that he was an acquaintance and I knew only that he was a reporter. They were looking for more than that. They told me that Jack was believed to be stealing documents from the shipyard and selling them to foreign agents. Even though I knew more than I was letting on it all seemed pretty preposterous. I started to worry about Jack. After they left and I watched them pull away, I called Jack but there was no answer.

I didn't risk calling Jack from work nor could I afford to be seen driving past his hotel. I started watching everybody at work again. I had gotten a bit lazy since the overtime had stopped and I knew that someone was watching me. I had to find out who it was or my own life might be in danger. Because I knew my job so well, I just lost myself in work. The time flew by and since my level of performance was high, no one would suspect me of anything. A delay in my own investigations would not affect the outcome of whatever was going on. It was big enough to be a continuous and extensive plot. I just wasn't quite sure what it was.

I called Jack when I got home, but again there was no answer. I was worried. My concentration was broken by the ringing of my phone. This time it was Mike. He hadn't called me in weeks. He said he had missed me at work that day and wanted to invite me to one of his parties. Just the same old crowd, he said. I didn't want to go but my curiosity was getting the best of me. I was sure that Mike was a key player but I had no proof. I thought that maybe one of his friends might get a little too drunk and speak a little too freely about what was going on. It had happened before. I told him I would be there and hung up the phone. It was the same old crowd. I recognized nearly everyone and they recognized me. Everyone was cordial and relaxed. I kept my ears wide open for anything that might answer my questions.

Bev wasn't there that night; although I knew she was a regular when we weren't together. I listened intently to every conversation that I could get close to and, as the night wore on, the conversations turned more and more to work.

I zeroed in on Judd Perth. He was pretty drunk and running his mouth. He wasn't talking loud but he was rambling on and on about this and that. When he started talking about receivers I gave him all of my attention. He talked about how he had found a foolproof way of opening up the units and exposing their components. He bragged about how he could seal them back up and even replace the manufacturer's seals, and that they were completely undetectable. And since no one would ever know that they were opened, no one would ever know that they were tampered with. I knew that Mike and he were in it together and I figured that there were more in the organization that were involved in the cover up and all of the other things that spies needed. They were probably all getting a nice payoff, as well. I knew then that I had to bust this thing up. I had a duty to myself and my country to stop any kind of actions that threatened national security. I tried to call Jack when I got home but still no answer.

I lay awake for hours trying to decide what the next step should be. I considered calling Bev but in the past, when I had brought up controversial issues, she had shunned them as if she found them distasteful or irritating. She showed no interest at all. I thought about Steve but figured with him having just gotten out of trouble he wouldn't be interested in plunging back into it. I was sure that there would be trouble. I figured that I had enough information, even though Jack had all my evidence, to present a pretty good argument. I thought about what level I would have to take it to if I wanted to get any action. I also thought about that visit from Naval Intelligence and calculated how much risk that would cause.

The picture was not pleasant, but I knew what I had to do. Monday morning I called Chuck and asked for an appointment, a confidential appointment. It was unusual for a worker to take a problem to his level without going through the chain of command. But this was not your everyday problem. This was big. He seemed both surprised and concerned when I sat down and began to outline the scenario. He listened as I presented all of the facts and linked them together. He asked a few questions but mainly he just listened. When I finished, he sat back in his chair and was silent for a long minute or two. That made an interesting picture. I may have mentioned that he liked to smoke cigars and in spite of all the efforts to ban smoking in the offices, he had hung on to his rights. His office always had that stale smoke smell lingering in corners. His secretary was always putting air fresheners around and he was always collecting them and throwing them away. I had the feeling that the game had been going on for twenty years but this time he hadn't smoked his cigar while I talked, he chewed on it. Then he leaned forward, looked me straight in the eye, and asked me if I knew what I was saying. He said he was wondering whether I had seen too many spy movies and just needed a vacation. He said he could arrange that. He asked me if I knew what it meant to yell espionage around a shipyard that was handling secret equipment. He asked me if I had any idea of what could happen to me if this whole scheme was true and the bad guys got to me first. At that point I didn't care and I told him that. It was my duty to report what I suspected and stand by my decision regardless of the consequences. He was not happy. Either he did not want to deal with the crisis, or he was in on it too. To this day, I still believe the latter.

CHAPTER VIII

WAKE-UP CALL

I never did figure out the communication lines within their organization, but I knew that news traveled fast. By the time I got back to the office from my meeting with Chuck Slater, the details of the meeting were already known. Evil faces looked at me when I walked back to my desk. Coffee had been spilled on my desk and papers. It was all childish stuff but they were letting me know that they knew and telling me that I better watch my step. Mike had left work suddenly for personal reasons. After an hour the tension hadn't let up. I too, left for the day. They certainly couldn't get on to me about attendance. It was the first time I had missed any hours since starting work at the facility.

I drove around for a while trying to convince myself that I had done the right thing. Of course I had. I had pretty much alienated myself from everybody at work but I knew I was right. I drove down to the coast and I drove up into the hills. I stopped and scanned the horizon at each point but none of it made me particularly happy. I remembered that Bev had not been at work that morning, so I ran by her house in the hopes of catching her there. I wanted to explain to her what I had done and see whether she was willing to understand. She wasn't home.

I got back home in the early afternoon and tried to ring Jack again. Still no answer. I was beginning to get worried. I wanted to go by his hotel room to see if he had skipped town, but remembering those

Naval Intelligence guys, I decided that staying put was the best move. They were on to him for something, and whether or not it was part of my plans, I needed to stay clean. I was worrying about having to go back to work tomorrow and deal with that childish mob. Although I wasn't really hungry, at about six I walked down to the corner and bought a pizza.

Early in the evening, Charles Slater called me at home.

He assured me that everything was being handled in the strictest confidentiality. He told me that he had filed a report with the shipyard security office and that they would be contacting me personally for more details. He said he admired my courage. He told me that he couldn't transfer me, so long as I wanted to work as an Industrial Hygienist. If I was willing to change jobs into another section, it would be at least a week so I would have to stick it out in the IH section for the time being. Finally, he told me not to judge those around me prematurely. On that kind of naval installation, breaches of security were very serious and things like investigations and inspections were hard on everybody. An employee, who "rocks the boat" is considered to be a very serious offender of unwritten rules. I thanked him for calling.

Later in the evening Mike called. He sounded really concerned. He was concerned about my safety. If I had really found something, he said, my life could be in danger. He suggested that I move back to his place for a while. Thanks, but no thanks. He assured me that the hard feelings would pass as soon as the investigating parties had made their rounds. He said he had seen these kinds of things before. He told me to keep up the good work and everything would turn out for the best. After ten minutes, I think I was actually starting to believe him. He was coming across as very sincere. But I remembered that he was also one of the leaders in this organization so he had to be a smooth operator. I thanked him for calling.

If there was one thing I learned in California, it was that life was not simple. Every time I turned around there was a new problem or a fresh crisis waiting. I was spending increasing amounts of time just trying to reason things out and sort through piles of data. I had always been a deep thinker but this had reached the point where it had ceased being enjoyable or stimulating. I hadn't identified it as survival instinct yet, but looking back I can see that it was brewing.

I thought long and deep about that day, about Chuck Slater's call and about Mike's call. I thought back over my conversation with Chuck and the hostility that greeted me when I tried to go back to my job. I didn't know who to trust. I was pretty sure of a few co-workers that I couldn't trust, though. I needed someone on my side, someone that I could talk to and someone that would help me reason this whole mess out. I thought that person was Jack but he had disappeared.

I went into work the next morning and tried to act like nothing had happened. I faced the same childish behavior from my co-workers. They ignored me except when they wanted to make some derogatory statement or gesture. I got out into the yard, as quickly as I could. I just had to get out of the office as soon as I could. Although I got a few strange stares, there wasn't any open acknowledgment that anybody knew what I had done, unless it didn't make any difference.

Bev found me about mid-morning and her basic reaction was that I was just looking for trouble. Her idea of doing your job was appearing to do exactly what the book said and keeping your nose out of everything else. They have guys whose job it was to snoop around and check for these kinds of things. She couldn't understand why I was prying into something that I had no business in. She said she didn't feel right being with someone who would do that kind of thing. As she walked away, I wondered if her words applied to the group behind all of this. She just seemed so damned naive.

While I was eating lunch, alone, Steve Bocco came up and stood next to me. He didn't look like he was sure of what to say, so I just shook my head and said something like 'another fine mess.' He laughed softly and told me that he admired my courage and added that he wouldn't have done it. He had devoted his life to staying out of trouble, not going out looking for it. I knew that this was someone I could trust but before I could really talk to him, he had to leave and slipped quietly off into one of the machine shops. Before he left he gave me two bits of advice, watch my back and watch my front. I wasn't sure what he meant by the second part but the first had been a favorite of Jack's.

Steve had acted as if he wasn't supposed to have been talking to me. He had sneaked in and out and had talked very softly which was very different from the night in the bar. He acted like he didn't want to be seen with me. That reinforced the notion I had that I was being watched. Obviously the word had spread very rapidly that I was trying to spill their plot. Considering the fact that I now had no friends left, I realized that there were two kinds of people left here; those involved in the plot and those who weren't involved but were afraid of its outcome. As far as I was concerned, that meant everybody was in on it.

As soon as I passed through the main gate heading home I started scanning my rearview mirrors. I knew they were following me. I just wanted to see how long it would take to spot them. A green sedan had been behind me since a block outside the gate. They were conveniently staying back a good 300 feet, so I couldn't get a glimpse of who was in the car. However, it looked like two silhouettes. I took a sharp, unexpected left turn into a residential area and stopped in front of a parked pickup truck. They turned in and stopped, waiting for me to proceed. I continued on and stopped again. They stopped. I quickly turned around and went back down the street past them. I intended to get a good look at my competition and I intended to let them see who they were dealing with. We each got a good look. They didn't follow me after that but I knew there were more out there.

I drove to my condo without stopping and there was a strange car parked out on the street. It looked like only one person was sitting in it. I was now certain that they would be watching my every move. It's funny but somehow that made me less concerned about where they saw me go. I headed for Jack's place. Jack had told me that he lived in a hotel. He mentioned once that he was financed by others, which gave him the freedom to move around without a great deal of pressure. As long as he produced the work they wanted, he lived well. His car was in the garage below the hotel so after parking my vehicle, I went up the back stairs to avoid notice by the front desk. His suite was on the fourth floor but didn't really have any view to brag about. I knocked several times but I heard no movement inside. I tried the knob and it was unlocked, so I cautiously walked inside. Obviously someone was still living there. There were personal articles and clothing lying around the room although no serious disarray. He had a word processor on the table by the window but there were no papers lying about. The rooms looked as if the occupant had just slipped out to run a few errands. I looked around a bit more then slipped quietly out and back to my car. When I got back to the condo, I found that the front door had been broken open. Inside, someone had turned just about everything upside down. I called the police. The first cop on the scene arrived in about 18 minutes. He was Officer O'Malley and he was right out of a TV show. The conversation went like this:

O'Malley said, "Are you Mr. Thomas?"

I said, "Yeah, that's me."

O'Malley said, "Anyone else here?"

I said, "No, just me."

O'Malley said, "Any idea who might have done this?"

I said, "No, I was hoping you would help with that."

O'Malley said, "Are you involved in any drug deals?"

I said, "Of course not!"

O'Malley said, "That's good."

At that point he decided to enter the condo and look around. He made a laughing comment that the place looked kind of like his kid's room. He called for the crime lab to come out and dust for fingerprints. He asked me if I knew what was missing. At that point, I realized that I had never looked around or even checked my own belongings. The few things of value that I owned were still there. He told me he had to leave and that the lab truck would be there in about an hour. He gave me his card and told me to call if I discovered anything missing or if any other information turned up. He told me to call anytime, as he had an answering machine. I had a great sense of security knowing that if I called this cop I would be able to reach him. The crime lab arrived about two hours later and proceeded to cover the whole place with dark gray powder. The only finger prints that they could pick up were mine and since I still hadn't found anything missing, they left a bit frustrated. I started cleaning up enough to get to my clothes and the things I would need for work the next day. I was not going to let them think they were getting to me. The next day at work was filled with smirks and whispering. I knew that they knew. But I was determined to go on. Like the previous day, I got out to the production areas as quickly as I could after getting in. I pursued my job as if nothing had happened. I worked alone. At lunchtime, I received another brief visit from Steve. He said only that the previous night had been a warning and then he slipped away again. I hadn't told anyone about the break in so that confirmed my suspicions. Near quitting time, as I was walking back toward the office to turn in my worksheets, I was approached by two big guys flashing badges. They were from Naval Intelligence and they wanted to talk to me about my allegations. I realized that these were the same guys that came to my house asking about Jack Dempsey. I found it odd that they started asking me questions right there in the aisle. They basically had me repeat most of what I had told Charles Slater and I began to think that their jobs were an oxymoron. When I finally got back to the office, I had a real bad feeling about that interview. The office was empty when I got there, the interview having kept me past normal quitting time. I turned in my worksheets and sat down at my desk to think for a few minutes. My desk was pretty much cleaned off since it was an easy target for pranks or other office foul play. I was startled out of a thought by Bev's voice. I didn't see or hear her coming but she was right there in front of me. She was smiling.

She said, "I am sorry for the outburst the other day but I was just concerned about me. There were a lot of rumors going around about what I was involved in." She was worried about me. She gave me a hug and a kiss. That felt good but I couldn't help wonder what she meant by what I was involved in. I wanted to question her about it but she slipped away as fast as she had appeared. I went to my car and drove straight home. The phone was ringing as I approached the front door of the condo. Feverishly opening the one small lock,

I realized that I was just a second too late. The ringing had stopped. I pushed the door closed with my foot and waded through the debris of the previous night and into the kitchen. As I stood there staring into the refrigerator evaluating the three or four choices open to me, there was a hard pounding on the front door. I hadn't locked the door when I pushed it shut and before I could get back to it to answer the knock, it burst open and four police officers came charging through, guns drawn, quickly scanning the living Room and any areas beyond. Before I could say a thing, their weapons were pointing at me and a voice, which displayed a lack of patience told me to put my hands up real quick and not to make any false moves. I was immediately hand cuffed and a very young policeman read me my rights. I stopped him midway through and asked what I did.

In a very firm voice he replied, "You are under arrest for the murder of Jack Dempsey." They actually weren't very far from the truth. While they weren't very far off at all, they had no idea of the magnitude of what was at stake. I knew then that it was someone at the shipyard, who had killed Jack. He was getting too close in his investigation and armed with the material I had taken, he was probably ready to drop the case on his boss' desk back to Washington but twenty years with the bureau reminded him that that move might not work out, as planned. To this day, I believe that one of the John A. Walker, Jr. spy gang had taken him out and was trying to pin the murder on me. I kept trying to decide if I should tell them the whole story. I figured that they would get a rundown on it from work when they investigated and, besides, they were civilian and would have no jurisdiction over it. Like I said, they went on for five hours asking questions and writing things down and recording stuff and asking me the same questions to see if I was going to change my mind. I stayed right with them the whole time and finally they thanked me and left. A uniformed officer came in and fastened the handcuffs. He led me down a short corridor and put me in a small cell. It was well lit and I could tell that there were three other cells, one next to mine and two across the hall. The door opened only to the corridor so I couldn't see if anyone was next to me. One cell across from me was empty but the other had a sleeping figure curled up on the cot. I sat on my cot for a few minutes and surveyed my surroundings while contemplating my predicament. All of the necessities were right here in front of me. There was a thin, but soft mattress on a metal spring and wire mesh cot that was fastened to the wall. There was another one above mine but folded up against the wall like a bunk on an old railroad Pullman Sleeping Car. I figured that was for crowded conditions. There was a small sink and toilet plumbing set-up separated by a shoulder height partition, as viewed by the person seated. If the other guy was washing his hands at the sink; then, the guy on the toilet had absolutely no privacy. Criminals don't deserve privacy, I reasoned. And like it or not, I was a criminal until someone believed my story and let me go. I laid back on the so called bed. The pillow was flat.

I was startled by the voice coming from the other cell. He asked me my name and what I was in for. I really wasn't sure what I should say in a situation like that, but I answered truthfully, Rob, murder. His name was Richard and he was a chronic car thief, who was actually fairly interesting to talk to. He knew about all kinds of cars and about the insides of all the county jails and prisons that dot the California landscape. This time he had sweet talked a young lady into letting him take a spin around the block in her Ferrari. Around the block turned into a joyride that lasted 24 hours. The next day he drove back with the intention of returning the car and quietly slipping away into the shadows. They caught him before he made it back to the Vallejo. His biggest regret was that even with a car like that, he hadn't gotten laid.

They gave me my one phone call and I called Bev. I asked her to get me a lawyer and to check out the condo. I doubted if the police had bothered to lock up. I suppose it was the lateness of the hour but she did not seem very eager to help me. But she said she would and there was a lawyer there to see me first thing in the morning.

Also that morning, they took Richard away. He said he was going to the big house, as he referred to Folsom Penitentiary, in Oakland. I realized that I might be following him.

My lawyer was in his fifties and although he appeared extremely disorganized, he seemed extremely intelligent. He told me that he was a friend of Bev's family and had a great deal of experience in these kinds of cases. The fact that he said "these kinds of cases" bothered me. I mean, how often does a law abiding citizen get thrown into jail for the murder of his friend when both of them were working together on a big expose' but I told him what I thought he needed to know and he seemed satisfied. I had expected him to outline his defense strategy but he never did. He just said to sit tight and he would get me out of there. Sitting tight was about all I could do in that cell.

Bev came in to see me a little later. She assured me that the lawyer was really good and would take care of everything. I believed her and it wasn't too long that he came back and the police officer unlocked the cell and said I was free to go. I figured that he had made my bail and I was sort of in his custody, although it would seem strange to let a murder suspect go. At the time I was just glad to be out. He took me aside and explained that he had cut a deal with the judge and since the case so sketchy anyway, I was free to go on my honor. I was to keep myself cool until the trial. That seemed simple enough but no less strange. He gave me a ride home. Sure enough, Bev had locked up like I had asked her.

Once inside my condo, I felt safe again. I knew the police wouldn't be back again and I looked forward to a good night's sleep. But I had to call Mike first. I was sure that he knew what had happened that previous night. Since he was my boss, I thought I should call him and let him know I was okay and would be in the next day. Our conversation kind of shocked me. Our friendship had become pretty weak in the past weeks but he had still acted like he cared about me. After explaining my ordeal, he stopped me and said not to come back to work---not yet anyway. He assured me that I was still employed but that my clearance had been revoked pending an investigation. It seemed like there must have been at least a dozen investigations going on at the same time that involved me. He told me not to worry, things were being taken care of.

The crazy part came next. Mike told me that a doctor, a psychiatrist, would be calling to arrange an appointment to talk with me. Again he said not to worry, that this was just standard procedure. I began to wonder what it was a standard procedure for. Just stay close to home, he said.

I didn't sleep very good that night. I knew something strange was going on but I was becoming more confused than ever. I had figured out what was going on at the yard and had reported it to the proper authorities. Now I was accused of murder, furloughed from my job, and waiting for a call from a shrink. Things were moving too fast and I couldn't get a grip on the whole situation. I needed time to reason the whole thing out. And apparently, now I had the time.

The next morning, I got some paper and a pen and planted myself on a lounge chair on the balcony where I had a good view and I started writing down the complete sequence of events for the last few days. This string of bad luck had begun shortly after I had told my story to Charles Slater. My apartment had been ransacked, I was being followed, and then this business about Jack. Somebody wanted Jack and me out of the picture. The wrong people obviously knew about my talk with Charles Slater. I still wonder if he had any part in any of what went on. Chuck always acted like he was in the dark about it all. But I was obviously too close to something really big. They had to quietly get me out of the way without attracting attention to themselves. Chances are they had been following me before I blew the whistle. They must have caught me sneaking around during those late nights on overtime. That was probably how they found out about Jack. They had seen him come over. By setting me up for the murder, I would draw so much attention to myself and my own situation that all attention would be diverted from what was going on at the shipyard. And if they were real lucky, this whole affair would discredit my story. Who was going to believe a murderer?

It was all becoming clear. I had played right into their hands. I was on symbolic house arrest, Jack was dead, and it seemed all of my work was going unnoticed. As I looked out in front of me, the haze over the city seemed to be trying to swallow me. My concentration was broken by the ring of the phone.

It was Dr. Goldman, the psychiatrist I mentioned earlier. He introduced himself and told me that he was working in conjunction with the lawyer, Mr. Simpkins, on my case. He said that the court was requiring that I receive a thorough examination by him if I was to keep my free status. Again, this just wasn't making sense to me. But I agreed to meet him at his office that afternoon. Minutes after hanging up from the doctor, the lawyer called to make sure that I had gotten the call from the doctor and that I was going to make the appointment. There was a strange urgency in all of that.

For the rest of the morning and up until I had to get ready for my appointment, I continued pondering my notes. I drove downtown to Dr. Goldman's office, however, traffic problems caused me to be twenty minutes late. I remember that because he made such a big issue out of it. He went on about how he had thought that I wasn't going to show and how he had called my home and was just about to call Simpkins.

The rest of the interview went very smoothly. He spent about an hour and a half asking me questions about everything from what it was like when I was five years old to how it felt to spend the night in jail. I looked at ink blots and some other shapes, and I played word association. He even did stuff like checking my blood pressure, heart and lungs. He checked my vision and I asked him if I needed glasses. I was expecting to put pegs in holes next but that quickly, it was over. He made it clear that I would be advised of his opinions in due time. For now, he told me to go home and relax. After just one day, home was beginning to feel confining, like a jail cell with no visible bars.

Again I was thinking about what was going on. I couldn't complain, because I was out of jail. But there was unmistakably something going on below the surface, out of my view. I knew that I had to be extra careful and extra observant. Traffic going home was worse than I had coming in. I was hitting rush hour, even though it always seemed like rush hour in California. As the cars crept along the freeway, I remember looking in the rearview mirror, scanning for unmarked sedans. About half the cars fit the description and even though I couldn't see anyone back there following me, I had the satisfaction that they were in the same traffic jam. I thought how funny it would have been if they had run out of gas and had to go back to wherever and explain. I glanced at my own gas gauge. I was sure they were back there somewhere but a red Porsche with a California blond driver averted my eyes.

I amaze myself sometimes with the amount of detail I remember. I suppose with all I have been through I developed a keen sense of observation. I have been watching everything around me and listening to everything I have heard since the whole thing started. I had to; my survival has depended on it. And besides my thorough notes, I have ingrained it into my mind so that I never forget what they did to me.

My empty condo was waiting for me when I finally made it home. I turned on the stereo and settled back on the sofa. I bent over to turn on the TV and it lit up. I turned the sound all the way down and put on a tape that I had recorded when I was back in Florida. It was a combination of rock from ten years earlier and some great blues songs from a record I had borrowed from my old college friend Birdman. It was a great feeling to listen to that old tape and think about the good times while the mindless sitcom characters moved silently across the screen. I fell asleep. The clicking of the end of the tape on the reel brought me slowly back to consciousness. I turned off the tape recorder and glanced at the TV again. There was an old movie on starring Humphrey Bogart. It seemed to fit the nostalgic evening I was having so I turned the volume back up and got a beer from the refrigerator. I wasn't hungry.

It was late, probably about eleven, when the phone rang, interrupting my peaceful hermitage. It was Bev. She sounded very concerned and asked if I was okay. She didn't say a word about the doctor's appointment. I thought maybe she didn't know. And that made me feel a little more comfortable about trusting her. She said that there was a lot of talk going on around work, none of it good. She said that Mike had called everyone together and diplomatically informed them of my unfortunate circumstances. I figured that he had to play it down, even if just for show. I had no idea how many people in our department weren't part of his organization. I wasn't searching for sympathy but I was glad that I had a source of information on the inside. I asked her to please keep me informed and she agreed to do what she could. She said that it wouldn't be a good idea for her to come over with the whole issue being so fresh. She told me to sit tight and do what the lawyer said. She repeated that he knew how to handle these kinds of cases. What kind of case was it?

CHAPTER IX

WADE SIMPKINS

Wade Simpkins called me to come to his law office the next morning. I got his call at nine and he wanted me there by ten. He was appearing before a judge and he needed to talk to me before he went. Luckily, he was not far away so even with the traffic I made it on time.

His building was one of those older structures that you see occasionally in this town. It was nothing to look at, just brick and peeling paint. Once inside, the halls were gloomy. I suppose for some of his clients, there was a hidden meaning in that. His name hung over a door on the second floor. Opening that door I found myself in a small outer office inhabited by six large file cabinets, a desk, and a young, but plain looking secretary. She addressed me by name and told me to go on in.

His office was only slightly plush. There were more file cabinets, plaques on the walls, and a beautiful framed print that looked like a Monet. His desk was large and made of mahogany. Its two most striking features were a marble desk set and a very new looking word processor. He was staring at a freshly typed page when I entered and he motioned with his hand for me to be seated. Once I was in the chair, he began speaking without looking away from the page and occasionally he pushed a button or two.

He started off by telling me that I was still in big trouble. It was his influence and their lack of firm evidence that enabled me to be released. He said that I was his responsibility. When he said that, he turned around and looked me straight in the face and asked if I knew what that meant. I wasn't sure what he was driving at but I nodded. He said that if I made one mistake or didn't do exactly what he told me, it would tarnish his reputation and send me directly to prison. He was more serious than I had seen him before.

He started by outlining what had transpired and where he was heading. They had found Jack's body with his head bashed in by some blunt object. He was found around midnight by a cleaning lady, who noticed the door to his room part open and had called hotel security. The security guard arrived and found the body. He called the police. The cops placed the time of death at about eight-thirty, which corresponded to the time I had been seen sneaking out the rear entrance. The crime lab found my finger prints, along with a lot of others, at various places around the room.

The body was taken to the morgue. Since he had no relatives in town, the positive identification was made by the hotel manager who apparently knew him well. Witnesses reported my presence, and that, combined with my finger prints and having been seen there before, led to my arrest. That seemed very clear cut to me and although I was definitely innocent, I could see how they drew their conclusions. Crazy stuff happened after that. First, the body disappeared. Someone with official looking paperwork walked into the morgue and drove off with Jack's body. They hadn't performed the autopsy yet. Simpkins had driven home the point to the court that without a body they had no case. He wasn't totally correct, but he was very persuasive. He didn't think that would hold up for long, but if I showed that I was behaving in his custody, chances are they would leave things alone until the trial. Also, fortunately for me, the newspapers hadn't gotten a hold of the whole story. Things happened so fast with the missing body and all that they just picked up the short crime beat blurb about an unidentified male found dead in a hotel room. That was not exactly a spectacular story in the big city.

But then came the part that just about floored me. If at the time we go to trial, and he assured me that we would, if the evidence was stacked against me, he was going to plead insanity. The first words out of my mouth were, no way. He ignored me and said he had to get to court and we would talk again soon. He told me to go home and stay there except for buying food or other necessities. I left there shocked. I might have had a few peculiarities, but I was not insane. I got in my car and drove away fast. Any other day, a cop would have had me for speeding in a second. I drove around for at least an hour before realizing that everything around me was boring. I went home and cooked a steak. The smoke set off the detector in the condo and that just irritated me more. I spent the rest of the evening sitting on the balcony. It was dark there and I could watch the city come to life as the sky turned a deeper black. Whatever direction I decided to go in, I would either get in trouble with the law or violate my own code of ethics. I knew that I would never be able to continue my investigation at the shipyard. I knew that I had turned it over to the Naval Intelligence guys there but I had already decided that I was going to continue my own surveillance. I didn't have enough faith in those guys that they would do a thorough enough job and really get to the bottom of it. I had planned to keep collecting evidence so that I could add clout to anything they came up with. Depending on how extensive those subversive forces were, the entire formal investigation was in danger.

This murder rap was sure to destroy my credibility. I was pretty depressed but I realized that it was the stuff I didn't know that was going to keep me hanging on. I really didn't know how much anybody else knew, or even what was going on outside a few feet beyond my view.

I would like to say that a feeling of sheer hopelessness had swept over me at this time but that was against my nature. 1 needed to develop a new strategy to fight back. I gave up on my thoughts of continuing my investigation. There were too many obstacles there. It seemed insignificant now. I refused to believe that it had all been in vain. I did what I knew was right and I was stopped by an evil force that was too large and too powerful to fight. But I had gotten so close to the real truth that the force had been obligated to shut me and my operation down. I held to a moral and ethical obligation to my country. They were devoted to destroying all of these things and they had recruited an army of followers that must have been enormous. They could not allow any outsider rock the boat.

Another striking truth hit me hard as I continued to think about things. I was sure that Mike had brought me out to California to recruit me into his band. It did seem odd, in retrospect, that he would have offered me a job after all those years and with such limited information about me. I figured that he had me pegged right from the start. That explained why he was so anxious to get me to stay at his place and hang around at all of his parties. Once I had gained the trust of all of his cronies, the transition would have gone smoothly.

He may have set Bev up as an insurance factor to keep me in line. At that point, I still wasn't sure about Bev. She seemed to fit into Mike's group, but she also seemed to genuinely care about me, which was behavior that I wouldn't have expected from a subversive out to destroy the country.

But those issues were becoming old news. I needed to get my own situation under control. I always managed to keep control and I couldn't let this be an exception. I spent a lot of time from that point on just thinking about everything. I knew that once I really understood the situation, I could plan the most effective action. And time was something I had plenty of. I followed everybody's instructions. I stayed home unless it was absolutely necessary that I go out, such as, to pick up things at the store, or when my cabin fever got the best of me. I was definitely playing it cool, as far as they were concerned and thinking things through before taking action. I arrived at some new conclusions. I figured that Simpkins, the lawyer, was a part of their group. He had to have been. He was supposedly a friend of Bev's family and he said he had worked on those kinds of cases before. Those kinds of cases might just have been ways of eliminating threats within a system that remained legal. He could have me put away in prison for a long time but I would still be able to talk and sooner or later someone might just listen. I was concerned about his reference to an insanity plea. That would leave a lot of uncertainty in the future. The psychiatrist seemed like a bit of a quack and I was sure he was a colleague of Simpkins. I guess it was kind of like that image of the man who was in the car accident and the lawyer, seeing an opportunity to make some easy money, sends the man to his own picked doctor to keep writing that his neck was still in bad shape. When the ordeal was over, the lawyer and his doctor friend split most of the settlement. The man was just the dumb fool, but he felt lucky as he counted his small share.

I was the dumb fool. They had gotten me into this seemingly impossible situation and they expected me to squirm and I'll admit I was starting to wiggle a bit. But I was determined not to let it beat me.

Simpkins called later in the week and told me that they had scheduled a preliminary hearing the following week. Again he suggested we talk. He also said that he had gotten the results back from my session with Dr. Goldman. My first thought was that this would be very entertaining.

When I returned to Simpkins office, I had decided to be a bit more observant than last time. The same secretary was in the outer office and, as coldly and official as last time, she told me to step into the lawyer's office. Again, Simpkins was seated at his desk, his eyes fixed on the typed page. Because of the angle, I couldn't see what was on it, but judging by the look on his face, I assumed he was studying some information regarding an important case. I scanned the room again as I waited for him to acknowledge my presence. I noticed that the painting looked authentic and that the plaques on the wall were mostly for marksmanship. The one in the center cited him as a Citizen of the Year for San Francisco from about fifteen years earlier. It sickened me to see that one when I thought that he was probably involved in this whole scheme.

I hadn't thought long about it when I heard him start talking to me. He repeated the charge and what had gone on so far. All of this, he had already told me. Then he told me about the upcoming hearing. It would be in front of a judge and the District Attorney would be presenting their case and their evidence. He told me that no one else would be there and from this hearing the judge would determine the next step. He said not to worry but to do and say just what he told me to do and say. He handed me a large manila envelope which seemed to contain about thirty or forty sheets of paper. He called it my homework and told me to learn everything in that envelope before that hearing. He intended to quiz me on it because that envelope contained the key to beating this rap. I didn't get a chance to open it in his office. He insisted that I take it home and study it. I needed to be able to absorb all of it.

I almost walked out without asking what the psychiatrist had said. Just then he looked at me and said frankly, that I was a schizophrenic.

CHAPTER X

THE LIBRARY

Again, I drove home in a daze. I thought that it had to be just part of his plan to get me off on the charge. He had some psychiatrist buddy pronounce me insane and then the courts would take pity and let me go but not out on the streets, that I was sure of. Before going home, I made a stop at the library to find out just what kind of nut I was supposed to be. Things were getting stranger by the minute.

Being the middle of a weekday, I was able to get a parking place right in front of the library. It was a flat, modern building with lots of glass and metal. The windows were tinted so dark that in the afternoon sun they looked almost like mirrors. I had been told once that libraries had to use tinted glass to protect the books from the harmful rays. It made sense. There was a large concrete plaza in the front with little trees evenly spaced, each one confined in a round opening in the pavement. I walked up the steps and entered the brightly lit foyer.

I had only been there once before and that was to return some books for Bev. I knew enough from my college days that everything was organized by number and a check of the catalog system would yield a particular book's location. I sat down in front of a small desk containing files of cards. Then I began scanning subjects: schizophrenia, insanity and the law, and psychosis treatment. They conveniently had little pieces of paper and short pencils, like the kind you always took from miniature golf courses, sitting by the files, so you could write down the numbers as you looked them up. I found that particularly helpful since I hadn't brought any with me.

I must have been thoroughly engrossed in my searching because I didn't hear anyone come up behind me. A voice startled me and I whirled around to find a smiling librarian asking me if I was finding what I needed. She said that she had noticed that I had been at the desk longer than normal and asked again if she could help me find something. I told her I was doing a college paper and the types of topics I was looking up. She directed me to the books I had written down and also suggested that I try looking in the periodical section. There I would be able to get the most current information on the topics. She added that professors really liked students, who used the periodical files.

I took her advice and spent the next three hours combing through the periodical guides and the vault of magazines and microfilm. She was right, there was a lot of current information there to supplement and update the books that I also checked out. Before leaving, I made a point of thanking her for her help. I took my checked out materials and walked out on to the plaza. Finding a vacant bench under a tree, I sat down and began reading through the book on the top of the stack. Although I was only thirty feet from the street, it was very peaceful there.

My new lifestyle had begun to distort my sense of time. I was supposed to stay at home unless a real need arose for me to go out. I had no job to go to, I had no friends coming by to see me. I had only my growing loneliness to deal with. I ate when the urge hit me. I played my stereo when I felt like some music. I laid in bed until I felt like getting up. I was becoming lazy and started to gain a few pounds. I read a lot in the books I had gotten from the library. I read the profile of a schizophrenic over and over but could not see myself fitting the mold. The more I thought about it, the more it seemed clear that I was being set up. And the more

I thought about being set up, the more I realized that I was utterly defenseless. Time was moving very slow.

I didn't hear from Simpkins for another week. I can only remember three other calls during that time. My mother called because she hadn't heard from me in a long time and naturally thought something bad had happened. I assured her that everything was fine. I had just been very busy and had lost track of how long it had been since I last called.

Charles Slater called one evening to tell me he was concerned about me. He assured me that my job would be waiting for me as soon as all of this mess had been cleaned up. He said some nice things that made me feel good. I thanked him for calling.

The third call was from Bev. She said she had been thinking about me and was wondering if there was anything I needed. She offered to run to the store for me or things like that. I told her that what I would really like would be for her to come over and spend the night or the weekend with me. She said she didn't think it was such a good idea right then but would keep in touch. She asked me if I still had her telephone number. I told her yes but I thought, what's the point.

Her call upset me. It seemed like for the entire time, since I met her, whenever I got upset, it was because of her. And at the same time I was crazy about her. I couldn't be with her enough.

Oh yeah, I also got a call from some guy trying to sell me the evening newspaper with free home delivery.

The call from Simpkins had been expected. I had been expecting it for days, actually. He just said that things were going along smoothly although the hearing had been postponed for a week. He asked me if I had studied the information in the envelope and I said yes. Actually, I had forgotten where I had left it when I walked back in that evening. I wasn't in a very cooperative mood and I think he sensed it. But rather than make a case out of it, he just let it go. After he hung up I realized that he hadn't asked me how I was doing.

That was just one more thing that made me think he really wasn't too concerned about my welfare. He was in it for the money and somebody was obviously paying him well. After all, he hadn't asked me for one penny. With the way my luck had been running, I figured he was being paid by the same guys who wasted Jack. I couldn't help but feel miserable considering how hopeless things were becoming. There was a time when I would have jumped right back and fought off any adversary. But like I said, I had been getting lazy. I was beginning to lie on the sofa and stare at the imperfections in the ceiling and think about how hopeless I felt. I would weigh that against my old desire to fight back and stand up for what was right. Hopelessness began to consistently win out and often I would find myself lying there with tears rolling down my cheeks and my breathing heavy laden. I just didn't seem to care anymore.

If I didn't really care anymore then it didn't really matter if I stayed home or not. What was going to happen to me was going to happen regardless of what I did to try and prevent it. Having finally reasoned that out, I decided I could use a beer and left for my old haunt near the yard.

As I approached the small parking lot, a sudden weird feeling came over me. This was the place where I had met Jack Dempsey. This was where we had met and talked about our plans. This is where he had agreed to help me blow the whole thing wide open. I stopped sharply but out of traffic. I couldn't go in there ever again. After about five minutes I realized that this was not the only bar in town and I drove off, heading back toward the city.

It felt good driving around because I had removed all of the chains that had been holding me back. After what that lawyer had said, I felt guilty walking to the corner for a loaf of bread. But it didn't matter anymore. Whatever was going to happen was going to happen. I was going to enjoy myself until then.

I found a club that was intensely lit in neon shapes that could be interpreted in many ways. I went in and squinted to find a table in the darkness. It seemed awfully crowded for a weeknight. There was a little jazz combo playing softly in one corner and crowded tables of people, mostly couples, spread evenly throughout the place. It was a really neat little place, nothing like the gaudy exterior implied. I found a free table off to one side, near the back, and sat down. The waitress was there in a flash and took my order for a beer and a bowl of pretzels like I had seen on some of the other tables as I walked in. I made myself comfortable. I was feeling good.

Everything about that place said "relaxed." The soft light, the soft music, and the soft, muffled sounds of the voices around me felt good.

The waitress returned with my beer and the pretzels and told me she would run a tab. As my eyes became accustomed to the dark, I began to scan the room, observing the people at the neighboring tables. They were mostly couples and mostly about my age. Everyone seemed to be dressed fairly well and everyone was totally absorbed in the jazz oozing from the corner. The combo was very good. Before long I was hypnotized by their melodic sounds.

I was brought abruptly out of my trance by the voice of a man standing next to my table. He was with a young lady, I assumed his date, and he was asking if they could share my table as the rest of the club seemed to be full now. I had no problem with that because I was in a good mood and he seemed like quite a pleasant kind of guy. And his girlfriend was quite attractive. They turned toward the stage and like everybody else in this most unusual place, became entranced by the music. It was only when the band stopped for a break did they turn around and speak to me. First, he thanked me for letting them sit there. I didn't see that as necessary since I had been the only one at a table for four. Then he introduced himself and his girlfriend. His name was Tim and he worked as an accountant for one of the big hospitals in the city. His girlfriend was named Erin and she worked in a record store, but she was spending a lot of time trying to get a break into movies. Not as an actress, though. She had spent her college days learning to be a director and she was trying to land a position on the crew of a major motion picture. I wished her well even though I was thinking that it all sounded like a far-fetched dream. She was so pretty that I figured she would have had an easier time trying for an actress role.

They had met at an outdoor jazz festival a few weeks earlier and this was their second time at that club. In spite of the vast differences between their occupations and dreams, they made a very neat couple. I didn't tell them the real truth about me, of course. I doubted whether they would have felt very comfortable if they knew they were sharing a table with an accused murderer. I told them that I was just a lowly government employee and was out on vacation. I said that I had stumbled upon that place entirely by accident and had been totally knocked out by it. They nodded. They understood what I was talking about. As we paused in our conversation, the combo took their places in the corner and began a set of Dave Brubeck tunes. The entire room was captivated. Before we realized it, it was closing time.

Tim and Erin asked if I wanted to join them for a bite to eat. They were heading for an all-night cafe two blocks down the street. They had the greatest omelets, Tim said. Erin agreed. I accepted their invitation and the three of us strolled down the street as if we didn't have a care in the world.

Since it was after two in the morning, the place was nearly empty. We got a booth in the back and we all ordered omelets and coffee. We didn't really talk much, just the continuation of the small talk from the Club, but I began to sense that something was not quite right. I felt like they were hiding something from me. Or maybe that they felt I was hiding something from them. When I had finished eating, I paid the check and politely excused myself, thanking them for a pleasant evening. They waved to me through the window as I walked down the sidewalk to my car. I hoped the rest of their evening met their expectations. I knew where I would want to have been if I was with a girl as fine as that. It did seem strange, though, that they were out on such a date on a weeknight.

The whole incident with the two of them seemed so insignificant. It wasn't like I was going to see them again. It had been a pleasant evening and their company for that brief time just added to my own enjoyment. We went our own ways and I didn't think anything of it until about two weeks later.

I was still on house arrest and I got a call about ten o'clock asking me if I wanted to see a big jazz/pop group that was playing downtown. It was Tim and he said he had extra tickets. I told him that I wasn't really feeling well and would have to pass this time. But I thanked him for thinking about me. What I didn't think of at the time was where he had gotten my phone number.

Even though it gave me a good feeling knowing that someone out there was thinking about me, I couldn't help but remember that strange feeling that had come over me in the cafe. I had just felt like something wasn't right. It was like they were covering up something.

After I hung up the phone with Tim, I started to think that maybe I should have gone just to try and figure out what their secret was. But I didn't know how to get in touch with either of them. I sunk back into a chair and continued listening to the Beatles' Abbey Road album.

CHAPTER XI

ERIN

About eleven-thirty, I was awakened by a gentle knocking at the door. It wasn't a pounding but a soft sound as if the person on the other side of the door was afraid of waking me. It took me a few seconds to get out of the chair. The position in which I had been lying had left my back painfully stiff and my left leg totally without feeling. I hobbled to the door just in time to catch a petite figure turning away. The light from my living room caught her as she turned to look back. It was Erin. She said she had just stopped by to make sure I was okay.

Tim had told her that I had not been feeling well. I invited her in and she sat on the chair across from the sofa. I fixed us drinks as she looked around my place. When I returned with the drinks she asked me to put on some soft music and for the next hour we talked and drank. She asked me about my job and I was pretty evasive until the liquor started hitting me. I'm not sure what I said after that but what I am sure about was that all of the sudden she wrapped herself around me and kissed me deep. I was taken totally by surprise but it felt too good to stop. I held her tight. Within minutes we were on the couch. Moments later we were naked. She made love to me unlike anyone ever had before. I lost consciousness about two-thirty. When I awoke the next morning, she was gone but she had left behind a note with a small silver ring folded inside. On the paper was a short poem that rhymed but made absolutely no sense to me. I don't remember what it said. But the silver ring is still in my pocket.

I went back to that club several times, both on weeknights and weekends. But I never saw either Erin or Tim again. At least I can't say that I ever recognized them again. I still see Erin in my dreams occasionally, though. The only reason that I bring it up is because it was probably the only good thing that has happened to me since the whole thing started. And yet, somehow it seemed connected. How did she know where I lived? Could she have been there to try and get information out of me? I don't think I ever passed out from booze before that. Could I have been drugged?

Simpkins finally got back to me and basically told me to meet him at the courthouse on a certain day and to make sure I looked clean and neat. Did he really think I would show up at a hearing about a murder charge looking like some kind of vagrant? I had lost a lot of things by that time but not my hygiene or common sense.

I met him outside the courtroom and he began briefing me on what to do and say. He told me that there were still some outstanding issues at stake and we had to proceed cautiously. He told me not to say anything unless I was answering a specific question and then, to glance at him for any signs. It seemed like I was playing a part in a movie. I told him I would do like he said. I told him not to worry. He didn't look like he was worried at all.

Other than traffic court for a speeding ticket a few years back, I had only seen a courtroom or a trial on TV or in the movies. I felt very vulnerable and somewhat afraid. I sat where I was told. I looked around to see if there was a crowd of spectators, but there were only a few young people that could have been law students seated towards the back. Just as I was about to turn back to face the judge's bench, the door opened and in walked Mike and Charles Slater. Then I felt embarrassed as well as afraid. In my mind I tried to guess their motives for being there. Maybe they were character references or maybe they just came to see me fed to the lions.

The room was called to order and the judge, an elderly black man, took his seat at the front of the room. He read the charges that I already knew and then read a list of objections that had been filed by Simpkins. It seemed that my lawyer had been busy after all. The judge called my lawyer and the prosecuting guy up to the front and talked to them quietly for what seemed like a long time. Even though they were talking in low voices so the rest of the room couldn't hear, I think I got the gist of what was going on. Simpkins had contested the charges because there was no real evidence, not even a body. Everything being used against me had been contrived to suit a half assed investigation and satisfy a demanding lieutenant. Simpkins had no intention of making me stand trial for murder under these circumstances. When he returned to his seat, he looked like it wasn't over, though. He told me that the judge was almost convinced but wanted to hear the evidence from each side before writing it off.

The prosecutor presented everything he had which consisted of the witness's statement that I was seen leaving around the estimated time of the murder, the fingerprint analysis, and the murder weapon. He also cited the psychological examination that Simpkins' buddy did. The judge seemed interested in that, and picking it up from my lawyer's documents, browsed it briefly. The prosecution rested.

The judge turned to Simpkins and told him it was his turn. He repeated what he had apparently said when he was up at the bench and asked permission to call a few witnesses which he was granted. The first one he called was Mike. After the initial name and relationship stuff, Simpkins asked Mike to briefly describe how I had come to California and what kind of work I did at the yard. He told it exactly the way it had happened, coming out from Florida and how I had transitioned into the job smoothly. Mike told the judge how I had blended nicely into the department and that he could not imagine me committing a crime like that. He then surprised me when he continued by saying that I had become antisocial lately and had been operating under some kind of delusion that there was a big espionage ring trying to sabotage things. He said that I had resisted his suggestions to seek counseling and after I had reported my suspicions, he had been very concerned with my safety and, ultimately with how I would be accepted back into the group at the yard. I knew that there was hate as well as astonishment in my eyes as I stared at him. Either he didn't notice or he didn't care.

Simpkins called up Charles Slater next and his testimony was not as strong as Mike's had been but his looks didn't hurt things. Chuck wore a tailored black pin-striped suit that was one size too small, which emphasized his straight as an arrow posture and compensated for the fact that he always leaned slightly forward. From the first day I met him, I thought that he looked like a domesticated African head hunter like Edgar Rice Burroughs depicted in one of his novels. I had always respected him. He talked about how thorough I had been on the job and how he always had felt fortunate having me on the team. He, too, said that he couldn't imagine I was involved in a violent crime like that. In fact he mentioned that I had once voiced my concern about working on equipment for ships that were designed exclusively for the purpose of destruction. It was, rather, my commitment to the safety of the submarine occupants and the welfare of our country that were my driving forces. Chuck was on my side.

Simpkins then asked him if he had read the psychological report and when Slater said yes, he asked him to comment. He really didn't want to answer that question and after a few minutes he responded that he really didn't understand all the scientific talk. But when faced with direct questions worded in simple form, he indicated that he had to agree with most of the points. When he left the stand, his head was hanging low. He didn't look at me as he passed. But then, even at work, he never really looked up at anyone when he walked.

In my own mind, it seemed that those proceedings had strayed off the mark. There had not been one mention of the murder in a long time and the prosecuting guys had not even cross examined. I searched my head for an answer as to what was going on but my long idleness had made me sluggish.

Simpkins obviously was picking up my concern and leaning toward my ear, whispered that we were doing fine and that the murder rap would be thrown out very shortly. Stay cool, he said.

There was another session at the bench and this time the prosecuting guy looked pretty sad. When he got back to his table, he started putting away his papers but he didn't leave.

The judge then spoke, ruling that there was in fact no evidence that could constitute a charge against me for murder. He therefore dropped all charges. But instead of stopping there, he went on to say that there was sufficient reason to believe that I possessed some degree of psychological imbalance and he was releasing me into the custody of a Dr. Samuel Goldman, a psychiatrist, who wasn't there. The judge stated further that he had briefed Simpkins on the procedures required. Again, I was more confused than ever.

Simpkins told me to just be cool and he would fill me in on what was happening as soon as the court was adjourned. I followed him to a small room across the hall from the courtroom that I imagined served as a consultation room. It had at least six chairs and a small conference type table. There were no windows.

He proceeded to fill me in on exactly what had happened in the courtroom. He figured that I didn't understand. He knew that the evidence the prosecution used was circumstantial and contrived. He had been about 75% sure that he could get it thrown out without resorting to other means. But because he didn't want to play games with that last 25%, he filed the psychological report as his backup. The report had been the deciding factor. Since the judge was a humanitarian, he had dropped all the charges in return for the promise that I would receive proper medical attention. Simpkins smiled and said we were home free. Then he started outlining what I had to do. I was no longer accused of any crime so I was free to come and go. Thanks, I thought. I would have to start seeing Dr. Goldman on a regular basis starting that week. He didn't know if the judge would monitor any of it but he said we had to play the game. We had to play the game? I asked him about going back to work. He made me wait a minute while he went out into the hallway and brought back Mike. Apparently he had been waiting outside for his cue.

Mike congratulated me as soon as he came in. He told me that nobody believed the charges. He asked who that Jack Dempsey person was, anyway. I didn't want to talk about it and sensing that, he changed the subject. He told me that my report at the yard had caused quite a stir. The FBI had been called in to work with the agents at the yard and they had really torn the place apart. They had gone through everything and had even searched the houses and apartments of my coworkers. Two technicians had been suspended without pay until they could be cleared. The atmosphere there was very hostile. People were not just mad at me for starting it all but they were also mad at each other. Morale was virtually nonexistent. He told me that luckily they hadn't found anything so the army of investigators was beginning to look other ways.

Mike said it would not be good to come back to work, especially in the health and safety office. He said that Charles Slater had been checking into openings elsewhere on the yard and at neighboring government installations. He wanted to get me back working as soon as possible but back at the same place was not possible. He never stopped smiling the whole time he spoke. I wondered how much of what he was telling me was true. I had gotten no information from work since I had left weeks ago. I couldn't believe that a real investigation would not have turned up anything at all. No wonder Mike was smiling. He was getting the best of both worlds, no investigation to hamper his operation, and me out of the way and discredited.

He assured me that he and Slater were doing everything that they could to get me back on the job. Then, as he was getting ready to leave, he told me not to worry about money. I was still being covered under the shipyard long term disability plan. He asked me if I had been getting checks mailed to my place.

I said, "Yes." The process would remain the same until I was back at work. He patted me on the back as he left. He was loving every part of this.

Simpkins had made a few phone calls while I was talking to Mike and then he took up the conversation. He told me to be at Dr. Goldman's office the following morning. I was going to be his responsibility then.

He said, "It's been a pleasure and I'm glad that it worked out like we planned." I thanked him. We walked out of the room together but then went in different directions as we headed for our respective cars.

I couldn't describe how I felt at that moment. I still can't describe it. But I did not see a sunny future.

I still don't know who paid Simpkins bill but I didn't. I never saw him again after we left that room. It's strange, looking back, how many people seemed to just disappear. I drove into the hills overlooking the city and just sat in the sun. On the way home I stopped at an Italian restaurant and had a splendid dinner complete with a whole bottle of Chianti. I was feeling no pain when I left.

It was dark when I finally reached home. I still wasn't walking real straight, so I was holding on tightly to the railing as I climbed the stairs. I could see some of my neighbors peeking through their curtains. I was wishing that I had something clever to shout at them but I was too involved in getting to my own place to worry about it. Most of them didn't even say hello to me anyway. Hell with them, I thought. My key found the doorknob keyhole and the one for the deadbolt lock easily even though I had not turned the light on when I had left. But then, when I left I had no idea that I was going to be late getting home. I switched on the living room light and spread out across the sofa, one leg hanging over the edge and resting on the floor. I had always heard that you should do that when you're drunk so the room doesn't spin. It seemed to be working because I fell asleep. I awoke about ten-thirty the next morning with an outrageous headache. I pulled a piece of paper out of my ·pocket. It was an appointment card for Dr. Goldman. My appointment was at ten.

CHAPTER XII

DR. GOLDMAN I PRESUME

When I called his office, Dr. Goldman was furious. He reminded me that I had been late to our previous appointment and that he could not tolerate irresponsible patients. When I told him that I was leaving right then, he said he had another patient coming and he was not going to keep that person waiting just because of me. I figured that he didn't care why I was late so I just said nothing. He gave me another appointment for four o'clock that afternoon. I knew what the first part of our conversation would be about.

I hung up the phone and went to the medicine cabinet to find something for my head. I was never much of a pill taker so I had to read the labels on some old prescriptions that were shoved behind my shaving gear. I found bottle with a half dozen tablets from when I had two teeth pulled. The label said "for pain" so I popped three of them. Then I went to the kitchen for something to eat. I had the sense of being a caveman satisfying my needs by priority.

For the past weeks, since all this started, I had not been eating very well. I could cook pretty good but I just had no desire to. I had been living on pizzas, fast food, and cookies. I remember squatting in front of the open refrigerator door and taking inventory of its contents. There were three slices of pizza stacked one on top of another on a paper plate. They were two days old and the top piece showed the effects of not being covered in the refrigerator. It was dried out and the cheese had taken on a translucent glow. More appealing was a container of macaroni and cheese, the boxed variety, that although was older, had retained its youthful, good looks. I grabbed for a carton of milk but poured it down the drain when I 'noticed that the "sell by" date had passed eleven days earlier. On a better day I would have smelled it first. I settled on a soft drink and began heating the macaroni and cheese slowly on the stove. My head was still pounding but I was incredibly hungry.

As I sat down at the table with the pan of steaming pasta, my head began to reel slightly. It had to have been the narcotic in the pain pills. I ate slowly and began to relax. The soft drink was an off brand grape soda and although the flavor was not as bold as the more expensive brands, it was satisfying.

I put the pan in the sink and retreated back to the living room. I clicked on the stereo and chose a record of big hits from the seventies that I had bought on a discount rack back in Florida. I liked most of the songs on it because they reminded me of college and good times. I stretched out on my back on the floor and let the music have its way with me. It felt good.

By two o'clock my headache had for the most part passed and I decided to head downtown to Goldman's office. The traffic had caught me last time and if I got there early, it could only be to my advantage in dealing with the shrink. He might see it as a reforming trend. The traffic was unusually light and I was parked on the lot next to his building at two-fifty. The day seemed bright in spite of the haze. I took a walk around the block to kill some time. Living and working where I did, I had never taken the opportunity to stroll around just for the sake of strolling.

The doctor's building was a massive concrete structure void of all character. There were no windows on the ground level and only thin strips of glass pointing to the sky above that. It looked kind of sterile. Maybe that was why so many doctors and lawyers had offices there. It was called the Downtown Professional Building. The name was as imaginative as everything else about it. I walked all the way around the block, and although it only met the street for about half way around, it was always looming over my head. Around the rest of the block were shops falling into four basic categories. There were at least six pornographic book and video stores, four massage parlors, three travel agencies, and three religious book stores. What impressed me most was the sense of peaceful coexistence that reigned over all. I wondered which of these shops was Dr. Goldman's favorite. He had to have frequented at least a few of them in the time he had been here. I decided he was the massage parlor type. When I reached the building entrance again, I went in and took the elevator to the seventh floor. It opened to the same bland hallway that had greeted me on my previous visit, not that I had expected anything different. I read the names on the doors as I made my way to Dr. Goldman's. They all seemed to be either oriental or Jewish.

The waiting room was similarly drab with pastoral landscape prints on the walls framed in gold painted wood. I bought a similar painting several years ago at Sears. Mary has it now, I suppose. There was a desk off to one side but, as before, it looked like it had never been used, except as a place for the mailman to put the mail. When I walked in, Dr. Goldman came out of his office almost immediately. He must have had some kind of signal wired to the door. Even though I was twenty minutes early, he had a foul look on his face.

He told me that he hoped my uncooperative behavior was not an indication of the way things were going to be. He said that he had been given responsibility for my rehabilitation and that he would not tolerate my insolent attitude. I had no idea where he was coming up with those crazy notions but he was too busy laying down the law to listen to my objections. He repeated that if I didn't cooperate with him, I would be turned back over to the state, and he was sure that I didn't want that. By now, I just wanted to get that session over with.

Finally we sat down in his office and got down to business. He started by briefly explaining what he had determined from my first, and only other, visit. Basically, he felt I was a sick man. He explained that everything I had ever done had a meaning.

I found that somewhat entertaining. To Goldman, there was a hidden meaning in every action and if he couldn't find a meaning in one of his books, he would make one up. At least he didn't try to tell me that I subconsciously wanted to screw my mother or anything.

Then he began to layout his plan for treating me. There would, of course, be many sessions in his office talking about every topic known to man except possibly baseball, I thought. We started right then and his first question was how I felt about the ordeal of the past weeks. I wasn't ready for such a direct question yet. After fumbling for words for a few minutes, I told him how I was sure that the whole thing had been trumped up just to shut me up and take the heat off the real guilty people. I told him that the investigation that I had worked hard to get started had lost all its steam now that I was discredited as some kind of loony. He was listening very intently. I told him how I hated sitting around my house on house arrest waiting for him or a lawyer to call and summon me to their offices. I guess I went on for well over an hour and I suppose I sounded pretty hostile because when I finished, he told me it was good to get all of those negative feelings out in the open. I personally didn't feel much better.

After a short pause while he wrote feverishly on his little steno pad, he told me that my time was up and that he wanted to see me again at the end of the week, same time. He had a pleased look on his face and that bothered me for some reason.

When I walked out of the lobby onto the street, I could see that traffic was atrocious. It would take me hours to get home in that mess. I decided to take a walk around Goldman's block again. I browsed in one of the adult book stores but I really wasn't in the mood for that kind of entertainment although I almost bought a copy of a video that I remembered watching in college. It wasn't worth twenty bucks.

I wandered into one of the travel agencies and picked up some information on Caribbean cruises. The agent on duty was a woman probably in her late fifties who was so helpful that I almost didn't realize she was there. She stapled her business card onto one of the booklets, the one she had been pitching and sent me on home like a teacher sending a student home after the first day of school. I almost dropped all the literature into a trash receptacle as I rounded the corner but I changed my mind. Ahead of me was a sign that said Bar and Lounge, which looked good. The place was small and not particularly dark but it was clean. The music was being supplied by the radio but the five other people in the place didn't seem to mind. I sat down at a table and a waitress asked me if I wanted a menu. I told her yeah and a beer. She was cute and very short. As I drank that first beer, I scanned the listing of sandwiches and salads. I ordered a triple-decker club, onion rings, and another beer. All arrived promptly just as the radio began a triple play of Beatle songs. I tried to flag down the waitress for another beer when I caught a glimpse of a familiar face sitting at the bar. It was a guy named Kurt who worked at the yard. He was some other type of technician and I had worked on projects with him maybe once or twice. As soon as he saw me, he laid a bill on the bar and took off for the door. I tried to call him but he had no intention of looking back. I didn't follow him but it made me think that maybe he was following me. Why else would he be downtown in the same block as my doctor.

I didn't think about it for long, though. My onion rings were getting cold. I knew they had been following me all along and I had just caught one of them off guard. My thoughts were interrupted by the waitress answering my call. Another beer arrived seconds later.

Again, I had drunk more than I should have but found my car without any trouble. I sat there with the engine running and the radio playing for about fifteen minutes till I felt ready to drive home. Traffic was much lighter then and I had no problems. I stopped at the market and picked up a few essentials and arrived home just as it was getting dark. I could hear my phone ringing as I approached the door but there was no way I could make it inside to answer it. It stopped ringing as I swung open the door. I figured if it was important, they'd call back and went into the kitchen with my bags.

I went back into the living room to close the front door when my eyes suddenly caught a sheet of paper that had been lying unnoticed for some time. It was the list I had started trying to recapture what had happened to me. It was now grossly incorrect. I had gotten off on the murder charge but now I was labeled a nut case. I was beginning to think that there were some things that I just wasn't meant to figure out.

Suddenly, the phone rang again. It was Mary.

CHAPTER XIII

BEV

Her voice on the other end of the line pierced my brain like a hot skewer. She was the absolute last person I would have expected to call me. Immediately I was bombarded with thoughts about how it had been before. I conjured pictures of her in my mind, her hair blowing on a bright Florida beach, her eyes flirting with mine as she handed me suntan lotion to smooth on her shoulders. For a second, I was back there. But when her voice spoke again, I knew I was not.

She asked me how I was doing and I told her fine. She said she had called my office that afternoon and they had told her that I was on a leave of absence. She asked me again if I was all right. I didn't really answer because I knew her well enough that if she suspected something, she would keep after it until I either told her or was rude to her. There had been times when she had wanted both.

I started asking her about how she was making out and even though I was sure she was lying, she said she was lonely. She had never filed any divorce papers after I had left. She said she thought I would come back. She wanted me back. Or at least that's what she said.

I told her that I thought moving here had been good for me. The job had worked out well and I was enjoying being a Californian. I knew she wasn't buying any of it but I kept laying it on. I was still feeling the effects of the alcohol and was probably a bit looser with my tongue than I would have been normally. I can picture myself sitting there on the arm of the sofa, with the phone receiver in one hand, nodding as I rambled on and on. I figured that since she had called me, she must have been willing to pay. She cut me off short after a few minutes. She said she could tell that something was wrong and practically begged me to tell her the truth. She was trying her teary eyed offense on me, and even though I had seen it a hundred times before, it was still beginning to work. The mounting tension was broken by a knock at the door.

I told Mary to hold and walked to the door slowly enough to slow my heartbeat down. When I swung the door inward, Bev was standing on the other side. She looked fabulous. She was wearing a black leather skirt that was well above her knees.

I suddenly became aware of the crisis before me. I had to either chase Bev away and get back to the phone, or invite Bev in and give Mary an excuse for a call back. I told Mary I would call her back later that night. I said I needed time to get my head clear after not having heard from her in such a long time. I didn't know what she really thought but I knew that I couldn't handle her on such short notice. At least with Bev there were no real secrets.

Bev didn't ask who was on the phone. She just said she was filling my request. The last time I had asked her to come over, she had declined. I figured that now that I wasn't a murderer, people could associate with me again. That kind of thing made me wonder just what kind of friends I had out here. But Bev was different. She didn't come to see me because she was told not to and she couldn't take the chance. But she had called and she seemed to really care. And now she was there in front of me looking like she wanted to apologize for all my troubles and offer herself as atonement.

My head suddenly felt like it was going to explode. In my entire life I had never been in a situation where there were two women in my life at the same time. I was never a great looking guy, just kind of ordinary. I didn't play sports in school. Oh, I could usually make the team but then I would sit on the bench the whole season and watch the game go by. I was a better than average student in my classes and actually did better in college. I was a good observer and a good organizer and that made my school work time efficient. It seemed like when a woman finally showed an interest in me it was because, they had seen the real me inside. I had always been glad of that.

Mary had been a person like that. We had met socially several times before she ever went out with me. And we spent a lot of time getting to know each other before we ever got serious. I think she understood me. She just couldn't understand the changes going on around us and how they were affecting our relationship.

Bev had never spent any time dwelling on the past but rather looked right into my soul and my heart. I think she also knew me well. And when I had needed and wanted someone, she had been there, up until a few weeks ago, that is. On that particular night, I chose Bev, because she was there and I knew that she would cause me no pain. I couldn't say that about Mary.

Bev had sat down on the sofa after tossing her jacket across the chair. Her skirt rode up so high, there was an immediate increase in my body temperature. She looked beautiful. I sat beside her and she kissed me softly on the cheek. Then she turned so she was facing me and shifted her weight away from me. She said she had been worried about me and had to know that I was okay. I thanked her for the lawyer and she just smiled and nodded. A friend of the family she said. I asked her how work was going and she just shrugged and said it was the same as always. I thought, how could it be the same as always if I wasn't around. She read my mind and added that she meant it was like before I came. I had little to offer her in the way of food and drink and I offered to take her down the block to a sweet little Italian restaurant. She declined, she had eaten before she came over. She seemed to be moving farther away from me on the couch. Sex was obviously out of the question. I asked her why she had really come over. She looked me straight in the eyes and said she just cared about me. Then she stood up, grabbed her jacket, and walked to the door. I tried to stop her but she wrapped her arms around me and kissed me hard. Then she was out the door into the night, her heels clicking on the concrete terrace. I didn't follow.

I called Mary about an hour or so later. I had to cool down and get my head back on track before I could do battle with her. The alcohol had worn off partially due to the elapsed time and partly due to Bev. Regardless, I was ready for her.

She answered on the second ring and all was quiet in the background. She sounded sweet as ever and we started our conversation again, but this time on my nickel. She didn't push the "what's wrong" angle this time but just talked softly about the good times we had had and how she missed them. She asked why I didn't I come back for a while since I was on leave. I declined the offer. The subject was changed and we talked about an hour more. Then she popped the question, could she come out and stay with me a while in California. She said she had vacation and some personal leave saved up and that it would give us a chance to get to know each other again.

The whole phone call had been setting me up for that.

She had been so nice that I had no solid reason to say no.

But I just couldn't save yes right then. If she came out here, I would have to explain my situation and I wasn't ready to do that with anyone. Most people that knew me out here had at least a basic knowledge of the past few weeks. I just didn't want to have to explain. She could tell that I was balking on her request and after a short pause, she asked if I was living with someone. I replied, "no." She took the hint and said that maybe we should talk again in a day or so. I thought that was a good idea and said goodbye, wishing her the best and thanking her for calling. After I hung up, I remembered that I had called her.

Throughout this whole ordeal, I had been spending much of my free time, which was most of my time, trying to understand everything that had gone on. It was all moving so fast and I just couldn't seem to catch up with it. The reality was that I was still out of work, although getting paid. I was being forced to see this psychiatrist who liked me about as much as I liked him, and my wife who I hadn't seen in seven months was suddenly trying to get back into my life. My normal thought process would search for connections since often things that happen in your life are linked. The job and the shrink were definitely related. I figured that when he decided I was sane enough, I would get a call from the shipyard telling me to come back. But the call from Mary was totally out of the blue. Maybe she was on the level and was lonely since breaking up with her new "boyfriend." But also, she might have been just being her conniving self. She possessed that character trait and if she wanted something, she would do whatever it took to get it. What did she want?

I didn't mention Mary to Dr. Goldman at my next visit. He would probably have come up with some Freudian interpretation that would have done my case no good. But at that appointment I was entirely cooperative, answering his questions in nice long responses. He seemed very pleased. I knew he would be. At the end of the session, though, he asked me why I was suddenly working with him rather than against him. I told him that the only way I was going to be able to go back to work was to stop fighting. I thought that was a good answer. He seemed less impressed but answered that he would see me the following week.

The next day was Friday and I was shocked to get a call from Charles Slater. Like he always did, he asked how I was doing. Then he said he had some good news for me. Dr. Goldman had notified him that I was ready to return to work and that the return to the routine would be good for me. He repeated what he had said before, that he would not put me back in the same job with the same people. He was afraid there might be too many lingering bad feelings there and he did not want to start new problems. He said he had found me a spot in Disposition, a department located in a satellite building away from everything and that was known as Uncle Sam's Garbage Can.

This was where every part or assembly that was rejected anywhere on the yard was brought to for disposition. This department would inspect and evaluate to determine what to do with the items. Sometimes they would send the parts back to the manufacturer for replacement. Sometimes the assembly would be returned for repair. And sometimes they would just throw it in the trash. Whatever was done with it, it was up to this department to decide. I had never been there although everybody knew of its existence. In my own mind, I could never imagine someone applying for a job like that. But now, that's where I was headed and I would have a chance to see, first hand, what kind of people handled a job like that.

I called Mary on Saturday, when the rates were lower. I told her that I was starting back to work the following week, so if she were to come out we probably wouldn't have a lot of time to spend together. I thought that my reverse psychology would back her off but it didn't. She took my comments instead as an invitation with limitations. I realized that I had planned this one poorly. She went on to say that she could explore a bit during the days and we could go out to dinner like we had in the past. No matter how much I worked, we would still have the nights, she said. She was excited. I was spiritless.

After hanging up the phone, I immediately called Bev.

She didn't answer. Mary would be arriving Monday evening. I could see that I was going to have a wonderful first day of work.

I reported to the north guard house at the yard on Monday morning. I was on time. All of my paperwork was apparently in order because I had no hassle getting through. I had to wait to be escorted to the building since for reasons that I didn't understand, this disposition area was a secure area. No one could enter without authorization. I was sure I would know soon enough. At exactly eight-thirty, a car stopped beside me and a guy about my age hopped out and strolled to my car. He asked if I was Rob and when I said yes, showing him my orders, he stuck out his hand and introduced himself as Willy Tate. "Follow me", he said.

This building was surrounded by a ten-foot fence with a gate that operated by a code that was punched in on a little pad. We parked right in front of the building which was definitely nicer and more convenient than before. Once inside the building, which also was code accessed, I realized that Willy was the boss. When we entered his office, it was also obvious that he was a Penn State alumnus. There were Nittany Lions everywhere. And Willy was one of the happiest people I had ever run into. I sat down across a large metal desk from him and he spent the next two hours telling me about the operation there. During that entire time, I never heard another person. He said that the stuff was transported to the warehouse at the back of the building and that once it came in, it was ours. We checked it out and we decided what to do with it. We generally had no deadlines and no pressure because we kept everybody else out. He was smiling the whole time. I asked him how many people worked there and he said, you'll meet them. I had noticed a few other cars on the parking lot when we pulled up. From there we took a stroll around the facility, which was certainly not designed to impress anyone. The furniture was old government issue stuff, big metal desks with the paint chipped off, file cabinets with bent doors and holes where the locks used to be. I began to think that all this stuff had come here for disposition and they had kept it all. I learned later that I was right in my assumptions.

The first person I met was an old guy named Rex. He supposedly had been an actor many years before and now was just working towards a pension from the government. He smoked a lot and laughed out loud when he worked. The second person was a maintenance guy, who was assigned to keep everything running. He could fix anything from a sophisticated testing device to the toilets in the bathroom. He never looked at you when you talked to him. I wasn't sure how to take these guys but as we walked to the testing labs, Willy told me not to worry, this was the greatest department on this whole base.

In the lab area I met a woman named Marie. She didn't smile much but rather seemed very dedicated to her work. She was kind of attractive and maybe ten years older than me. There was certainly no romantic interest here but I felt that she was more like me than anyone I had seen so far. There was only one other person in the building and he was an sailor who worked the receiving dock in the back. He was from Georgia and took an immediate liking to me, asking about towns and attractions that he particularly liked. He seemed pleasant enough.

It struck me that this was an unusual group of people stuck out there away from everything and everybody. I thought that maybe that was why I was being assigned to that group. I wasn't sure whether I should be happy about that or whether I should resent it. Willy seemed overjoyed to have me on his team. He spent the entire day giving me my orientation. When I asked him what exactly I would be doing, he just said that there would be plenty of work for me soon enough. I didn't ask him about it anymore.

By using the north gate, there was no backup getting off the yard at quitting time. That seemed like it cut ten minutes off my commute time. And that was good that first evening since I wanted to get home and straighten up a bit before I had to leave to pick-up Mary at the airport. San Francisco International Airport was not a place that I enjoyed. I actually hated going anywhere downtown, so I was glad that the interstate would take me around the city. I was really happy that Mary decided to make the trip, so I just grinned and drove south. It wasn't really that far, it just seemed that way.

I arrived about a half hour before her plane did, which was forty minutes late. I positioned myself towards the back of the crowd and watched for the gate to open and the people to begin streaming out. Mary was one of the last people off and was carrying two overstuffed carry-on bags. It made me feel good that the guys still watched her as she walked. She had lost a bit of weight but her jeans were fitting tight. She almost looked frail, as if the bags were keeping her balanced. It was a humorous sight, silly actually. She must have known it too, because as our eyes met we both burst into laughter. We embraced and then both burst into tears.

CHAPTER XIV

TOGETHER AGAIN

The next morning at work was real tough. I was having a hard time concentrating on the stuff that Willy was showing me and I kept thinking about the night before. We had sat up until four in the morning, drinking herbal tea and talking about whatever had come to our minds. It had been a wonderful evening. But that morning I was paying for it. I couldn't keep my mind focused on any one thing and besides my eyelids having grown extremely heavy, I had developed a powerful headache. During a break, I slipped into the bathroom, there was only one in this building, and scoured the medicine cabinet. I grabbed about four extra strength pain relievers and gulped them down with a paper cup of water. Looking further, I came across some pills marked for mental alertness. I took a few of them. If that didn't perk me up pretty fast, then I figured it would make me sick and I could go home and rest.

It did pick me up but it didn't get rid of the headache or make me sick, so I worked through the whole day. About an hour before quitting time I got paged for a phone call. That was kind of strange because in just two days there, I had realized that the phones never rang. The motley crew that worked there never seemed to be on the phones. By the time I reached the phone I had figured out who it was. I was right, it was Bev. And as I had anticipated, she asked how I was making out on the new job and things like that. I told her that I really couldn't talk right then and that I would have to call her when it was more convenient. She didn't ask when that would be and she didn't ask to come over. I still liked her but she had become so distant in the last few weeks that I decided I really didn't need her. Besides, Mary was in town and I felt like I had a chance to get back on track.

As I also had anticipated, Mary had cooked a fancy dinner for us. It was complete with candles and wine. She must have gone out to the store to get all that stuff since I certainly hadn't kept it in my kitchen cabinets. With the fancy noodles and stuff, she couldn't have gotten them at the corner store. I figured she must have taken a cab to some gourmet grocery store in the area. She had a knack for finding those out-of-the-way offbeat places. And she had told me that she had brought enough money with her that she wouldn't have to depend on me. That was okay because in spite of not having missed a paycheck in all this time, I always seemed to be on the verge of broke. I wasn't doing much eating in those days but I was spending a lot of time attached to a beer bottle.

I liked having Mary around those first few days. I had always felt good when we had gone out together. She was a striking lady and I always felt proud to be with her. But this time there was a little less pressure. She was on her own time and had her own money and she could come and go as she pleased. I went to work each day and when I got home she was there with dinner prepared and a story to tell about her adventures in California. She seemed full of life and that was good. I wasn't sure whether I would be able to keep up with her. When the weekend came I was ready. That week of work had been difficult and trying and draining. I knew driving home that Mary would be expecting us to sample some of the city's night life. Since I was off for the weekend there was no excuse not to party like a fool, just like old times. I almost dreaded coming home that night. I bought two roses from a girl on the corner and started formulating my defense for staying home.

I was shocked when I walked in. Dinner was set as usual and Mary was reading a magazine on the sofa dressed in jeans and a sweatshirt. She didn't look like she had any intention of going out. I was relieved as I handed her the flowers. She hugged me tightly and kissed me on the lips. In the four days she had been here, we had not been intimate. We had hugged a bit and given each other light kisses but we had not made love. Even though we were sharing the same double bed, we had not touched. She was sort of like a tenant sharing my space.

But that night caught me by surprise. She had every intention of staying home and trying to seriously discuss us. Her dinner was simple and delicious. There were two six-packs in the refrigerator. Sitting at the table, she talked while I ate. She wanted us to put the past behind us. We had both made mistakes, and we needed to try and start again fresh, armed with the knowledge of what had gone on before. I found her totally logical and had no reason to dispute her except for the one fact that I wasn't sure I wanted to go back with her. Commitment had become a four letter word with me. I had been alone for a long time and whether or not a person liked being alone, they always knew who they could depend on.

As I helped her clear the dishes, she talked about how she missed the things we did together. She included the way we made love.

Suddenly she stopped. She had forgotten to give me a phone message. Mike had called. She asked me who Mike was and I told her that he was the guy that had helped me get the job out here and that now that I was transferred to a new department, I hadn't seen him in a while. She said I was supposed to call him. She also said that she would like to meet him sometime.

I called Mike then so I wouldn't forget and also just to get it over with. As I suspected, he wanted to congratulate me on being reinstated and getting back to work. He said he was very happy for me. He also wanted to invite me to a party at his house the following night. Nothing big, he said, just a few close friends, all people I knew and people who were glad I was okay. He added that I should bring Mary along. Of course, if he had called earlier and talked to her, he would know she was here.

I joined Mary on the sofa. We had an incredible evening.

We watched an old movie on TV, we told silly stories about our college days, and we ended our moratorium on intimacy. We slept in

STINGRAY THE RUSSIANS ARE LISTENING   **137**

each other's arms and rose together in the morning to the sound of chirping birds.

I felt a little uneasy about the party at Mike's. I was committed to going and Mary seemed excited to meet Mike, he being the person that not only had pulled me away from Florida, but also the one who had given me the opportunity to start again out here. She seemed real enthusiastic and all day she kept asking me questions about what he was like and about my other friends. I told her what she wanted to know although my enthusiasm was noticeably less. We went shopping for most of the afternoon and while she was trying on clothes in one place or another, I had a most interesting thought. Now that I was free, I could pursue my investigation into Mike and his organization. Certainly after what I had been through they wouldn't expect me to continue. Their warning had been very clear. But I could not let it just drop. I had made it my duty to stop that insurrection. They had tried to stop me because I had gotten too close, closer than anyone had dared to get. I just had to be more careful this time. I knew I would have to learn their ways even if it meant joining them for a time. Suddenly the idea of going to Mike's party seemed better and better.

Although Mary had bought quite a bit of overpriced clothes, she dressed in jeans and sweater for the party. I was glad because that was the Mary that I had fallen in love with and that was the way I liked to see her. Other guys liked to see her that way too but in the past I had always known she would be with me. As Mike had said, there were only a few people there, two of my old co-workers and their dates, Judd Perth, and two girls who I had been seen somewhere around the yard. I had actually expected to see Bev even though I thought it could have made things awkward. Mike seemed really happy for me, not just for getting the job, but for being back with Mary. He seemed especially pleased to meet her.

In the course of the first few hours there, everybody made a point of coming up to me and telling me how happy they were that things were back to normal. I wasn't considering things to be back to normal, but since everybody was being so sincere and all, I didn't bring it up. I really hadn't explained the job situation to Mary and still hadn't felt any need to, but with all the fuss being generated over me, she was sure to suspect something. As I looked across the room I saw her listening to Mike as he apparently was running off with one of his stories. As I looked, they both looked back. Mike waved and smiled. He was telling me not to worry, everything was in good hands.

I found out later that night from Mary that Mike had told her that I had gotten a nice promotion and that was the reason for the party. And, of course, everyone wanted to meet her.

I accepted my congratulations graciously despite their suspicious origins. I drank a few beers and ate some of the food. At one point, around midnight, I looked but couldn't find Mary. I strolled around the house peeking here and there. I did know that place pretty well. I walked out onto the back porch and found them sitting on the bench, talking. They were close but not touching. I immediately began to swell with anger. Mike was trying to put the move in on Mary. He was smooth and I suppose he figured I could just go back to Bev and let him take over here. I was determined that whatever happened between me and Mary would be worked out between us, not by someone else. I told Mary that I wanted her to meet some people. We went back inside.

Back into the light, I suppose she saw that my face was flushed. She knew how I got at times. She immediately assured me that Mike was just entertaining her very gentlemanly while I was receiving all the praise. I tried to believe her but I didn't trust him. He was behind the whole conspiracy and he had already demonstrated to me what his power and influence could do. I was starting to hate him but I knew I had to get back in his good graces if I expected to do more digging. Mike was also the one who could open up the door for me. I knew I had to just grit my teeth, and keep him away from Mary.

The rest of the night was uneventful. The party had not been loud or rowdy or even very drunken. It had been an extremely enjoyable time. When we got home neither of us were particularly tired and both of us were relaxed and happy. We sat on the sofa with our arms around each other and watched a late-late movie. It reminded me of our college days where we would have marathon study sessions then collapse onto that old beat-up sofa and watch some all night movie in black and white. I had a color TV in California.

We awoke still dressed on the sofa although, by then, slumped over with her on top of me. My arm was asleep and our hair looked a mess. Once we had our eyes open, we both began to laugh hysterically. We held each other and kissed. We made love on the floor as the sun burst through the window into my eyes. We were not the couple that I had left behind in Florida. At the time, I thought it was the California sun.

CHAPTER XV

SESSIONS

When I told Dr. Goldman about Mary, he seemed both pleased and concerned. He, of course, asked me how I felt about it and I tried to answer as best I could even though it was still a bit early to make any real judgments. I told him that I was just going to proceed slowly and with caution. That was sort of the truth but I also figured it was what he wanted to hear. I was sure that his concern stemmed from how her sudden appearance would affect my recovery. I tried to give him the right answers. I wanted to get the session over with so I could get home to her. I'm sure that in spite of my politically correct answers, he could see right through me. But he smiled at the end of the session and reminded me of my next appointment. He still hadn't let me live down those first two meetings.

Willy, at work, was aware of my situation, what I had been through, and the fact that I had to see Goldman twice a week. I scheduled my appointments for mid-afternoon and would take off right after lunch. With the distance I had to go downtown and back, he didn't expect me back afterwards so I just went home. In my second week on the new job, Willy admitted that several of the workers there were also involved in maintenance sessions. Since I had only met three other workers, I figured it was all of them. I didn't ask them why because I really didn't want to go explaining myself to them. We all worked okay together and that suited me fine. I had specific responsibilities and I did my job. They did their jobs and the chatter was kept to a minimum, partly because we seldom ran into each other aside from lunch time, and partly because this was not a very talkative bunch, except for Willy. When I looked at the bunch in that building, I got the impression that they all had a story similar to mine and, like me, they didn't want to talk about it.

I didn't get home any earlier after my sessions because of the traffic. At first I wasn't going to tell Mary about them but just go on like nothing was happening. I was falling hard, again, for Mary. She was doing and saying all the right things. But if it wasn't meant to work out, I wasn't sure just how much of the other things I wanted her to know.

Two more weeks went by smoothly. Occasionally we would go out at night for dinner or a few drinks and music. She seemed to have an exceptional supply of cash. On weekends, we started planning trips up into the mountains or up or down the coast. These trips promised to be exciting for both of us since I had never been out of the bay area since moving there and I had a growing sense of adventure. Something was very different about her, though. Something that I didn't remember from before.

Although I kept trying to plan how I would continue my investigation, opportunities never presented themselves until the fourth week after Mary arrived. Willy told me that there was a shipment of parts, mostly small components, that had' been rejected over in one of the main assembly areas. Because it consisted of three full pallets, he wanted me to go over and check it out. He told me to take the equipment I needed and if it was bad, to instruct them to ship it back to the manufacturer directly from there. It seemed straight forward enough since I had spent most of my time in that department evaluating similar material. He added that the shipment was located in the area that I had worked in before.

I told him that it didn't bother me and since I was now in disposition, this was just part of my job. Since he figured it would take the rest of the day, he told me he would see me in the morning. He added that he really wanted to see it done that day if at all possible. I promised to get it done even if it took all night. We both laughed. There was my chance to get back and look around.

I met Mike at the office and he thanked me for coming over so soon. He explained that the parts in question had arrived a few days earlier and were rushed right to the assembly areas with only minimal inspection. Production was behind and there had been a lot of pressure to keep moving. But repeated failures had triggered them to re-inspect. As he left the office to head out to the assembly floor, I ran into Bev coming into the office. She smiled, as she always did, and gave me a hug. Then she kept on walking.

The pallets of boxes had been moved to an out-of-the-way location by a wall, maybe forty feet from where the operators were lined up at their stations. I'm sure that they all remembered me and most of them waved. The foreman was a guy named Ripley and we had known each other fairly well before. He came over had the right stuff, then I checked the vendor who had shipped this stuff in. There were computer terminals located around the areas which held the database for these kinds of things. My password was still good so I went in to the system and ran a routine check. There was nothing unusual except that this was a major supplier and they had been hit several times for quality violations. They were called Skepco Electronics and they were a distributor of specialized components. When a place needed parts that were not exactly off-the-shelf but rather with slight modifications that didn't quite warrant custom design, Skepco would have existing parts customized to fit the requirement. Companies like that had greatly reduced costs for the government over the years. That was why repeated quality problems tended to be overlooked. Their good to the government outweighed the bad.

I started sampling parts from boxes and found that many parts seemed to be just the stock stuff. They were mixed in with obviously customized parts as if an incoming inspection person would have only a limited chance of spotting them. And even if only a few were detected, there would not be enough to reject the shipment. This seemed like a pretty slick and bold move by a vendor. If they got away with it, they would get paid for the added work to customize the parts and the rework would have to be done at the base at the government's expense. And if a few of the parts were pulled out, they would just be scrapped by us because the individual dollar value was so low. The chances were very high that this type of thing had been going on for a long time but there had never been cause to look into it. I was ready to start digging.

I copied down all the information that the database had and then went back to the components. I had to get my work done first. I had some freedom of movement during the day but I needed to get into the quality records after everybody went home. I was sure that the Skepco thing meant something. I figured I would check out the reports on their past problems. That day's incident didn't quite warrant a deep search by a guy from disposition.

I did my work on the pallets and recommended that the shipment be sent back to the vendor for sorting and reshipment. I figured it would take three days to get the parts back so I got Ripley and one of his workers to select out enough good parts to hold the assembly people for the time. I had just started filling out my reports when the workers began heading out. I took my time. Ripley thanked me and left with his jacket over his shoulder. About a half hour later, I walked down the hall to the men's room that was located just outside my old quality control office. The lights were out inside, so I propped the door open, so I could see to wash my hands at the sink and planned my next move. I carefully closed the door and quickly walked back into the general office area. I knew where they kept the vendor records and I went right to the file. It wasn't locked because vendor records were not considered to be classified in any way. Skepco had a big file. They had been a supplier for nearly eight years. Their record really wasn't much to worry about, just a lot of minor citations for trying to slip things past the government inspectors. Every violation had been checked and filed, and all had gone without penalty. That I found a little bit unusual. I noticed that each of the citations was signed by Mike.

This did not appear to have any correlation with the scheme that I had found before but once again, Mike seemed to be involved. I copied down all the information that I needed and rushed back to my reports out on the floor. But before I left, I plugged Skepco into the computer again and copied down their address. They were located not far away, in the Napa Valley.

Mary sensed my excitement when I got home. She had gone shopping that day and was anxious to show me what she had bought but she knew that look. When I had that look, don't stand in my way. She was just hoping that I would tell her why I was feeling so good. I just told her that I had had a good day at work. I wanted to take a ride up to the Skepco facility but Mary had plans for us that night. She put on one of her new dresses and told me that she had made reservations at a particularly nice restaurant not far away. She said the prices were lower during the week, because it wasn't as crowded. I was already dressed so we left. We had a delightful evening but I could still sense something different about her. At times she would seem like she was trying to pry into what was going on with me. She really wanted to know why I was so excited that night but she wouldn't come out and ask me directly.

The next morning I called Mike to tell him what I had recommended on the Skepco shipment but he had called in sick that day. I was told that they had gotten my report and that the parts had been moved back to the shipping department already. I felt good about having dealt with that problem and since I had an appointment with Goldman that afternoon, the morning flew by. The day outside was beautiful and I was looking forward to letting the breeze blow my hair as I was cruising down the freeway. Five minutes before I was to leave, the doctor's office called and canceled the appointment. I think Dr. Goldman had been taken ill. I left anyway. I decided to surprise Mary.

As I pulled up in front of our building, I noticed Mike's car, or, at the time, what I thought was a car just like his. He had a small sports car and it was painted a unique shade of blue, soft yet bold. I was up the stairs to our door and inside in a flash. I had wanted to surprise her. I'm actually glad that I didn't. As I stepped inside, Mary stepped out of the bedroom, a sheet draped around her, looking almost horrified. Then it all clicked, that was Mike's car and I had caught them in bed together. Then I snapped. I ran for the bedroom, ready to tear him apart. The next thing I remember was waking up on the bed with a plastic bag full of ice pressed against my head.

Mary was sitting beside me on the bed. She was fully dressed and was holding my hand. In a soft voice she told me how worried she had been. She told me I had slipped on the wet kitchen floor that she was scrubbing when I tried to sneak up on her. I had hit my head on the counter edge and had been knocked out cold for nearly five minutes. She said she was just about to call an ambulance. My head hurt so bad that I didn't want to try to think about it. But I knew what I had seen and it wasn't a wet floor.

I was feeling better by early that evening and I told Mary that I had to run out for a few minutes. I told her that I didn't need her to come along. I hopped in my car and took off for the Valley.

Skepco was one of those typical flat, modern office complexes that had sprung up all over that part of California. It was mostly a combination of white stucco and glass. I imagined it glowing in the midday sun. But now it was evening and the shadows were beginning to hide the building's features. I rode through the parking lot, checking it all out. There were a half dozen cars still parked there, all up close to the front entrance. Among them was Mike's sports car. Now I understood, Mike was in on the whole thing, probably making a mint. I thought I had proof before about his involvement, but now I had seen it with my own eyes. I couldn't let it go that time. On the way back to my apartment, I called the FBI.

CHAPTER XVI

REALLY BIG

As I sit here now in this still room, I realize that I am not afraid anymore. I did what I had to do and I suppose I have been paying the price ever since. Back then, though, I was afraid. I knew I had come across something that was really big and I knew I had to put a stop to it whatever the cost would be. Back then, I never knew what was going to happen next, and even after it happened, I usually wasn't able to figure out why it had happened. I was always off my guard.

When I got back to my apartment I had one of those kind of happenings. Mary was waiting as I had expected. She didn't try to hound me for information about where I had been and she didn't explain what really had happened a few hours earlier. When I walked in, she gave me a hug and a kiss and began examining my head, which although not cut, had risen into a noticeable knot. She went into the kitchen and made an icepack and applied it gently to the source of my pain. We sat down on the sofa and she wrapped herself around me. It felt good.

After maybe a half hour, she got up and went to the medicine cabinet to get me some pain killers. I had a hard time imagining that woman in bed with Mike. But then I had had no warning signs in Florida either. Even now, I still love her. Even though it seemed that she had spent most of our life hurting me. I still love her.

I guzzled down the tablets with a full glass of cold water. It tasted good even though I knew that water wasn't supposed to have any taste. I settled back on the sofa and she put on a tape of Vivaldi. The next thing I remembered was the sound of the phone ringing. It started very soft and became louder as if cutting through the veil of sleep. I saw Mary pick up the receiver. She looked at me as she spoke in a voice just below my ability to hear. I realized then that my whole body was numb. I knew I had been drugged but my mind was too jumbled to be able to figure any of it out. I tried to reach out to her and ask her why she had done it, but I couldn't.

The next image that I remember was Mike standing over me. He looked very calm and friendly and he began speaking to me, first to be sure that I could understand him, and then to give me his message. He said that I was being very stupid. He said that I was putting my life in danger by pursuing these crazy ideas. He said I was suffering from delusions and that he would have to call Dr. Goldman. He probably said some other things but I really don't remember. He finally asked if I understood what he was saying and I must have answered or nodded or something, because he said, good, and got up and walked away from me. My vision was far from clear but it looked like he said a few words to Mary and then left. He didn't kiss her. This whole part is real fuzzy. It took me a long time to piece it all together but the pieces fit. It was almost like a dream. A really bad dream.

Obviously, I didn't go in to work the next day. Mary called in for me and spent the day trying to nurse me. I wasn't really sick except for the intense pounding in my head. She kept applying cold compresses and giving me aspirin. I checked them and they were the real thing. She fixed me something to eat when I was hungry and generally stayed right beside me.

I probably wasn't a very good patient because with my terrible headache, I couldn't tolerate any music or other sounds. I wrapped a pillow around my head to block the noise but it didn't make much difference. Mary finally said that if I wasn't better in the morning, she was going to call a doctor.

I ate only a few bites of food all that day. What I was suffering from was a ravenous thirst. I kept drinking and drinking, mostly water but occasionally some tea. I forced about half a piece of veal Parmesan and some broccoli at dinner and retreated back to the chair in the living room that had been my roost all day. I couldn't lie down or my head would throb. I noticed after a few minutes that my headache had faded considerably. As I looked up, I saw Mary coming in from the kitchen. She had put away the leftovers. She knelt on the floor in front of me and rested her head on my lap. I told her that I was feeling better. She looked up at me and asked if I remembered Mike being here the night before. I said yes. She asked if I understood what he was saying. I said yes. Now I knew that she was in on it too.

Jack Dempsey had told me before that if I was going to get involved in this kind of stuff that I had to learn that I couldn't trust anyone. That seemed like a long time ago and I missed him a great deal. He was the one that I could trust in all this and he was dead. It just didn't seem fair but regardless, I was on my own again, alone. I took off the rest of the week and I did finally go to a doctor. He said I had received a mild concussion but due to the time since the injury, there was no danger. He just prescribed rest and aspirin. I thanked him and paid my bill. Mary looked relieved. I drove home, my first time behind the wheel since the "incident." I was very relaxed.

Mary decided that since I was doing okay, she would head out to one of the malls for a few hours of shopping. She told me what she wanted to get but I've forgotten now. As soon as she had pulled away from the apartment, I called a taxi.

I told the driver to take me to the hotel where Jack had lived. At the time I had no idea why but I knew that I had to go back there. I figured it was some strange cosmic calling drawing me to the scene of the crime. Maybe I was going to get some revelation or maybe Jack was going to talk to me from beyond the grave, or wherever he was, and give me some critical information. I was sure that he had been killed because he knew too much. And now it seemed like I was getting close enough that the bad guys were beginning to worry. I wanted to make them worry.

From my several trips there, I knew my way around the building pretty good. I slipped in the back maintenance door when the coast was clear. I used the back stairs that were usually deserted, because they were dark and eerie. The place seemed empty even though it was mid-afternoon. I instinctively tried the doorknob, but it was locked. I'm not sure why I had expected it to be open. Too many movies, I suppose. Then, for some odd reason, I looked under the doormat. There seemed to be a force calling me. A shiny key revealed itself to me. I grasped it and quickly slipped it into the lock. In a second, I was inside and pushing the door closed.

The shades were up so the room was flooded with light. As I looked around, I realized everything in the room was the same stuff that Jack had in the room. But it had been weeks since he had been killed.

The room was warm from being closed up and I began to perspire. It was not dusty and did not smell musty. It actually looked as if someone was living there. Maybe the person that killed Jack, I thought. Fear swept over me and a touch of panic made me bolt for the door. I peeked into the hallway and seeing that it was clear, I eased the door shut. After a half second hesitation, I slipped the key into my pocket and made for the stairway. When I stepped out into the street, I felt like I was white as a ghost. I had a strange sensation when I was in the room. I felt like someone was watching me even though I had checked it out and knew that there was no one there. It had felt the same way in the hallway.

There was a small lounge sandwiched between a dry cleaners and men's clothing store in the next block. I stepped into the darkness and found a seat at the bar easily. One of those talk shows was on TV. The bartender brought me a beer and went back to the show. I didn't want to talk anyway. I used the phone at the back, next to the restrooms, to call a cab. I was back to the condo before Mary. I snooped around in the bathroom trying to find any unusual drugs. I was sure she had given me something, and I was also sure that she wouldn't have been so stupid as to leave something out but I had to check anyway. I found nothing. I took two aspirins and settled back into my chair. I reached over and clicked on the radio. I turned the volume down low. My head didn't hurt then, but I had some serious thinking to do and I thought that might trigger another pain.

Mary came back about six and carried in a bag of Chinese food along with several other bags displaying the names of some of the finer stores. For the first time in days, I was hungry and was quick to get the plates and the food on the table. I devoured a heaping plateful and then realized that Mary was eating only an eggroll. She remarked that she had eaten several slices of pizza not long before that and had stopped for the Chinese, because she knew I liked it. She was trying to be nice to me but I knew she was in on it. I knew I could play their game and bring them down. In reality, it kind of went the other direction.

When I had seemed to have gotten my fill, she turned towards me and asked if I remembered what Mike had said the other night. I said yes but asked why she was asking me such an unusual question. She didn't say anything right away, but after a pause, she said it was just important that I did. Her voice did not show any real concern for me, just that she wanted to make sure I was following orders. I thought to myself that Bev would never talk to me that way.

I got very drowsy again after dinner and I was sure that Mary had drugged me, probably in the Chinese food. That would explain why she hadn't eaten any. As I was fading out, I saw Mike come in through the front door and, along with Mary, they stared into my face. I wanted to spit but my mouth was parched. I know what they were doing while I was off in Never Never Land.

CHAPTER XVII

The Office

It dawned on me as I was lying on the sofa that Saturday that I had never heard from the FBI. In my mind, I suppose I had expected agents crawling all over the place a few hours later. But if they had, I would have heard about it and Mike wouldn't have been still stopping over. I wanted to call them back but I just wasn't feeling clear headed enough to explain, which I was sure I would have to do. Besides, Mary was sticking close to me all the time, under orders from Mike, no doubt.

Knowing that I would be going back to work on Monday, I let my concerns fade. When I got to the office, I could make my calls without interference. The group there had no interest in my personal activities. They were each hung up in their own world of trials and tribulations. They were always nice enough, and often would talk on and on about anything or nothing, but they were very private when matters of their lives were concerned. They were not threatening but not really allies either. I knew one thing for certain, whatever happened to me, it would have no effect on them. There was a strange comfort in that.

When I arrived at work that next week, I was met at the door of our building by Willy. He smiled as he always did and asked me how my head was. I smiled back and nodded. Then I gave him the slip from the doctor that would allow me to come back to work. I followed him inside. As we reached our office area, he stopped and said that he wanted to talk to me after I got settled back into things. He said there were a lot of phone messages and loose ends to tend to. He did not have a particularly concerned or troubled look on his face, just the look of a boss telling a subordinate what to do. That didn't bother me.

There were a lot of phone messages as Willy had said and most of them had his initials on them which indicated that he was the person who had answered the phone. There were two from Bev; she apparently hadn't known about my little "accident." There were two from Ripley, the foreman who had had the defective parts. The first was just a message thanking me for taking care of the whole thing. The second, from Friday, was asking me to call him back as soon as possible. I called right away but someone on the other end of the line told me that Ripley was out sick.

The other important message was from an Agent Morris.

The phone number was in San Francisco and I noticed my hand shaking as I dialed the number. I had to leave a message for him and then went to Willy's office to see what was on his mind. He saw me coming and signaled me to come in and sit down. He motioned for me to swing the door shut even though there was nobody else in the office at that time. I remember not liking the look on his face. It was about one half troubled and the rest sinister. He stared past me for the first few seconds and then focused right into my face. I felt naked. He asked me why the FBI was calling there but before I could answer, he went on that he didn't like the FBI calling there because that meant they would be visiting there. He rambled on like some kind of lunatic. It was really scary. He kept asking me questions but not giving me a chance to answer them. Finally he spun around in his chair and looked at the wall behind his desk. He was sweating. So was I, so the next five minutes were dreadfully silent. I didn't dare get up to leave and I was afraid to try talking to him. I spent that time scanning and surveying his office. I had only been in there twice before.

The room was small and simple like most of the low level supervisors had on shipyards. It reminded me of one of the offices that I had spent an hour in that night at the police station. The walls were painted a shade of institutional gray. It was the kind of color that did not go well with anything you would choose to hang or display. Three of the walls were adorned with the Penn State stuff I had seen before. The wall behind Willy's desk was covered almost entirely with photographs in frames, none of which matched. There were autographed pictures of baseball players and one from former President Nixon. There were two that might have been pictures of his family, an attractive woman and two small children. But like the others at this place, he never spoke of his world outside of Mare Island. Finally, there were a half dozen scenery photos that might have been taken by him. He was staring toward one of them that showed a sailboat breezing past a rock jetty. It was too far away to see very much detail in it, but there appeared to be a fisherman sitting on the edge.

Willy finally turned around back toward me slowly. His expression had changed back to what I had always considered normal. In a soft voice he said he was sorry for the outburst. He mentioned that he had had a bad time with the FBI a few years earlier. With that, he let it drop. He said he was sorry again and told me to be careful. Then he stood up behind the desk. That was his signal that he was through and I should get back to work. I rose and turned to leave. When I reached the door, I turned to him and said thanks but he had turned back to his pictures.

The office was still empty and as I sat at my desk, I couldn't help but wonder what had been with Willy. I had never seen him act that way. He was always so even tempered and calm about things. Even when he was upset about some project or evaluation, he was calm. I proceeded to file away reports from the past week since I had no particular project assigned to me. Even though I hadn't been in this office very long, I had picked up on the routine. Whoever was not "gainfully employed" took care of the clerical duties for those that were. It was one of those unwritten laws that I think all offices work under. I didn't mind, it gave me a chance to think.

Marie arrived about ten-thirty. She had been out on an investigation at another part of the yard. Interestingly enough, the complaint was about a shipment from Skepco. They were totally different kind of parts than what I had been concerned with and they were in a different area of the yard. But the circumstance was the same. She, too, had directed them to be returned to the shipper. But as far as she was concerned, the issue was ready to be filed. She handed me the folder and went out to the loading dock to take a smoke. I read the file before I placed it in the cabinet.

The FBI guy called back just after lunch and since he was in town, we arranged to meet that evening to talk. With Mary at the condo, I knew that was not a good place. He suggested I come to his motel. I told him I would be there. I called Mary to tell her that I had something to take care of after work but I wouldn't be late. She, of course, asked what it was but I just gave her the vague reassurance that I wouldn't be late. When I hung up the phone, I suddenly had this weird feeling that there would be a car waiting to follow me when I left the yard that afternoon. I had been followed before, so I knew how to spot them and to take care of myself.

It was a miserably slow day with nothing to do but file and answer phones. And with all the time to think, I started to worry. I can't say that worry had been one of my feelings up to that point in time. I knew that I had things under control but the scope of what was going on was swelling. The more I looked, the more I seemed to be finding out. And now I would be going to see an FBI guy to blow the whole thing wide open. I knew that I was putting my own life in danger but that wasn't the reason for the worry. I had much earlier accepted the danger. No, it was more of a case of worrying that no one would believe me. I know it probably sounds funny but with the exception of Jack Dempsey, nobody ever really took me serious. The bad guys considered me more of an inconvenience or they wouldn't have just kept up the threats. They would have killed me and set someone else up or made it look like an accident. I wasn't worried about that. I just couldn't seem to get the why part straight. But I remembered what Willy had said to me, "Be careful." I knew he meant it even though it seemed totally out of place at the time.

Marie pretty much ignored me the whole day. She had subtle ways of telling you to stay away. She would sit at her desk with her body turned slightly more to the left than normal, so you had a full view of her back. When the phone rang, she would ignore it as if she was deaf and let you grab it. Usually she had it on the first ring. She had a small radio on her desk that she normally kept very low. She liked her country music. On that day it was loud enough that she could pretend not to hear you if you talked. By mid-afternoon I needed a break from it all and slipped out to the dock area to talk to that sailor from Georgia.

When I was working, I usually ran into him at least once a day and he liked me. It was like he was expecting me to give him news from home. He always gave me straight answers when I asked him questions. He wasn't quite as weird as the others in this place. I suppose it was because he was Navy and the rest of us were civilian.

I tried to ask him if he knew what was bothering Marie. He said that the people in that department were there to get away from all the hassles and that they were under the impression that I was going to start up trouble. He added that Rex was pissed also. I was caught up on the clerical duties and since the sailor didn't seem to be overly anxious to get back to whatever he was doing, I decided to see what other information I could get out of him.

As I had expected, everybody working in that building had been placed there to get them out of the way. They had all gotten into trouble somewhere along the way, even Willy. They were all still given the opportunity to do a good job and they all took it very seriously. But they all held some deep resentment. But more importantly, they all wanted to be left alone. I was starting to rock the boat. He gave me one caution. There was nowhere else to go except out the door. And he had seen a few go that direction in the four years he had been there.

They had been like me, he said, hot shots who couldn't accept their new station in life. Sometimes they just had bad attitudes, sometimes they just kept stirring up trouble. I was being pegged as the latter. There was no room for negotiation there. The whole yard was run that way. You either joined the team or you were thrown out of the ballpark. He spoke like an old teacher counseling a young student, patiently and understandingly. More and more, I was beginning to realize that this was what everybody had been trying to tell me since

I had started there. They just wanted me to join their team, because their team was the only one that was allowed to win.

The sailor could see that I was beginning to drift off in thought so he ended his lesson. He told me to decide whether this team was right for me and if it was, then to join it. If not, he told me to get out while I still had a choice. I thought that was a strange way to put it, but I thanked him for his enlightening words. He smiled and went back to work.

I strolled back to the office, not realizing that over an hour had passed. Everything was quiet. I finished up some additional filing from Marie and briefly skimmed through two cases that Willy had apparently put on my desk for follow up. I decided to get started on them the next morning and prepared to leave for the day. Marie was a few steps ahead of me and as she passed my desk on her way to the door, she said goodbye. I grabbed the hotel address for Agent Morris and went to my car. I didn't see any unusual vehicles parked within sight.

CHAPTER XVIII

CONSPIRACY

I spent most of the twenty minute ride to the motel trying to beef up my courage. I knew this might be my last chance to get someone to believe me and to do something about the conspiracy. I would have to be so convincing and have enough proof that they would act fast. If not, and the word got out, well, I didn't want to think about what would happen. For the last few minutes of the ride, I got my facts straight in my head.

I pulled up in front of his door and before I had a chance to knock, it was opened and he beckoned me in. He was obviously a no nonsense agent because he flashed his badge, introduced himself as Agent Tad Morris, and got right to asking questions. He wanted facts, he said, not my opinions. I told him what I knew and what things could be verified with paper work and things like that. He didn't seem very impressed but took notes the whole time I was talking. After his first few questions that were obviously intended to get me going, he eased back into his chair and listened, interrupting only to clarify an occasional point and talk I did. I spilled everything I knew and everything I thought about how the loose ends tied together. After an hour he was tolerating my editorializing. He kept writing all the same.

I was exhausted when I came to the end of my story. He looked at his pages of notes for several minutes before he started talking to me again. He told me that my report warranted investigation and that he would initiate appropriate action once he had a chance to look over his notes again. He verified my address and where I could be reached during the day and thanked me for bringing this to his attention. He told me that the investigation was now entirely in the hands of the FBI and that I should not talk to anyone else about it or attempt to continue my own snooping. He said that would only hinder the Bureau's efforts. I understood what he was driving at and I agreed. When I walked out of that motel room I felt better than I had in weeks. I even bought a dozen roses for Mary on the way home.

She was shocked out of her head when I handed them to her. Before she could ask why, I kissed her and said I felt better. Inside my head I was wishing I could be there when she tried to explain it to Mike.

Mary had prepared me supper and had arranged it on an oven proof plate so that I could heat it up. Microwave ovens were not available to the public in those days. She slipped it into the convection oven before I could reach it and fifteen minutes later I was eating a meal that tasted great. And I don't even remember what it was. That night it didn't matter. I was feeling great.

I remember it so well because the feeling didn't last very long and, in fact, it just might have been the last good night of my life.

Except for tonight, that is. Sitting in this small room forcing myself to bring it all back has been soothing. A few hours ago I was tense, waiting for my impending fate. But now I can see that I wasn't to blame. I did what I know was right and the fact that I have been paying for that decision since then. The street out front has been quiet for a long time, the only movement being the bugs attacking the street lamp. I can feel myself smiling with satisfaction but I don't dare look in the mirror. Nor do I want to know what time it is. It is still dark and that is a reality that no one can distort. When the light comes, it will be morning.

When I went to work the next day I was feeling good. I made a point of apologizing to Willy although I wasn't sure just why. But I needed to assure him that everything was okay with me. I even stole one of Mary's roses and gave it to Marie. I think she accepted it as a sort of peace offering. She felt better and that made me feel better, not to mention it helped our working relationship. I needed her help that day with one of the cases I had been given. I was concerned about precedents that had been set and she was the one who would know. I didn't see the sailor from Georgia, though. But the word spread throughout the department of my changed attitude, because when I ran into Rex after lunch, he asked where his flower was. His sardonic laugh filled the loading dock.

My near wonderful day was shattered when I went to my car to leave that afternoon and found two of my tires flat. I called a local service station for road service and then called Mary. Willy was the only other person there and as he was about to go he asked if he could do anything. Since I had everything under control, I told him no thanks. He left and I went out to wait for the tow truck alone. It was still light out but I didn't notice the car coming towards me until it was almost there. Maybe it was because it was a neutral color or maybe my mind was just drifting off somewhere, but it startled me. Two guys jumped out and walked over to my car, surveying my predicament. I had never seen them before and although I didn't think they were going to rob me or anything, I knew this was not a social call. The bigger of the two had red hair and he just kept shaking it and saying something like 'Gee, that's a real shame' and then asked the other guy what he thought. The other guy agreed and added that that was what happened to people who caused trouble. Again, pieces started to fall in place. These guys probably worked for Mike and had probably poked the holes in the tires. When they looked at me, they both laughed. I felt saved when I saw the tow truck heading for the parking lot. They hopped back in their car and sped off. I think a stone from their tires put a tiny crack in my windshield.

The service station repaired both tires although the service guy suggested I buy two new ones since they had been punctured at the edge of the tread and he said he couldn't guarantee that the plugs he had put in would hold too long. I paid him and went home. I didn't buy any flowers.

Mary had some dinner waiting again but she was not as cheerful as I had expected her to be. She didn't know the circumstances of the flat tires but she was acting like she knew something just the same. I ate my dinner alone in the kitchen. I had an uncanny feeling that Mike had been there before I had gotten home. It's funny how I keep calling it home. It seemed that ever since Mary had come out west, I had lost that place that I called home. It wasn't that she had taken it over or anything, but rather like I had been pushed out. Our condo had been a place for me to escape the pressures of the world. Mike and even Bev had thought I was weird because I didn't like to go out and party. I used to like to stop at that little bar near the yard until the whole thing with Jack. But that wasn't a party place, just a quiet little harbor in the storm, a place to drink a cold beer and not have to impress anyone. I think they thought I was crazy. But they left me alone and didn't push it on me. It seemed strange to say Bev's name again.

When I finished eating and had rinsed off the dishes in the sink, I went into the living room where Mary was sitting. She spoke first. She asked what was wrong with me but she wasn't looking for an answer. She kept on talking. She said that she didn't understand why I was acting so crazy. Back in Florida when she got like this, she would be fighting the tears as she spoke. But this night she had raw determination in her eyes. She showed the anger of a child, who has been told she can't go out to play. She pounded her fist on the arm of the chair and said, coldly, that Mike would be back shortly and talk to me. I laid on the sofa and I tuned her out.

It was an hour or so later when Mike arrived. He opened the door and when he came in he wasn't smiling. There was no happy-go-lucky California playboy in the living room that night.

For the next three hours I listened. He was blatantly honest to the point that it shocked me. But I just kept listening.

He started by telling me how when he had met me in that bar in Florida he was there checking out another old friend from the Navy in regards to recruiting him for a job out there. That guy had turned him down, not wanting to move his family three thousand miles to earthquake country. It had been a coincidence that we had met but he had made the same offer to me just the same. When I accepted the job, he thought he had recruited another player for his team. It hadn't worked out that way. That created a big problem for him. If I wouldn't join the team, he had to kick me off the field. Where had I heard that before?

Mike told me that he had tried to tell me to back off, but I wouldn't listen to reason. He had tried to convince me by using what methods he had at his disposal. He said that he was convinced that the psychiatric reports were right and that I was suffering from some delusionary disorder that inhibited my ability to discern right and wrong. I had gotten this distorted idea that things were going on that were harming the country when, in reality, it was just some simple business game where everybody won. The defense guys in Washington liked to see the budget being used on a worthwhile program, the subcontractors were making a tidy profit, and the team members at the yard were skimming off a nice commission. I didn't believe he was telling me "all of it." He was incriminating himself before my very eyes, I wished that Agent Morris had been there, as I had a burning desire to ask him a question.

I said, "Why did you kill Jack Dempsey?"

Mike said, "I didn't."

I said, "Then, who did?"

Mike said, "You did!"

My mouth dropped wide open. Then he clarified that comment.

He said he had tried to tell me to stop but I insisted on giving information to Jack, information that should not have gotten out of the office. He said that it was unfortunate about Jack but it would have been more unfortunate if that information had gotten out. He didn't care, I could see it in his face. Then he got to the punchline. I had broken my word before and he had gone easy on me but I had used up all my favors. He was very blunt, if I got in his way again, it would be over for me. Again, I was shocked. I could not believe that I had heard all of those things that night. Then I looked at Mary. She didn't look shocked or surprised. She was looking at Mike. I realized then that my suspicions were correct. I got up from the sofa and walked to the window and stared out into nothing. In the reflection of the glass I saw Mary and him looking at each other and mouthing words. They weren't watching me at all. She had been part of that whole scheme. She had suckered me in and then made a complete fool of me while acting as an informant to keep them abreast of my comings and goings. But the final blow came when I determined that she was sleeping with the enemy. She had betrayed me. And she would never admit it.

I walked out of the room and sat in the kitchen, leaving the two of them alone in the living room. I couldn't see them and couldn't hear any talking. I imagined him beginning to run his hands over her breasts. First over her shirt, then slipping a button open and sliding his hand across her skin. I knew what she liked. Now I wondered how many others knew.

I reached in the refrigerator and grabbed a beer. I noticed that there were three more left. I was not much of a drinker after Jack died. Just an occasional brew to relax to. But that night I felt like drinking. I guzzled the first one down and grabbing the second, I propped my feet on another chair and leaned back. I rested the top of my neck on the padded top of the chair and it was remarkably comfortable. As the cold amber liquid of the second bottle slid down my throat, I strained to hear a sound from the other room, but still only silence. Yes, he was very good with women. When I thought about how sexually damaged she was when I met her; it somehow gave me pleasure to know that she actually found a partner. By now he was kissing her neck gently while gliding his hand over her jeans, between her legs. She was staring at the ceiling, closing and then opening her eyes. She was trying painfully not to moan with pleasure. She was about to give herself to him for what may have been the fiftieth time. It didn't matter how many because I knew she would crawl back to him again and again. I was squeezing the glass bottle so hard that I expected it to shatter into a thousand brown pieces. I grabbed a third beer. What I really wanted to do was to walk in that living room and slam Mike over the head with one of these bottles and then grab Mary and screw her so hard that she screamed for me to stop while enduring multiple orgasms. But what would be the point in that, I thought. I heard walking; then, the door open and close. There were no words spoken. I heard Mary's footsteps on the uncarpeted tiles near the hallway. I stood up and pulled the last beer from the refrigerator. My head started to spin slightly. She walked into the kitchen and looked at me with pitiful eyes. Her shirt was unbuttoned. I thought about slapping her hard with the back of my hand but why?

CHAPTER XIX

THE GOOD DOCTOR?

One of the first things I did at work the next day was call Dr. Goldman. I had been seeing him all during this time but had been concentrating on saying what he wanted to hear rather than talking about what was really going on. I had been able to figure him out fairly easily. He was concerned with maintenance, that is, keeping me stable now that he knew what was wrong with me. He really wasn't interested in hearing about new problems. That might have indicated a resurfacing of the old problem. Or worse yet, a new problem that would force the good doctor to have to think about what to prescribe. He wasn't being paid for that. He was being paid to rehabilitate me. Yeah right!

But I called him, like I said, because I seemed to be confused. I knew what was going on even before Mike told me. He just filled in the missing pieces. But I couldn't understand why I couldn't get anyone to do anything about it. I hadn't been able to do it alone. I thought maybe talking to him, a third party, might help, as he did sound concerned on the phone. He arranged to extend our appointment for that day to a full hour. Next I tried to call Agent Morris, but I couldn't reach him. He had checked out of the motel and his office said he was in the field and took a message.

To avoid any repercussions from Willy, I plunged into my work after that. Since his outburst, he seemed to be watching me when I was on the phone. My morning calls had taken close to a half hour. But he knew that I could work circles around Marie if I put my mind to it. I had to keep working just to keep from thinking about everything. No one called me that day and when I left to go to Dr. Goldman's office, I didn't have any flat tires. Traffic was unusually light and I got to his building earlier than usual. But rather than walk around outside, I went straight up to his office. Everything looked as it always did and I sat down and grabbed a magazine. I knew that he knew I was there, but figured that he had another patient. After just a few moments, he poked his head out of his door and said he would be with me shortly. He was on the phone.

Those were some real long minutes, because I know it was twenty or twenty-five minutes before he called me in. No one came out so he must have been there alone on the phone. When I sat down I remarked that the call must have been about a real serious patient. His look said it was none of my business but his words just said yes, very serious.

I used up the whole hour telling the story to him and I felt like I had to summarize most of it. But I did spend more time talking about the past week or so and about the threats and what Mike had told me. He listened intently and I don't think he interrupted once. What bothered me was that when the hour was up, he didn't comment or offer any advice. He just had that "END OF SESSION" look on his face. It said thanks for coming, see you next week. That wasn't what I had gone there to see or hear. I needed someone to tell me where I should go next. I had already gotten the phone numbers for the FBI and Department of Defense in Washington. Sooner or later I was going to get someone to listen. But on that afternoon I was looking for Dr. Goldman to stare over his half glasses and tell me what I wanted to hear. I finally asked him what I should do, as he put his pad back in his desk drawer. He stared off into space and then replied that he didn't know and that even if he did, it would still be up to me to decide for myself. It all sounded like double talk. Seeing my distrust, he shook his head and told me that I had to decide if the risk was worth it. Was the crime so bad as to risk my own life to expose it? He suggested that I should talk with a Psychologist and he would recommend someone to me next week.

That didn't seem like his characteristic reply and I thought maybe it was another of those subtle warnings that kept sneaking up on me. Either way, he sounded like he cared, which was uncharacteristic in itself. As I walked to my car, I didn't feel any better. And when I got there I felt worse. The two big guys who had paid me a visit while I was waiting for the tow truck were leaning against my fenders, one at the front of the car, one at the back. I gave then a "fancy meeting you here" kind of greeting and they responded by grabbing me and slamming me against the car. The wind was knocked instantly out of me. As I gasped for air, a fist caught me in the kidney and my knees buckled. One of them grabbed me by the hair and turned my head to look into his face. He told me that I wasn't as smart as he had thought I was or else I would have let things go.

He laughed and said "last warning." With that he threw my head against the side of the car. If I hadn't have turned my head slightly, it would have broken my nose. I slumped to the ground and heard them drive off. Boy, did I hurt.

I drove home, stopping only to buy a cold bottle of soda, which I held against the side of my head for the rest of the trip. The condo was dark inside when I opened the door. The drapes were open and the lights were off. I let the late afternoon sun touch the floor and walls. Mary was gone.

I suppose I had expected it. I had picked up on her little game and she could not go on knowing that I had something over her. The place actually looked exactly like it had the day before she arrived. And that felt weird. It had felt like Mary had been here for months. I guess she had controlled all of my time away from work so completely that I had forgotten what it had been like before. I had wrestled with feelings of love and betrayal, hate and compassion. I felt relieved that she was gone but at the same time missed her dreadfully. I opened the soda in my hand and took a big gulp. I felt that I was missing a hunk of my life.

I tried to call Dr. Goldman back to complain about the security in the parking garage and to let him know about Mary but all I got was his answering machine. He often stayed at the office late but I guess that was not one of those nights. I walked around the condo and I could almost detect an echo. She had not taken anything of mine. I went from room to room and realized that she had put everything back exactly as it had been before. It was uncanny. There was no trace that she had even been here. I sniffed for a faint lingering of her perfume but there was none. I decided I liked the way things were and I clicked on the stereo. I bumped the volume up slightly.

I next morning I went to work with a mission. I got into the files and started rereading everything on Skepco that I could find. I had a suspicion that they were somehow associated with Bectech but found nothing in the file. There were lots of reports of discrepancies over the previous few years. I had driven out there once and it did not look like anything special. The verdicts were always the same, send the stuff back to them but there were no reports showing that the stuff came back in a second time bad. That way they had kept off the government's list of bad suppliers. They were clever indeed but the real discovery came when a booklet fell out of a file from the previous year. It was Skepco's annual report.

There were some slick black and white photographs in the front part, which had a three page summary of what the company did. I already knew what they did. In the back were pages and pages of financial figures that maybe if I had taken more business courses in college, I would have understood. The part that really mattered was the middle section. This was where the booklet listed the company officers and the Board of Directors. The third name down was William S. Regal, Vice President. I knew what Mike's given name was but at that point I would have bet anything that William S. Regal was an alias. Also of interest was a name on the Board of Directors, Wade Simpkins and he was supposedly a friend of Bev's family. Things were getting entangled and at the same time clearer. I went back to my desk and called Agent Morris again but he was still unavailable.

I began to plan my next move. I knew that I would have to be very careful, very quick, and very profound. I figured that if I decided to act in some way, I would get just one chance. All I had to do was decide what I wanted to do and come up with a plan. I put all the files back in their proper places and sat back at my desk. I was caught up on my own work so Willy couldn't complain if I looked like I was drifting off into outer space. Besides, in that building we were all nut cases.

At lunch, I sat outside under a large tree that shaded the front door of the building. In my mind, I could see the Occupational Safety and Health building where I used to work. I wondered what was going on there. I thought how Mike had his own company supplying defective parts and then covering up the whole thing. And he was making a bundle. He got a salary at the shipyard, a salary from Skepco, and probably some kind of commission on all the parts. And he had built an empire so tight that anyone who threatened its existence was exterminated. All of his team, as he called them, probably got some sort of kickback for keeping the heat off the operation. As I said earlier, that's where Mike had gone wrong. He thought I would join like all the other traitors.

I didn't play that game. I was not going to defraud my country or my countrymen. I had to fight them in whatever way I could. I had to be willing to take the risk. Jack would have; then I thought, what would Jack have done. Now I was looking at things from a different perspective. If I could think like Jack, I could work out a plan.

As I started driving home that afternoon, I found myself drawn toward the valley where Skepco had its headquarters. And driving, I felt that special sort of freedom knowing that there were no expectations of me. There was no one waiting for me to arrive home for dinner. There were no friends waiting for me to call them to arrange a night out. I was alone again. But there was a certain exhilaration in that loneliness. I was basking in freedom and I thought that it might have been how our country's founders had felt when they were signing the Declaration of Independence. It was elation with a bit of apprehension about the consequences that the future would hold. I knew how they felt.

Skepco was just another flat building in this land of flat buildings. I drove past it once, surveying it as I drove. I continued down the road past a half dozen other structures. I didn't even look at their names, because I was here to see just one. I turned around and went back towards my target. I parked by the curb and watched across the parking lot. As before, there were only a few cars on the lot, all up near the building. I figured that the workers had all left for the day and these were the cars of the big bosses with reserved parking spots. Everything around here was still, which kind of surprised me a bit. This was the Napa Valley, this was wine country. That day it seemed to be sleeping.

A car entered Skepco's lot and stopped near the other cars. I didn't recognize the car but I did the driver when he got out. It was Mike. No surprises there, after all, he was a vice president. He hurried to the door and used a key to get in. I suppose he had some late night decisions to make. Another car appeared carrying two passengers. Although it was still light out, they were partially blocked from my view but I had a hunch they were the two guys that had assaulted me. They also entered using a key. Realizing that I was sitting pretty much in the open, I thought I should move to avoid suspicion. I drove away and began heading back to the city.

I parked my car just down the street from the condo and walked to the corner to buy a pizza and some beer. I decided to eat there, although the thought crossed my mind about how attractive it would be to go back there, kick off my shoes and leave them on the living room floor. I wanted to toss my tie, which hung loosely around my collar, across a chair. I would be home, I thought, and safe but not now. I devoured most of the pizza and drank three of their beers. It was about ten when I walked in the condo. I looked at the notes I had written.

I stood there looking at the papers for a few minutes and then began reading again. I never wrote anymore on them but I still have them. They are in my coat pocket. I have read them so many times that I know it all. But that night was special because I decided what I was going to do. I was going to do what Jack would have done.

CHAPTER XX

SKEPCO, INC.

The next morning I called in sick, or actually left a message on Willy's answering machine, since no one was in that early. By seven I was parked across the street from Skepco.

I found a spot in the parking lot of the building across the street that gave me a good view of Skepco's front door. There were plenty of cars on the lot that early in the morning so I figured I had good cover. I had brought along an old pair of binoculars and my camera even though I didn't have a telephoto lens. Some things just seemed standard in this spy business. I chuckled to myself.

Cars began straggling onto the Skepco lot soon after I was parked. None of the people looked familiar nor did they look suspicious. Just regular people going to their regular job, unaware of what was really going on. I felt sorry for them. At just about eight, a big car arrived and parked up close to the door. I put the binoculars to my eyes and focused on the car. The driver was a short, bulky man, probably in his fifties. He was dressed well and took a precautionary glance across the parking lot before strutting through the front door. I couldn't say that I had ever seen him before but there was something strangely familiar about him.

A moment later a small car pulled in and out stepped a girl that I had seen before. She used to work in the same building that I did at the yard. I never got her name but the word was that she had quit for some high dollar job. More people arrived until at about nine, the movement ceased as suddenly as it had started. The parking lot was far from full, in fact there might have been cars in only one fourth of the available spaces. There didn't seem like there had been enough people to perform the work needed to ship all of the parts to the yard or yards for that matter, as I did not know the full scope of the operation. Everyone, who had gone in had looked more like office workers than shop workers. I considered the possibility that this was the administrative headquarters for the company and there was another production facility located elsewhere. But this building, which was not huge by anyone's standards, was too big for just an office complex. I thought maybe it might be a warehouse also. I finally admitted to myself that I didn't know what was inside that building and I also admitted that I wanted to find out. I put the binoculars under the seat and started the engine.

I wasn't dressed particularly well but I wasn't too shabby. I pulled my car across the street onto the Skepco lot and found a place not too far from the door. I thought to myself that I must be crazy. I got out of my car and began walking toward the door. In my mind I was trying to decide what kind of job I was going to be applying for.

The reception area was very open and bright. The entire front was glass and the sun, although low in the morning sky, blasted the whole area. Each of the other three walls had a door in it. None were labeled and none had windows to give me a clue what was behind. There was a receptionist, a stern looking middle aged woman, seated behind a heavy oak desk. She had been watching me since I had entered. She asked if she could help me when I was still five feet away from her. I said that I wanted to apply for a job and before she could ask another question, I added that I had heard that they were accepting applications for inspectors and electronic repair technicians. I told her that I had experience in both areas. She smiled and handed me a clipboard with an application and pen attached. She motioned to a small seating area in front of the glass wall. The chairs were very soft to the point of being uncomfortable for anything except sleeping. I filled out the form very seriously, using my real information and experience. I thought that would be more impressive and it would be days later before they could verify any of it, if they would, that is. I just wanted to look good enough to get a chance to see what was behind those doors. I needed one chance to look behind the scenes there.

She smiled when I handed her the completed form and I watched as she scanned over it checking key entries. She asked me to have a seat and as I walked back to the chairs, I looked over my shoulder and saw her call someone on the phone. A few minutes later a tall man wearing a gray suit came out of the center door and picked up the application form off of the receptionist's desk. He, too, scanned it over and twice he looked up toward me. When he had seen enough, he walked over to me and introduced himself as Mr. Cappelli, or something like that. He said that my application looked pretty good and asked if I had time to chat about it. I said yes, of course, and followed him through the center door.

As I would have expected, the door opened into a corridor, which appeared to go straight to the back of the building. Every door that I saw along this hall was closed. I imagined they were locked also. We only went a short distance when he motioned for me to enter an office whose sign said 'B24.' It was a small suite that appeared to have three offices opening into a common reception area. It was very bright from the lights overhead. There was no one at the reception desk although it had obvious signs of being lived at. There was a man sitting behind a desk in one of the offices. He seemed engrossed in his work and paid no attention to me. The second office had the door shut. The third office was apparently Cappelli's.

I sat across from him and waited patiently as he read over my application again. He talked a little about what they did at Skepco, all of which I already knew. In fact, I think I probably knew more than he did. He said they were in the need of a few good inspectors. He added that they would, of course, have to run a quick background check since they dealt with mostly government work. He added that it was just routine and I certainly had nothing to worry about. Again, I knew more than him.

I was amazed when he offered me a salary that was easily 25% higher than what I was making at the yard. I accepted the job contingent on the background check. He seemed pleased and assured me that I would hear from him in a few days. He escorted me back out to the lobby and shook my hand. I said thank you to the receptionist and began walking toward the front door. I heard the side door open and I stole a glance through it but it was only a sterile corridor like the one I had been in.

Once back in my car, I looked at the building again. I tried to map out in my mind what the layout must be inside. I ran over in my mind all that I had seen and heard while inside. I was sure the three doors inside had some sort of locks on them like the ones on the internal offices. If I could get some sort of master key I would probably be able to move freely inside, I thought. But where would I get a master key. And besides that, I had no idea how I was going to get inside in the first place. Suddenly, feelings of stupidity and hopelessness swept over me. I was sitting in my car at a place I shouldn't have been, trying to devise a plan to break in and find what; then a sense of worry hit me as I realized that Skepco was going to be checking into my background and I had given them my real name and address. You can't imagine how utterly stupid I felt.

I pulled off the lot and started driving back towards the city. I was not going to go back to work and I didn't feel like going back home. So I just engaged in what had become my favorite pastime when I needed to think or feel sorry for myself, driving around. I always kept my gas tank pretty full, maybe for that unconscious reason.

In San Francisco, I picked up the Pacific Coast Highway toward Los Angeles. I had driven that road once before when Mary had first come out. A part of me deep inside wanted to see the beach. And that was weird, because I had never liked beaches as long as I could remember. Unfortunately, I had a fair complexion and had a very low tolerance for the sun. The sun hurt my eyes and it burned my skin. I was always the guy at the pool or the beach that never took off his T-shirt and tried to stay in whatever shade he could find. I always had those tan lines on my arms but I figured that by wearing a shirt all the time, nobody would notice. Mary, on the other hand, worshipped the sun. Her skin had a natural golden glow about it and she only darkened in the Florida sun. I was sure that California would be good to her too. Where my body was mostly without shape, hers was a work of art. I used to say that they designed the bikini with her in mind and she made a believer out of anyone who saw her. Even as I was driving down that highway, I couldn't stop thinking about her. I hated her but still wanted her.

It was warm and the breeze felt good through the open car window. It was the right time of day, so that the water looked bright blue. The beaches were not very populated, just the normal regiment of surfers and walkers. I pulled over into a small picnic area just above the beach. It would have been a great place for a picnic with the view, the breeze, and the quiet. But I didn't bring anything along. I sat on the picnic table and gazed out over the ocean. I knew that Hawaii was out there somewhere. I sat there at least two hours and the amazing part about that was that no one disturbed me or even came near me. It was almost like I was invisible. All I could think of was how stupid I had been. I had played my ace. In a day or so they would be on to me and I would be probably getting an unpleasant visit from a couple of Mike's heavies. I didn't know why I had gotten the idea to go inside and apply for a job. Had I really thought that I would be shown something that would have mattered? For a while, I thought about taking off somewhere and leaving it all behind. Just disappear and that would be the end of it. But then I kept thinking about how Jack had said you had to be resourceful and clever. He said you had to look deep into everything, because there was always something else lurking there that you really ought to know about. I knew he was right but I just didn't feel like the right person to go through with it. I got back in my car and pointed it for home.

As I was approaching San Francisco, on a stretch of road that was surrounded primarily by state park areas, I saw a few small buildings with white painted siding. There were only a few parking places out in front and I pulled into the first one. The first building was a little restaurant whose sign said that it specialized in Chicago style pizza.

It had a redwood deck off to one side that was cramped with round tables and wooden chairs. They offered a terrific view of the bay and the ocean beyond. In the center of each table was a large umbrella, although they were all in the down position. All of the seats were empty. I would have thought the place was closed if not for the front door of the restaurant being wide open. In the middle was a small hardware store. It had a sign in the window that said it was closed. By the looks of it I figured it had been closed for quite a while. It looked dusty, in fact this entire little group of buildings reminded me of some old western that I might have seen on TV. I felt like I should be hitching up my horse rather than parking my car. Hanging in the windows were things that looked like old farm implements. And just inside, off to one side, was something that looked like a wagon wheel. It made me think of the antique shops I had been in back east.

The last building in the short row was a locksmith. That building was much smaller than the rest, not just in width but it was only one story high, whereas the others had two floors. It, too, looked deserted but its sign said open.

I decided that rather than just sit there for the rest of the day, I would see what Chicago had contributed to pizza. As I suspected, there were no other customers in the place. I looked around and saw that there were more tables inside, as well as a counter that ran the entire length of the side wall. At one end was a sign that said, "Place Your Order Here," and at the other end, one that said, "Pick-up Your Order Here." The area between the signs was taken up by stools with red vinyl seats. As I stood there reading the menu which was painted on huge boards hanging behind the counter, I sensed that the guy behind the counter was staring at me. He asked if he could help me. He didn't sound as if he really cared one way or another about what I wanted, but rather had memorized the line after years of working in little places like this. Behind him sat a girl eating a hamburger and drinking what was probably a soda. She took no notice of me.

I ordered a small pizza with sausage and onions and a beer. He handed me the beer right away. He didn't make me go to the sign for pickup. With the cold bottle in my hand, I walked around the place passing the twenty minutes it would take for the food to finish cooking. He went about pounding out the dough. The room was decorated in a mixture of bad Italian looking scenery shots and pictures of Little League baseball teams. The teams had names like the real ones, Dodgers, Red Sox, Orioles, and, of course, the Giants. There was a row of trophies on a shelf high above the floor. Apparently this restaurant was a sponsor. I wondered if the team got free pizza after each game or just the ones they won.

Near the door was a bulletin board that was maybe half full of index cards and scraps of paper. There were things for sale, houses to rent, and two cards looking for a ride to San Diego for a weekend that had long past. The pizza came quickly and it was superb. I did have to go to the pickup counter that time and I got another beer while I was there. I sat at a table and looked out the one window at the back at small waves slapping the sand at regular intervals. It had a strangely calming effect. I was still thinking about what I had gotten into and how I was going to get out of it or at least I had to figure out what to do next. It was an hour before dark when I finally walked to my car. I had kept the pizza shop entertained for a while with stories about the beaches in Florida. The girl who hadn't noticed me when I came in had noticed that I had a slight accent and had questioned me about where I was from. Neither of them had ever been out of the area except on family vacations and then not very far. I learned that they were boyfriend-girlfriend and that they liked working here, because the boy got to drive the girl home which meant they could stop at one of the little beach spots for some private time. Private time was his phrase. I always called it making out or getting laid. They also said that there was never any business on weeknights so they tended to close early. The owner came in to open in the morning and got what little money they had made out of the safe then. I figured that gave them a little more private time. By the time I left, they weren't acting as if I was an inconvenience anymore.

As I started my car I looked up again at the hardware store and the locksmith, both now closed. At that moment I knew what Jack would have done.

CHAPTER XXI

No One In Sight

I drove down to the airport. There was a classy lounge in an adjacent hotel that I had taken Mary to on one of our nights out. They had a live band on weekends and I thought I would take a chance that night. There was no band but the place was hopping to a DJ playing a mix of songs spanning a couple of decades. The place was fairly crowded with business looking people. I suppose it was a combination of passengers coming and passengers going. There were several flight crew members scattered about. They stood out in their tailored blue uniforms. I found a table easily and ordered a good imported beer. I figured that if I had to wait, I would wait in style. The waiter brought me a bowl of pretzels. I sat there alone and no one approached me the whole time except the waiter who earned a nice tip. I didn't want company. I just wanted time to finalize my plan. At about eleven-thirty, I paid my bill and slipped out to my car. I was on the Pacific Coast Highway in minutes, heading for the site where I had enjoyed that Chicago pizza earlier in the day. I was relieved to see that the restaurant and its neighbors were dark, closed for the night. There was not even a neon sign to catch the eye of a passing motorist. About a quarter mile up the road on the opposite side of the street, I parked my car on a small pull off whose only distinction was a pay phone situated under a street light. I waited for the traffic to pass; then, I cautiously crossed the street and ran down the beach until I was directly behind the hardware store. The three buildings were a ghostly gray in the dim moonlight. I crept up to the store and pressed my back to the wall, scanning the area. There was no one in sight. Satisfied, I tried the back door. It was locked, of course, but seemed flimsy and there was no deadbolt. I guess people were just more trusting out there. I gave it a nudge and it creaked and almost sounded like it was beginning to split. I imagined that the sea air there must take its toll on the wood. I gave it one hard push and it splintered open. I listened for an alarm but heard none. All the same, I moved quickly. I found a flashlight on a desk near the door so the rest of my search went smoothly. I grabbed what I thought I might need: a crowbar, the flashlight and some extra batteries, a knife that looked like something you would clean fish with, and a small case containing several screwdrivers and a socket wrench set. I was back out the door in less than five minutes. I listened for sirens and peaked around the building to look for lights. There were none.

Encouraged by my success, I boldly moved to the locksmith shop. Its owner obviously believed in using what he sold. There was no way I could have broken in that door. I walked around the building looking for an alternate approach, my pockets bulging and the cold metal of the crowbar pressing against my leg. I guess I must have looked like some kind of amateur burglar, but then again, that's precisely what I was. On the wall that faced the hardware store, the windows were way too small and about 18 inches beyond my reach. The back had none. On the open side, the same small windows stared at me from above. The front was all glass, two large picture windows flanking a glass door. Everything was framed in wood with paint starting to peel. My only way in was going to be through the door, so I checked both directions, listened for the least sound, and wrapping the crowbar in my jacket, I knocked out the glass a piece at a time. I amazed myself at how quietly I had accomplished the feat. With the exception of having to duck into the shadows twice when cars went by, I seemed unchallenged. I stepped inside carefully. With the flashlight I located several large rings of keys. Looking at them quickly, I saw the word 'master' stamped in several of them. So that was how those guys could come out and unlock things so fast! There was a master for everything. I found four rings of keys. One looked like it held only car keys, so I left it there. I took the others with me. I was accumulating too much stuff. It was getting heavy and noisy. While I was fumbling with my assortment of tools and keys, I spied a tan canvas bag hooked by its shoulder strap over a chair. I grabbed it, threw in the keys and other stuff, and slung it over my shoulder. It felt good to take the knife out of my belt.

I slipped outside. It was so quiet that I could hear every wave as it slapped the shore and slid back into the sea. It was a repetitive slap, then hiss. Like a shadow, I was back in my car and heading for Skepco. It was twelve-thirty. I remember looking at my watch and seeing my hand shaking. Everything around Skepco was as quiet as it had been back at the shops. All of the buildings had outside lights and most had at least a few interior lights shining through their windows. In the lobby at Skepco, the lights were very subdued as if they were on a dimmer switch. I parked across the street again in a place where I was completely engulfed in shadows. I ran across to the front door and rummaged through my rings of keys. I grabbed a ring that clanked with heavy duty building keys and started trying them one after another in the keyhole. Some would go in, but none would turn. I tried the second ring and my hands began to shake again as I kept looking over my shoulder at the deserted street.

Finally the fifth key of the third ring slipped smoothly into the slot. I wasted no time turning it. The lock slid back into its keeper with a dull thud. I slipped in the door and kept a low profile as I made my way to the center door. I left the front unlocked for a fast getaway. I assumed the center door was a shorter path to the shop area from my earlier survey. The same key unlocked that door. I listened for alarms. I looked for flashing lights. All was still.

Once the inside door had shut, I ran to the end of the hallway, past closed doors, which probably hid offices. At the end of the hall was a door wider than the others with a glaring off limits sign. This, I thought, must be the place.

The lock on this door looked very different but surprisingly, the same key worked as it had on the previous two doors. Beyond the door, even in the limited security lighting, I could see that I had entered a huge warehouse area. From the outside, the building hadn't looked big enough for all that space. I walked along one side looking down rows and rows of pallets of boxes. I quickened my pace, trying to find some clue that would make this trip worthwhile. I had no idea what I was looking for but figured I would know it when I saw it.

Along the left side of the warehouse area, there were work rooms which were obviously assembly stations. There were windows running from just above my belt to just beyond my reach along the entire wall between the rooms and the warehouse. The lights in the warehouse softly illuminated each room. I recognized most of the equipment in the rooms, because it was the same type used on the yard. There was a lot of test equipment and dozens of soldering stations. I was looking at a pretty sophisticated operation, easily as well outfitted as anything the government had to show. I didn't see whether the other side of the warehouse contained similar rooms but, considering how symmetrically everything was arranged in this place, I'm sure there were.

The components in that first room were pretty ordinary. It appeared that Skepco was doing preliminary assembly work for some customer other than the Navy.

The next room was almost identical to the first except there was a different assembly on the tables. I recognized them from an evaluation I had made a few weeks before. But again, this wasn't what I was looking for.

The third room, though, seemed to be more of what I wanted. The outer double doors were metal with a cipher lock and the frames of what must have been the windows facing the warehouse had been filled in by plywood or something. I had no time to try and figure the combination to the lock, so I took the screwdriver set out of the bag and started disassembling it. There were screw heads on the outside which I thought would let me remove the outer plate, and then just a little tinkering and I would release the catch. I once had to get into my condo that way when I locked the key inside.

Everything was working well. The outer plate came off and even though I had to contend with an inner plate, I probably got the door open in less than fifteen minutes. It was dark beyond the door so the sudden intrusion of even the limited lighting from the warehouse identified shapes. There was a crate sitting near the door and bags of packing materials stacked against the wall. The work benches were covered with an assortment of parts and things that I could easily identify even in the dim light. I felt for the light switch and pushed up. As the fluorescent light flooded the room, a strange feeling twisted my insides. I had seen this stuff before. Those were transmitters from the shipyard. Once they were delivered, they were not to leave the yard unless they were in a boat. They were top secret. What would Skepco be doing with the transmitters, I wondered. They must be tampering with them, I thought. Everything was fitting together. It had almost been too easy.

In my momentary lapse into thought, I had let my guard down. I didn't hear them behind me, but felt the stick hit the back of my legs. I came down hard on my knees, groaning with pain, my teeth grinding together. The barrel of a gun nuzzled my ear. Frantically looking around, I noticed the video camera in the corner near the ceiling. Damn! Why hadn't I looked there? With the soft light I hadn't noticed any cameras. They had probably been watching me every step of the way, waiting to see just how far I could get.

A heavy hand shoved me flat to the floor, face down. A voice said "Don't move." The gun barrel relaxed. There were other footsteps approaching, but my head was looking the opposite way. I really wasn't in the mood to try turning it right then. It didn't matter anyway. I was caught.

The next few hours reminded me of a previous incident. The handcuffs, the questioning, the cell, it was all so familiar. The facilities at that police station, however, were better than those downtown. This time I had my own toilet and considering the crime, my treatment was a little less severe. Breaking and entering didn't carry the same esteem as murder. Even three breakings and enterings in one night, although the police never mentioned the other two. I always wondered what the record was. That guy must have been real good. I'll bet it was like six or seven.

I actually felt a little disappointed by the whole thing. The last time, the cops were prepared to drag me out of the condo. This time they were very polite. It was the private security guys at Skepco that overreacted. I had always feared being face to face, so to speak, with one of those rent-a-cops. I just never considered them as real police. It bothered me that they carried guns with bullets. But when the real police got there, it was okay.

I found out that the front door of the building had a silent alarm to a control station not far away. When I tripped the alarm, they began watching my actions on their video screens. There were video cameras in every room in that place. I had an audience the whole time and didn't know it. How rude

The control station had dispatched the two big thugs to intercept me and then they called the local police. They also put in a call to some of Skepco's big bosses. I woke up a lot of people that night.

I found out later that there was a big hassle out front, because the Skepco security guys didn't want to let the police into the building. The two cops who took me to the station were talking about it in the car. I don't know how far it went except it was the local police that picked me up off the floor. The rest, like I said, was pretty anticlimactic.

They helped me into the squad car and even played a decent radio station on the ride to the station. Nobody pushed me around or threatened me. They talked about a lot of things from sports to women to what a bunch of shitheads the Skepco guards were. They weren't talking to me but they didn't make any effort to conceal what they were saying either. I leaned my head over the seat back and watched the stars and street lights through the rear window. Once at the police station, they asked me for a statement, which I gave them, although not in any detail, and they put me into a cell. I didn't use my free phone call, since I really couldn't think of anyone that I wanted to call. At that time I had every reason to be sitting there feeling sorry for myself but instead I was actually feeling pretty proud. No one would listen to me, in fact everyone resisted me, and I had been forced to take things into my own hands. And I had done it all myself. But the most important thing about that night was I knew that I was going to make people listen to me. When they asked why, I would unload the whole story, under oath, to the authorities who would have to investigate it. With all that I had been through, during those previous two weeks, there was nothing else that they could do to me there. I laid my head back onto the pillow and immediately fell off to sleep.

CHAPTER XXII

Not Exactly As Planned

As I sit here in this hotel room, I can't help but remember how good I felt that morning when I awoke in the jail cell. I was so sure of myself that I was borderline cocky. After the horrifying weeks that had preceded that morning, I was suddenly feeling like I had taken on the world and had won, at least a battle. I had carried out my plan with hardly a hitch. Being arrested was only a minor inconvenience. I had achieved my goal by getting the goods on Skepco. I needed only to wait until the questions started and I would spill my guts about everything I had seen. Then I would watch the authorities clean up all the loose ends.

I realized that I had done the right thing. But the days that followed didn't sustain that feeling. It was just a momentary elation because, as usual, things didn't go exactly as I had anticipated. I should have expected trouble when I saw Mike walking toward my cell door.

He was accompanied by a police officer and when they reached my door, the officer unlocked it and swung it open. He said I was free to go. I looked at him puzzled. Mike told me to come on along. I was shocked. I followed him out to a counter where another officer handed me my personal belongings. Mike didn't talk but merely pointed to the door that led outside. Standing on the single concrete step out front, I asked Mike what was going on. I told him I wanted an answer right then and there. He just said that Skepco had dropped all charges and he continued walking to his car. He said he would give me a ride back to my car. It was still parked where I had left it the night before. I didn't believe what I was hearing. All of my carefully laid out plans had been a waste, because no one was going to ask me the questions that I needed to answer. I must have been shaking my head pretty vigorously, because Mike nudged my arm to snap me out of it.

He said to cheer up, I was off the hook again. How would I be able to convince anyone that everything I had seen was all part of some evil plan? I knew he was laughing deep inside where he knew I couldn't hear.

As he pulled alongside of my car, he said I should go home and call him later that evening, so we could talk. I told him that I had nothing to talk to him about, but he countered by saying that I certainly did. Probably more than I imagined, he added. I got out of his car and slammed the door shut. Thinking how good I had felt just an hour earlier made me nauseous. I drove my car directly home and phoned the office since I had not called in to work that morning.

When Willy answered the phone, it was obvious that he already knew what I had been up to. He told me that he would be forced to terminate my position at the yard. He said I would be receiving a registered letter explaining how my irresponsible actions had made me no longer employable with the government. Of course, I had the right to appeal. It didn't seem to matter that I had been released. Again, I was flabbergasted. His tone of voice was very cold and almost robotic. He sounded like an old west hanging judge reading the sentence. He ended the conversation by saying, "I'm sorry, good luck." I heard the phone click on the other end. I grabbed a beer out of the refrigerator even though it was morning. I sat on the sofa, resting my shoes on the coffee table. That hopeless feeling began to creep over me again. I was still shaking my head when I felt the tears running down my cheeks. I figured that I had played my last ace and lost just about everything, my job, myself respect, my sense of honor. At least everything that mattered. I sat there for several hours and probably wouldn't have gotten up then, if I hadn't needed to go to the bathroom. I dropped the bottle in the trash and realized that my muscles ached dreadfully. I was also incredibly tired. I suppose that being up the whole previous night was the cause of that. After emptying my bladder, I decided to take a walk around the block to loosen up and get some air. I did that from time to time, as I found that most days and evenings were pleasant in this part of California. However, before I made it to the door, the phone rang. It was Mike. He didn't sound particularly agitated that I hadn't called Him.

Mike said, "I thought that you wouldn't call. Rob, I told you that it was extremely urgent that we meet and talk. There are things going on that you don't understand even though I had tried to explain them to you once before. You are putting your own life in danger as well as those around you."

I asked, "How is Mary?" He didn't answer. He went on telling me that I had to meet him and listen to what he had to say. I think he could sense that he wasn't getting through to me.

He finally said, "Look, I need your help."

That was the shocker of the whole conversation. The concept of him needing me for anything just didn't exist in my brain. As long as I had known him, from back in our Navy days, he never needed anything. He had the cars, he had the girls, he had the money and now he needed the help of the likes of me. I didn't believe him but I will admit that it got me wondering what he was up to. I figured he was going to try to sucker me into another scheme, as the fool, no doubt. But still, I just had to see how he was going to try to sell it to me.

I finally agreed to meet him if he bought me some dinner and bought the beer. He said to meet him at a place called O'Leary's in a half hour. O'Leary's was a neat little bar that I had been to a few times before but never with Mary. My mind always conjured up an image of a cow wandering the streets of Chicago but beef was not one of their specialties. They had a great selection of imported beers and a great menu of soups, sandwiches, and appetizer kinds of things. Their jukebox was stocked with mainly great oldies from the 60's. The place was all decorated with wood and brass like the bar on that TV show. Even with changing my clothes, I was there in twenty minutes.

Mike was waiting inside the door. We took a table over on the left side and the waitress brought us two Heinekens along with a menu.

Mike suggested the club sandwich. I ordered, instead, the grilled chicken breast. I didn't need him telling me what to do. And besides, he had said he needed me for something. I sat there sipping the brew, waiting for him to lay it on me but he just kind of turned away and stared off across the room. A Beatles' song filled the room. My sandwich came in what seemed like just a few minutes and as soon as I had taken my first bite; Mike turned to me and told me to listen.

He told me that I had been on the right track about things going on at the shipyard. Yes, Skepco was a front for an operation that was skimming a lot of money off of government contracts. I took another bite but using his finger to drive home the point, he stressed that there was no tampering done that would jeopardize the function of any unit or compromise the safety of any person. All Mike and his merry band were after was the money that could be made by double and triple charging the huge military bureaucracy for various subcontracted tasks. Since he had everybody in the whole QC organization on board, he could make sure that things ran smoothly. He had to pay more people off but the income was enough to keep everyone happy.

I was the hitch, the problem, the wrench in the works. I hadn't bought into his group and that had caused real problems. Not at first when I was naive to everything around me, but later when I started to get curious. He hadn't wanted to hurt me, because I was his friend but he knew he had to get me out of the way fast. That's when he mentioned Jack Dempsey. He said only that Jack wasn't, who I thought he was and motioned for me not to talk as he continued.

Yes, he had set me up for Jack's murder and then had arranged to get me off, so I wouldn't spend any time in jail. He knew that would get me transferred to another job at the yard and he had hoped that I would've gotten the message to back off.

Mike said, "But you had kept on prying and that had caused more problems. By breaking into Skepco, you had actually done us a favor." I had been made to look like some kind of lunatic. I was under psychiatric care and now had been totally discredited. I had really helped him out there. When I asked why Skepco had dropped the charges, he replied simply that there was no point in pursuing it at that juncture. I was beginning to understand. I had become my own adversary in this game. Everything I had been doing was just making my own position weaker. Mike was just sitting around waiting for my next move, which promised to be more entertaining than the previous. I remembered that Mike had said on the phone that he needed me for something. So far, his narrative had been just the telling of what had happened to date and how stupid I had been. I started to ask him but he cut me off again. He ordered two more beers.

I had finished my sandwich and we were on our third round of beers. I was feeling good and the music, which was now much softer in the background, made a pleasant backdrop. He was obviously evading some issue. I figured that he just couldn't bring himself to ask me for a favor. I munched on some of the nuts that were in the bowl on our table. They were unbearably salty but I knew that it was a common practice for drinking establishments to serve complimentary snacks which made you want to drink more. Just good business, I suppose. Besides, Mike was buying.

He seemed to have a really strong interest in my activities, though, considering that he had made every effort to assure that I had become a nonentity. I appreciated Mike's tone of voice and the way he carried the conversation as if we were good friends. It made the evening very comfortable. I asked him, again, what he wanted but he went back into his narrative. This time, though, he wasn't talking about me.

He started off trying to sound real generic but it quickly became obvious that he was talking about himself. He talked about being contacted by a John Walker, who told him that he had friends in high places and he was looking for sharp guys to work in big government facilities and look for ways to skim some of that fat off the top of the budgets. He offered big incentives for hard workers. Mike had become one of his operatives mostly, because he had such a hatred for the Marine Corps and Navy. Also, his curiosity and love for money caused him to accept the offer, just to see if it really could be done. Mike did well at everything and at the shipyard he was made supervisor in just nineteen months. He had earned everyone's respect and trust, so he moved freely. He saw many ways to skim the fat and with the help of three business associates, he helped set up Skepco as an outside support facility. Mike simply set them up as a preferred vendor, which was within his power to suggest, and the games began. He, of course, had to recruit a lot of his staff in order to ensure the smooth workings, but that hadn't been hard. Money talked and he was quickly realizing that the potential was astronomical. He wouldn't say how many he had on his payroll even though I asked him sort of indirectly.

Years had gone by and he had steadily grown, not just in size, but in dollars in his pocket and dollars being sent back to the big guy. He got so big that John Walker started sending around auditors to check out the operation. Just an honesty check, you understand.

Up until about a year earlier, Walker and his associates had been satisfied and reportedly sent a messenger to their big bosses in Moscow to report the good news.

Mike said, "Until that announcement, I had no idea that someone in the Soviet Union was connected to the operation." During the past year, they had been extra critical about everything. Walker asked for information that Mike had felt he didn't need to know. He showed Walker all the books with all the journal entries.

He showed him all the things he needed to see to be sure that the big bosses were getting their fair share. Mike figured that he was getting too big and Walker was getting worried that he might decide to take off on his own. Having a competitor that knew so much was not good business.

For that year, Walker, who said that he lived in Los Angeles, had also been sending private investigators to spy on him. Mike had his own tight security network and they had pegged three different guys poking around. The first two had been picked up fairly quickly. They just didn't fit into the lifestyle of San Francisco and the wine country. Also, they were pegged as outsiders right from the start. Mike's group was trained to spot anyone or anything that was out of place or out of the ordinary at the yard and in the city. As soon as those two guys started asking questions, the word went out and operations shut down. They would find nothing to report. They both left as quietly as they had arrived. Mike cracked a slight smile when he talked about those two guys. He saw them as bumbling idiots and wondered if they were all Walker had to offer. If it was the case; then, all Mike could say was bring them on.

It was about the time that the first of the investigators had come to town that Mike made another startling discovery. There was an attractive woman that worked in Mike's office that never really bought into the plan but also never got in the way. She just went on in a world all her own, a world that was totally alien to him. Mike had tried to get at her a few times but she deflected all of his advances. It became obvious that she would not become one of his conquests but might become one of his friends if he would get his head out of his pants. He needed her as a friend and compatriot to keep the operation running.

Mike said, "Her name is Bev and she was a friend of John Walker's son."

It felt good hearing that Mike had never made it with Bev. I suppose I was less threatening to her. She had been a good friend to me, so much so that I felt like rushing to a phone and calling her but I wouldn't have known what to say. Mike noticed that I was drifting away and nudged my arm. I snapped back sharply and he went on with his story.

The problem was the third private eye. He was good, real good. Mike figured he had been snooping around for about six weeks before he found him. But more importantly, he had developed some contacts within Mike's organization. Mike could not afford to be vulnerable. His only chance was to eliminate the threat by whatever means it took.

Mike said, "With extreme prejudice," all he needed was the right set-up. The guy's name was Jack Dempsey.

CHAPTER XXIII

GUESS AGAIN, MISTER

That name cut through me like a razor blade. Deep inside
I felt the urge to call him a liar but I knew he had been straight with
me up until then, so I held back. I was beginning to realize that he
was bombarding me with all that information to set me up for the big
favor. As yet, I had no idea what it was going to be but I felt myself
beginning to brace myself in the chair.

Mike went on saying that Jack had become too dangerous to his
organization. He was on the verge of uncovering a number of projects
that were in the works and these projects were things that Mike wasn't
ready to share with anyone.

Mike said, "Then you dropped into the picture." All of the stuff
that I had given to Jack was essentially meaningless and worthless but
the fact that he had gotten it from me showed Mike that I was a risk
that had to be dealt with immediately. He said that he knew I had been
snooping around all along. His security guys had been tailing me. Of
all the people Jack had gotten to, I was the one who was closest to
Mike and his inner workings.

So I had set myself up to take the fall. One of Mike's goons had
taken care of Jack just after I had left that night. Since the staff at the
hotel had seen me come and go, I was easy to identify. I would have
bet that the guy that did the job probably even dressed like me. Mike
had taken care of two problems at once. But he didn't want to punish
me too much, because he figured he might still need me. And he felt

we were still friends. He just hadn't anticipated that I would start up my own investigation so soon afterward.

Anyway, he got a lawyer who was affiliated in some way with his organization to handle the defense and then arranged for the body to conveniently disappear. It was all very smooth. The insanity plea was intended to partially discredit me and therefore discourage any further snooping on my part.

I thought, "Guess again, mister." As I sat there in that bar, I knew I still wasn't through. At that point I finally managed to get a question in.

I asked, "Why didn't you suspect Bev, if she was close friends with John's son and he seemed to be out to get you?" He didn't really shrug off the question but replied that Bev was okay. Then he repeated that Bev was not a problem.

Mike said, "I can't understand why you are so committed to bringing me down."

I said, "It was because you are being dishonest with our country and that I couldn't accept that."

Mike said, "Don't you realize that you are just as guilty as the rest of us with your break-in at Skepco and all the classified information you have stolen from the shipyard?" His voice was sharp but I didn't let it intimidate me. I knew that I was right. I had just been complicating his life, and inside of me I could sense a faint smile at that thought.

At that point we both took a break from the conversation to order another round of beer and a medium pizza. I wasn't really hungry until I looked at my watch and saw that three hours had passed since my sandwich. I think we also needed that break, because we were reaching an impasse when the conversation became two-sided. I didn't much care what he thought about my ideology or my methods of execution. And somehow that brought me to my next question which, I'll admit, came out of the blue.

I said, "Why did you steal Mary away from me?"

It came out pretty strong but it didn't shake him. Mike was almost always Mister Cool, and I could see him switching into that mode to respond to that question.

Mike said, "You can't lose what you never had Rob." Then he went on to tell me that he had called Mary to come out here from Florida. He had even paid all her expenses. He said he needed someone to keep an eye on me, someone that I would trust. She had served that purpose for as long as she had been needed or more accurately, for as long as I had let her. Then it was over; end of story, back to where it had been before. He drank the last half of his beer and signaled for more. I couldn't think of anything to say back to him.

We were quiet again. And I have to admit that I kind of believed him. He had nothing to gain by lying about it. He was right, our marriage was at best on the brink of going bust.

I remember burning my mouth on my first bite of pizza.

I felt really stupid sitting there with molten cheese draped over my lip, grabbing for a napkin. I could see Mike laughing without making a sound. It brought to mind a similar scene from back in our Navy days except that time, the roles were reversed. I think we reached a strange yet slightly shaky understanding at that moment. For a minute we were buddies again. I knew that he was ready to ask me for the favor. And I guess I knew that I was going to say okay before the words left his mouth.

I always considered Thomas to be a heroic name. It has a sort of swashbuckling sound to it, like a British character in an old movie. But it is also dignified, like a member of Parliament. It might have been the name of a famous lawyer or statesman. Instead, it was the name of a salesman and his son, a patriotic worker who tried to find justice in a corrupt environment. But I had a duty to my country and myself. That I knew for sure. After all, my ancestry had been traced back to the Mayflower.

The favor was not really anything difficult and I certainly had the time in those days, being unemployed and all. Mike wanted me to do surveillance work, spying on people that he suspected as being "eyes" for his boss. After the disappearance of Jack Dempsey, he was certain that his operation would become a prime target. In fact, he was sure that there was at least one person snooping around at that time. And if Jack had been one of the best, then it was also certain that more would follow.

In spite of all my seemingly refutable adventures, I had gotten virtually zero press coverage. Incidents like murder and breaking and entering just didn't carry a lot of power in the media in those days. So outside of those directly involved, nobody really had much knowledge of what I had been into. My name was not a household word. Mike figured I would be able to move around very freely that way. He would give me a fake name and a fake occupation and I could try and gain the confidence of those snoopers while I pried them for information. Basically, I was going to become a Jack Dempsey. Just keep reporting back to Mike and my financial situation would cease to be an issue. It all seemed very simple and I already knew that I would say yes. It was that power that Mike exerted over everybody. If he had chosen to be a salesman working on commission, he would have been the richest man in California. His four hour presentation that night sold me. We drank one more beer to symbolically close the deal.

I knew I was staggering as I walked to my car, fumbling for the right key. Mike offered to drive me home but I declined his offer. He did not appear as if he had had even one drink.

I thanked him and assured him that I was okay. Other than suffering from information overload, I was. I needed time to think. I let my car idle on the parking lot for probably fifteen minutes before starting for home. In spite of how much I had eaten that night, I felt compelled to pull into a little burger drive-in. I really just wanted something cold and sweet to drink but ordered a hamburger and fries along with a large Dr. Pepper. I surprised myself when I ate all of it. I was wide awake thinking about all that Mike had said.

His comments about Jack Dempsey and Bev had me wondering.

His answer about Mary didn't. Anyway, he had said he would call me the next day to work out the details. It seemed so clear cut and simple, just the way Mike ran everything. One side of me was ready to jump at a chance to do some meaningful work, regardless of what side it was on. The other side was searching for a way to make the scoundrel Mike pay for all that I had been through. The extra food, the night air, and the twenty minute break sobered me up. I went home and went right to bed.

Noises outside woke me up the next morning. It turned out to be just one of my unruly neighbors arguing with the girl from the front office. But I couldn't get back to sleep even though I was pretty tired and a bit hung over. Fixing myself coffee, I thought again about Mike's proposition. I decided to take him up on his offer but to keep my eyes open, not just for him, but for things that I could use in my investigation. I was not going to be pushed out of the picture that easy. Mike had actually given me a new chance, a chance to prove what I was capable of doing.

I laid around the condo the rest of the morning watching the sunlight move slowly across the living room floor. Its path followed an odd diagonal shape, which seemed to fight the natural lines of the room. I had never noticed it before but it fascinated me of that morning. I just drank my coffee and sat with my legs draped over one chair. It was the beginning of a strange day.

Mike called a little after and seemed in a real good mood. I guess he thought that he had snagged the one fish that had eluded him for so long and I guess he had snagged me in one sense. I was now part of his organization. But unknown to him, my motives were different.

He talked pretty freely considering I assumed he was at work. He told me about a guy that he was pretty sure was snooping around. He gave me the guy's name, description, address, and any other information that he had. He told me to follow the guy around a bit, without being detected, of course, and to report back to him each day. He said not to try to contact the guy until he said to. At that time I was going to just be a spy.

Mike said, "Once you demonstrate that you could do our kind of surveillance work, I will get you more involved through some of my security guys." I had met a few of them already and although my memories were not particularly pleasant, I could hardly believe that I was actually being given the chance to get into the real inner workings of Mike's organization.

Needless to say, that was exciting to me. I listened eagerly; then Mike talked about compensation.

He said, "If you go a week without a hitch, I will make you full-time and salaried at $500 per week, tax free, of course, plus your rent and utilities will be paid in full." I was lucky that I wasn't taking a drink of coffee when he said that. His package was more than double what I had been making at the yard, so without hesitation, I asked him when do I start. He said that day.

I was pretty sure that the guy that Mike had me following was one of his own security guys. Mike was too cautious to send a rookie like me out after a real bad guy. He was going to spend that first week without pay as a test of both my abilities and my loyalty. I was convinced that I was going to win him over. I was going to do it right. I was actually starting to feel good again.

I hung up the phone and got dressed. I found some left over pizza in the refrigerator and ate it cold, an action that normally made he feel ill. But I was feeling good that day and even that cold pizza tasted good.

Mike told me that the guy, whose name was Mario, tended to stop at a certain bar near the yard almost every afternoon.

I was glad that it wasn't the same place where I had met Jack but not real pleased to know that it was a biker bar. A lot of them hung out there and it had a reputation in the local paper for spectacular fights. I was sure that Mike was planning a good show for my first day.

CHAPTER XXIV

CHILI DOGS

The bar was called Bud's and there were six Harley Davidson's parked out front. I parked across the street under the shade of a big oak. There were several cars there, too. I sat in my car for the better part of an hour planning my strategy. I knew I had to blend in if I was going to do any spying. I decided to watch who went in and out of the place for a while, taking particular note as to how they were dressed. It was lucky that I did. In that hour I watched maybe twenty people pass through the front door of the place and all but one of them were wearing jeans and some sort of loose fitting shirt. Even the one girl that went in was dressed in that style. This was not a hangout for office workers.

I decided that I had better go home and change, since I was wearing khakis and a polo shirt. When I returned, I parked in front and walked right in. It wasn't very crowded, so I took a seat at the bar and ordered a beer, the same brand that everybody else at the bar was drinking. I studied the rows of bottles lined up just below the mirror behind the bar, just the normal assortment of spirits. The bartender looked like a Bud and he wasn't very talkative. The whole place was actually pretty quiet. I found that a little odd but I wasn't there to ask questions.

There was one thing I had learned about bars several years earlier. If you sat at the bar near the center, you could survey almost the entire room through the mirror behind the bar. Normally the area back there was so cluttered that the rest of the patrons couldn't pick your face out looking at them. I suppose to them you just looked like an antisocial drinker, who wasn't looking for company or sympathy. I had used this technique in my early college days to discretely survey places for good looking women. This time I was searching for a guy named Mario. No one there fit the description.

The bartender slipped a laminated card under my change.

I noticed that it was a menu with about six things on it. He said the cold cuts were fresh and walked away again. Mid-way through my second beer, I took a look at the card and ordered a ham sandwich "through the garden." I thought that was a particularly clever way to say lettuce, tomato, and mayo, as I chuckled to myself.

I called out, "Bud," as I held my right hand in the air, Bud nodded and he scribbled the order on a scrap of paper that he handed to someone behind the swinging door at the far end of the bar.

A few minutes later my sandwich arrived along with a third beer. I motioned to Bud that I was moving to a table off to the side. I had surveyed the place through the mirror and decided that it would be better for me to eat at the table rather than at the bar. Everyone sitting at the tables were eating something, so I fit right in there. I hadn't seen any waitress or customers coming up to the bar to order but I just let that pass for then. The table I sat down at gave me a good view of the front door and the whole inside of the place but at that moment my attention was focused on that sandwich.

It was monstrous. I could have cut it in quarters and eaten for four days. I was glad that the cook had cut it in half and he even put a mound of potato chips on the side. I was contemplating how to pick it up for that memorable first bite, when a guy matching Mario's description walked in the door, motioning to Bud. He sat at a table with two guys that probably belonged to two of the bikes outside. Both were dressed in leather and wore many tattoos. He was in greasy looking jeans and sweatshirt. One of the bikers called him by name. Although I couldn't make out much of what they were saying, they seemed to be acting like old friends. Bud brought a beer out to him, which was the first time I had seen Bud come out from behind his bar. My first bite met my expectations, as it was delicious.

The three of them spent the next hour drinking, laughing, and making crude gestures at several of the other patrons.

The other people either left after a few minutes of it or gave it right back. It reminded me of the way kids tease each other in elementary school. They didn't seem to take any notice of me. But I was noticing everything about the three of them.

They all looked pretty tough, so I had to make sure that I didn't attract any unwanted attention. They didn't seem to be searching out non-regulars but just out to have some fun and get a little drunk.

They looked almost enough alike to suppose that they were brothers. They had the same dark, blackish hair as well as the same uniform and their ages could have been staggered a bit with Mario being the middle kid. I figured that I was drifting too far off my mission and refocused my attention on Mario. For the entire time he was there, he made no move that would have caused me to suspect him of anything.

I finally had to slip off to the men's room. When I got back a few minutes later, Mario was gone. He had apparently left although his two buddies were still there. I paid my own bill and quietly slipped out the door and walked to my car.

I scanned the parking lot for Mario's car, which Mike had told me was a late model Corvette. There was only one car on the lot that fit that description. It was parked opposite me and about eight cars down. Even though it was a long way from the nearest lamppost, its silver color stood out in the night light. As I got into my car I saw that there was somebody in that car.

I figured it was Mario; then, I noticed that there was somebody sitting next to him. I could only see silhouettes and the occasional flash of match to cigarette. I started my car. The person in the passenger's seat got out and disappeared behind the building. It looked like a girl. The driver turned on his headlights and pulled off the lot. I followed at a safe distance. Since it wasn't too late, there was enough traffic on the streets that I could follow very discretely.

The car just drove around for about an hour, mostly toward the city; then, he started heading back out into the valley and in the direction of Skepco. He pulled into a Holiday Inn. I pulled past the driveway, parked, and ran around the building to see where he was going. Sure enough, it was Mario. He had parked in front of a first floor room and used a key to open the door. Apparently, he had been staying there.

I looked around to get my bearings. I had learned my way around the small town that surrounded Skepco, so I felt comfortable sitting there in my car. My learning how to get around always came from driving from one place to another; although, I always had a good map in the glove compartment.

I decided to get out and buy a coke from the machine under the stairwell and propped myself against the ice machine next to it, so I could watch Mario's room for a while. After about twenty minutes I started to get a little self-conscious.

I began to feel like some kind of peeping tom that would be noticed before long. I started strolling along the row of units opposite where he went in and I saw his lights go out. I went back to my car.

Suddenly, I was overwhelmed by this feeling that he knew I was on his tail and he was just waiting for me to leave, so he could continue on whatever mission he was on. I turned my car around and pulled it further away from his room but parking where I still had a good view. The lights were still out and Mario's car was still there. I waited. I felt like I should be eating a donut. Within ten minutes he slipped out of the darkened room and into his car. My hunch had been right.

I realized then that my task was going to be a bit harder.

We were in a less traveled area and there were fewer cars on the road than before. I pulled out after he had turned left onto the main road. I saw him ahead as I turned.

He seemed to be driving at a higher rate of speed than before, and although my car would have been no match for his in an all out race, it had no problem in those city conditions. He was heading toward the valley again and again I thought of Skepco. Was this guy spying on Skepco or for Skepco. I was sure this guy worked for Mike and was supposed to give me a workout that night. I was determined not to let him get away and, to the best of my abilities, not to let him know that I was following him. Maybe he thought he had given me the slip at the motel.

He went right to the Skepco building and pulled around to the loading dock. Again, I kept my distance. I didn't pull in; I watched from the road with my binoculars. There was a van parked at the dock and a man got out when Mario pulled up.

This guy had a package under his arm that looked a little larger than a shoebox. They exchanged a few words and the man handed the package to Mario, who quickly got back in his Corvette.

He stood there appearing to watch Mario pull away. I knew it would be hard to turn around and follow him again without being seen, but I had to give it a try. Without turning my lights on, I backed up into a parking lot entrance. I hoped the glowing of my brake lights didn't give me away. If Mario wasn't looking for me, he probably wouldn't notice me. I don't think he did. He drove right on by. I waited a few seconds, then followed with my headlights off at first. In my rearview mirror I saw the van pullout but go the other direction.

At a stop sign, Mario had made a right turn. I clicked on my lights and followed. I felt comfortable knowing that we were back in a little bit of traffic. I felt like I had some cover. He was heading back for the motel. Again, I drove past it, turned around, and pulled in just as he was opening his door, package under his arm. I parked and bought another coke. I realized that this surveillance stuff was getting expensive. The lights were on in the motel room.

I was just taking a big swallow of the soda when a hand rested on my shoulder. I choked. It was Mike and he remarked that I was good, real good. Now I knew who Mario worked for.

Mike told me to rest the next day and he would call me with the next assignment. I realized then that it was nearly two in the morning.

I was asleep seconds after hitting the bed but my dreams kept it from being peaceful. For that entire night I had the feeling that something wasn't right. I wondered what was in that package that Mario had picked up. Mike hadn't asked for a report of what I had seen, he seemed to just assume that I had seen what I was supposed to have seen. And on top of all that, there was something familiar about that Corvette.

I woke up about noon. I was ravenously hungry and thirsty. I ate the last piece of cold pizza and drank a glass of milk that was OK but going fast. I started to feel better. It was bright and sunny outside and I tried to think of better times. Suddenly, a name and a face popped into my mind, Bev.

I called her at work since I knew she never went out to lunch. She answered on the first ring almost as if she knew I wanted her to. She sounded really glad to hear from me and asked how I was doing. I didn't tell her I was working for Mike but just that I was doing okay. I think she knew what I meant. She could always see through me. I wanted to ask her out again but it had been so long that a question like that would have been out of place. That's why it felt so good when she invited me up to her house for dinner that weekend. I had the feeling that better times were coming. When I got off the phone, I laid across the couch and smiled.

CHAPTER XXV

LEAVE TOWN?

Mike called around four o'clock and told me to take it easy that night. He added for me to get some rest the next day, because I would probably be up all that night. I didn't mind working like that, I was willing to do what he needed. My only concern was what I would do for the next eight or ten hours. I was wide awake.

Grabbing a jacket, I hopped in my car and took off looking for that one thing I felt like eating. That thing turned out to be chili dogs and I bought three. I drove out by the local airport to a place where I could pull my car onto the side of the road and watch the planes take off. I sat there, as I wiped the chili running down my arm and chin. The airport runway was only long enough to accommodate small jet business traffic but I was feeling the force, as several jets took off one after another and climbed into the sky. I once saw the space shuttle being carried on the back of a 747, which was a real thrill, so you know that this sight was an adrenalin rush for me. I pulled off the road just as one passed overhead. I took a picture, which I keep with me to look at today.

I sat there until just after dark and then drove down the road until I found this Ben & Jerry's ice cream shop. Besides, this was another great spot for sitting at an outside table and looking at the air traffic. I sat there for a little while before heading for home.

As I parked my car, something told me to look across the street. About sixty feet up the street was a parked Corvette that looked just like the one I had been following the night before. Immediately my mind went into overdrive trying to rationalize why that car might be there. I got out and closed the car door quietly. There was no one in the Corvette. I slipped into the shadows and started toward the condo. My door was still locked tight and there was no sign that anyone had tried to break in. Things were just their normal level of noisy for a Thursday; then, I heard the shuffling of shoes on the concrete but before I saw anything, the sound and whoever it belonged to were gone. I went inside and switched on the lights. Everything was just as I had left it that afternoon.

I grabbed the last beer from the refrigerator and tried to decide whether I was just being paranoid. I looked through the living room blinds and saw that the Corvette was gone. I didn't sleep very well that night.

Mike called about ten the next morning and gave me the assignment for that night. I was to follow Mario again but this time I was to take special notice to who he met with and whether he went to see them or if they came to see him at the motel. Mike didn't give any other explanation and I guess I knew what he was getting at. I dug an old steno pad out of my desk and threw it and a couple of pens into a beat up leather backpack that I still had from my college days; then, I went back to eating dry cereal out of the box, as the milk had turned.

I decided that I would try and get a fix on Mario earlier than the previous time, so I wouldn't have to play games at Bud's place again. A stranger strolling in there twice in one week would surely draw the attention of any of the regulars, Mario included. I also decided to stock up on food and drink in case I was stuck in the car for a long time. By the sound of things, I was sure that I would be. I dressed in darker clothes, too. I had seen enough movies to know that part. By noon I was ready to hit the road.

My first stop was the 7-Eleven, where I bought some crackers, cookies, and pretzels. I also grabbed a few apples from the display on the countertop. In the same block as the 7-Eleven was a deli where I ordered three cold cut subs. I bought a half dozen bottles of fruit juice from them. I figured all that stuff would keep in the backpack without the need for refrigeration. I was proud that I hadn't bought any candy bars.

Next I tried to remember how to get to the motel, where I had left Mario the other night. All of my running around that night had been after dark and things obviously looked a little different in the daylight. As my sense of direction is good, I had no trouble retracing my path. The Corvette was parked at the front of the room.

I parked my car in an inconspicuous spot out of sight of the office and hidden enough from Mario's room that unless he was specifically looking for me, he wouldn't have a clue. I took an apple from my pack and bit in. It was sweet.

I positioned myself, so that using the outside and inside rear view mirrors I could check any movements behind me and to my right. It really didn't need to have Mike surprise me again. I was very cautious not to draw any attention to myself, so I didn't play the radio or move very much. I remember thinking that I had everything covered except going to the bathroom. I suppose that is why on cop shows they always had two guys on a stakeout. Knowing my body, I knew that I would not need to take a crap for hours and I could use an empty juice bottle to take care of the other need.

After about an hour, I became more observant of the motel itself. There was very little movement anywhere around the place even though there were plenty of cars. I rationalized that it was past checkout time and too early for most travelers to be checking in, so these were the parked cars of those guests who were out and about. It made sense to me.

I saw the drapes open in Mario's room but didn't see any head peeking out. I was still sure that he was checking the parking lot for unauthorized vehicles. I was hoping that my cover was working. But with the angle that I was situated at, he probably couldn't see me anymore than I could see in his window. The drapes closed again and a minute later he came out to his car. I put down my bag of pretzels and started my engine. I saw the vapor from the Corvette's tailpipe and knew that he had done the same. When he got to the street, he turned left. He was heading toward Skepco, I thought.

We hadn't gone far when he stopped next to a Taco Bell and made a phone call from a pay phone on the side of the building. I had pulled over at the curb four cars behind him. I hoped that the high traffic volume would keep him from drawing his attention to my car. I wondered why he hadn't called from the motel where it would have been free. All sorts of different things went through my mind right then. Maybe he had someone else in the motel room that he had to keep from hearing the call. Maybe he was afraid of someone tapping his line from there. Maybe he was just making sure that the call wasn't traced. Maybe I was just trying to read too much into it.

Finishing his call, he drove off again toward the valley.

Despite his flashy car, he drove extremely conservatively. He was obviously making no effort that would draw attention to himself. Most guys with fast cars like to show off just how fast and noisy they can be but he made it fairly easy to follow, even in my old blue Maverick Sport Coupe.

I was right, he drove to Skepco and parked out front.

There were still several cars on the lot scattered randomly but Mario used a key to open the apparently locked door front doors. Of course, I remembered working my way through those doors. He was only inside for a few minutes when he came back outside accompanied by another guy. Fortunately there was enough daylight to allow me to take several photos of them.

The two men talked for another minute or so then shook hands. They looked as if they had reached some sort of agreement. Mario got back in his car and drove back to the bar from the previous night. I hoped he wasn't planning on making a night out of it. The next night was my date with Bev and I really wanted to be sharp for it. And that would be difficult if I was up all night chasing this guy.

Bud's looked the same that night as it had when I was there before. It might have been the same cars and motorcycles out front too. Mario parked on the side of the building as he had done. I took a spot closer to the door for better visibility. I wasn't sure just then whether I wanted to go back inside but since Mike wanted to know who Mario was talking to, I knew that I couldn't get out of it. I waited for Mario to go inside and then waited about ten minutes more. I didn't want there to be any suspicions that I was following anybody.

Mario had corralled a pretty girl off to one side and was obviously putting the make on her. I grabbed a beer and sat at a table off to the side, on the opposite side of the room as the last time.

Just as last time, the evening was uneventful. He stayed about two hours, talking to the half dozen people that approached him as if he was an old friend. I made notes of their descriptions. When he left, he left alone and drove around a while before heading back to the motel. The lights in his room stayed on until past three in the morning.

At around four, I left and went home. I fell right into bed and slept peacefully for about five hours. Mike called about noon as I thought he would. He didn't sound very happy. I gave him my report of everybody that had been around Mario and I even told him about the phone call from the taco stand. But he sounded like he was preoccupied with something. I knew from experience that when Mike got like that, he could go out of control in an instant. At the end of a long string of what sounded like muffled voices, he said he wanted to see me in his office at Skepco. He told me to ring the bell when I got there.

I really didn't like the sound of his voice and the fact that he wanted to see me. I had my date with Bev that night, so I didn't want to get detained or find myself running another errand for him; however, I needed Mike's financial help if I was going to stay in Vallejo. Of course, Mike was responsible for me getting the boot from Chuck and for that matter, any prospects for other employment there. It was obvious to me that it wouldn't take much for him to make things happen one way or another in your life.

I figured that was what Mary liked about him. He made things happen; while I followed directives and waited to see what would happen.

I got dressed and drove out to Skepco as fast as I could.

There were about a dozen cars on the parking lot and I grabbed the parking space marked "Reserved: President." I rang the bell and after what seemed like a long time, a guy in jeans and UCLA sweatshirt came out to the lobby and opened the door. I had no idea where Mike's office was, so I was glad that the guy said to follow him. He led me through corridors that made me feel like a rat in a maze. We were on the opposite side of the building from my previous visit and the hallways bore no resemblance. The irregularity of it all distorted my usually good sense of direction.

A door opened into a reception area in a suite of plush offices. Only one had the lights on. There were no windows. The guy looked inside and finding no one, instructed me to have a seat and that Mike would be right back. From my chair in the waiting room I could see a sliver of Mike's office.

It was mostly cluttered with folders of papers and other boxes of unidentified stuff. The light flowing from that open office door kept making me feel like a moth near a flame. I wanted to move closer so that I could get a better look at what was inside but a little voice kept telling me not to.

The room that I was sitting in was not very fancy. It looked like every other waiting room I had ever been **in.** I started to look at three month old copies of <u>People</u> and <u>Sports Illustrated</u>. But before I got too involved in surveying the place, I scanned the ceiling and walls for cameras that were watching every move I made. There were none to be seen. I stood up and slowly crept around the edge of the room, looking at the furnishings at each point. In a few moments I had reached Mike's door and I stopped and listened, straining to catch any sound. It was dead quiet. I peeked in the door to get a little better view and found that the whole room was cluttered with boxes of files. Either Mike was a lousy housekeeper or he was digging into old files trying to dredge up some information. I scanned back and forth across the room but nothing had any familiarity to me. That was, until I looked close at a photo in a small frame on the credenza behind his desk. It was a picture of Mary. It was not a new picture of her but one from about two years earlier.

My ears picked up a warning this time and I sprang over to a grouping of landscape paintings just as the door opened. It was Mike and he was alone. His first words were a reference to the fact that the paintings I was looking at were originals. Then he asked me for what

I had on Mario. He asked me to sit down. He studied the notes that filled two handwritten sheets but he looked more disappointed than pleased with what he was looking at. He asked if that was all, as he dropped my sheets into a pile of other assorted papers. I had written down everything that had happened, everywhere he had gone, and described everybody he had talked to. Mike asked, "Why haven't you gotten close enough to hear what Mario was talking about when he was with those people at the bar and at the loading dock."

He was starting to piss me off but after a few seconds I realized that he was a lot madder than I was so I backed off. I explained that I thought I was doing what he wanted. But he just went off. He started yelling and pounding his fist on the desk and every minute or so he would fling a couple of papers off into Skepco space.

Finally he seemed to calm down and with his new found composure, he told me that I was fired.

He said, "You're just not cut out for this type of work, Rob, but don't worry about money, because I will continue to take care of your expenses for a while, so you can get started again in California or somewhere else." He told me that he was doing that as a friend.

We both stood up and he led me back to the front lobby.

He didn't say another word to me and I had nothing to say to him. He wished me good luck as he unlocked the front door.

CHAPTER XXVI

FOUL PLAY

I just couldn't figure Mike out as I was walking the thirty feet back to my car. I had seen him in some weird moods but that had been one of the strangest. One thing that pleased me was that I wasn't bothered by the picture of Mary. That lack of sensation would have made Dr. Goldman very happy.

My next thought went immediately to Bev. It was only about three o'clock and I wasn't due at her place until at least six. I took the leisurely route home and again surveyed my situation. Again, I was bouncing on the bottom. Again I was without a job and discredited from getting another around here. I stopped at a liquor store and bought a six pack for me and a bottle of wine for that night. By the time I had gotten home, I had narrowed my alternatives down to two.

Once in my living room, I popped open a beer and thought about it. I could leave town and put this whole California experience behind me. Or maybe I could go back to where my parents lived in Georgia. I hadn't spoken to them about Mary and me but I thought it might be a good place to start fresh from after she and I divorced. My other choice was to stick around and run Mike's hospitality into the ground, getting in his way whenever I could. I have to admit that that one definitely sounded more attractive to me at that particular moment in time. I didn't see where I really had very much else to lose. Whatever I was going to do, I knew that I had to think about it carefully. But I wasn't going to think about it that night. It was time to get ready to go over to Bev's.

It always seemed that there was a lot of things going on that I didn't know about which eventually would catch up to me. Mikes comment about Bev's friendship with the Walker family was working on me. I was always in the background of a dozen different plots and schemes and as my attention was always diverted to investigate one scheme, I always found out about the other schemes under adverse circumstances.

It seemed my entire adult life had been a testament to that.

My mind kept rolling back and forth over that idea, during the entire ride out to Bev's house. I suppose that was why I probably looked a bit spooked when I walked up to her porch.

Bev was sitting out front with a glass of wine that was almost empty. She had been waiting for me. I smiled and handed her the wine I had brought. She asked me what was wrong.

I shrugged and said, "I had been fired again that afternoon. I wanted to keep it low key but I also knew that she would get the details out of me before the night was through. She stood up and gave me a kiss on the lips. She motioned for me to come on inside and I followed willingly.

There was that familiar herbal scent in the air of the living room. I remembered it from before. The only thing different from the last time I had been there was the way Bev was dressed. Before, she was dressed in tight jeans or "that dress" when away from work. But tonight she was wearing an unusual robe that could have been African or Mid-eastern or something. The pattern on the fabric seemed almost random and the colors appeared to dance around her. I found myself becoming hypnotized. Bev just laughed. I think she knew what effect it had on me. She explained that her uncle had sent the robe to her, having picked it up on a recent trip overseas.

She said, "I'm not sure whether I like it, but judging from your reaction, it has promise." We both laughed out loud.

That was the first time I had heard her talk about her father's brother, although she really wasn't talking about him. Everything I had heard about him had been from Mike. I dropped the issue from my mind.

She had prepared a simple Chinese dinner complete with floor seating. She looked strange with her legs crossed, and only the faintest outline visible under the flowing robe. She began inquiring about my afternoon as we ate. She seemed very interested in what had happened. She knew that Mike had "hired" me to do some surveillance work, but she started to pry, as to who and why. Luckily, since I knew very little, I had very little to say. She seemed to understand.

Bev asked in a very serious tone, "What are you going to do next."

I shrugged and said, "Actually I have two choices that I had arrived at." She giggled at my idea about pushing Mike to the limit. That was something she would like to see, she said. The conversation was beginning to go in a direction that I had not intended it to go, so I tried turning it around. She caught my drift and brought up the topic of the robe again. She said it was from Morocco and supposedly quite expensive. Her uncle Claude, told her that it was the garment of a woman of breeding and substance. That seemed appropriate to me. She told me that there was a custom that went along with it. The woman was not to wear anything under it.

At midnight, we were in each other's arms, wrapped in a blanket of soft cotton. She had followed the custom. The dishes were still on the table in the morning.

I felt wonderful as I drove home the next day. It was a perfect Saturday and we had arranged to meet again for dinner on Sunday. Bev had a way of making me feel good about myself. She was not threatening and she had no unrealistic expectations of me. If I decided to stay in California, it would be mainly to be near her.

At that time, I hadn't made up my mind what I wanted to do or where I wanted to do it. My whole California experience had been a bummer over all. The job turned sour and everything else in my life had seemed to go down along with it. True, Bev had been a bright spot in all of it. She alone had stood behind me when everybody else had turned away. If only I could get her to move away with me somewhere, I thought. But that was unlikely at best.

There really weren't too many places I could move to either.

I wasn't ready to go to another strange location without friends. I also wondered what kind of reference would follow me in my search for a new IH or quality control job. I thought again about going back to Georgia and moving back in with my parents until I could get settled into a new routine. But like I said, we hadn't spoken about the recent developments between Mary and me. Today, I know that they liked her more than me. I wasn't sure I wanted to go through the humbling experience. It would be the return of the prodigal son except I would not expect to be showered with gifts or sympathy. It was hard to see myself in that role.

But there was one consistent thing in my life, during those times, my luck. When I walked up to my condo door, I noticed that it had been pried open and was pulled closed until it just met the frame. With my shoe, I pushed it slowly open, scanning the living room for a hulking figure. Everything was quiet and seemingly deserted. I stepped inside and pushed the door closed but the lock was hopelessly busted. I knew it would be tough to get a maintenance man up there on a Saturday. I grabbed a beer from the refrigerator and started surveying each room for signs of things out of place. Things were in slight disarray in every room. Even the medicine cabinet had been violated.

I felt I was fortunate that the burglar had been, at least, neat. I could find nothing broken but it was obvious that whoever had broken in had been looking for something in particular.

At first inspection I was unable to determine anything missing. As I grabbed my second beer, I called the police. They asked if I thought anyone was in the apartment. I told them that I had checked every space but didn't scare up anyone. They didn't sound like they were in very much of a hurry to respond, so I took a frozen lasagna dinner out and heated it up for lunch.

It had just come out of the oven when the police arrived at the door. I could see them from the kitchen. They knocked and then slowly pushed the door open. The first officer called, **"Mr.** Thomas?" He was followed by another uniformed officer and a guy in plain clothes.

I greeted them and began to explain how I had found the door broken and things in slight disarray. But the plain clothes guy, who identified himself as a detective Ernest Ropper, stopped me short.

He said the officers would take a full report but he had some other questions for me first. He asked me if I knew Nobel and I, of course, answered yes. He asked me stuff like when was the last time I had seen him and were we friends?

I hadn't asked why he was asking that stuff, because they hadn't tried to arrest me and it seemed just that he should be in trouble with the law. I told him that I had worked for Mr. Nobel and had just recently left his employ. The detective didn't seem overly interested but jotted down notes on a little pad that fit nicely in his pocket.

The more I looked at this detective, the more I felt I had seen him before. He hadn't been involved in my previous exposures to the criminal system but I was sure I had seen him around. The other two cops just looked like cops.

The shock came when he asked me if I knew a Mary Thomas.

I suddenly wanted to know what all the questions were about. He must have noticed my voice rising in pitch and volume. He told me in his cold, impersonal tone that there had been a car accident the previous night and that a Mary Thomas had been injured but released from the emergency room this morning. He was investigating the accident to rule out foul play. I figured what I had told him up to that point had made me a suspect.

When he finished with the questions he rose to leave.

He suggested that I not leave town for the next day or so and told me to notify him if I had anything to add. He handed me his card and directed my attention to the two uniformed officers. One of them had the forms out to register the break-in. The other went to the door, as the detective was leaving and began inspecting the damage. They were very efficient and after the last policeman I had spoken with, very courteous.

They seemed very concerned about what, if anything was missing. I told them that I hadn't determined if something was gone but if I noticed anything missing, I promised to call them.

They handed me a copy of the report and left quietly.

I called the front office. The girl sounded shocked to learn about the break in and she told me that the door would be fixed today. I told her that I did not want to leave with my front door open for anyone that should happen by. At that moment, I turned, and with the phone still at my ear, I saw where something was missing, a small medal that was imprinted with the words "World's Best Husband."

It was a silly thing and maybe the only thing I had salvaged from our marriage. Mary had given it to me at a time when I know that she really meant it. It was also a time when the Olympics were on TV every night and she bought the medal, because it resembled the gold medals that were given out there. She made a real production out of presenting it, too. She even had me stand on our picnic table and bow to her, as she hung a red ribbon with the medal hanging from it around my neck. She really did love me and I loved her too.

I had kept it hanging over the corner of a framed picture taken of us on our wedding day.

It reminded me of an innocent time. It was the sunlight reflecting on the area of glass that had been under the medal that caught my eyes. The rest of the frame was slightly dusty and discolored.

I put down the phone and walked over to the picture. I wiped the dust off the face of it with my sleeve. It was a good picture. I always thought that the photo captured the kid in each of us. Kids, who were not thinking about our abused childhoods or our futures. It was taken at just the right angle to capture the best sun and to show green rolling hills in the background. I took that photo with me everywhere.

I found myself thinking about her accident. I became impassioned with finding out more about the accident. Was Mike or someone else in the car with Mary? Did they leave the scene of the accident, because they did not want to be found with Mary? Mike told me that Mary returned to Florida on a flight that left the evening of the last day we were together. I called Bev to tell her about the break in. She seemed sympathetic but less than sincere about it. I also told her about Mike saying that Mary left on a plane earlier but the police questioned me about knowing Mary, who had been involved in a traffic accident yesterday.

She said, "Rob, I thank God that you did not confront the intruder," but nothing about Mary and her accident.

I picked up the last bit of information when I called the police station back and tried to reach the detective Ropper. The officer, who took my call, paused for about 30 seconds before telling me the detective was not available to take my call. He said that he would leave my message for Ropper. I never heard back, so I began to get the feeling that they were not going to share their information with me. It became apparent to me that the detective suspected foul play in Mary's accident. I found myself beginning to believe that I was more than a suspect in the eyes of the detective. It was business as usual in the life of Rob Thomas.

CHAPTER XXVII

A TRIANGLE?

Bev called me later that afternoon. She, too, was concerned about the implications of a triangle. She didn't seem shocked about it. I told her that the police had already questioned me and that I wasn't particularly worried. Hearing her talking with little sympathy made me realize that I was not really upset either. It was a kind of relief, as Mike was as suspect as me. When the detective found out about his illegal activities, he would be arrested and others would appreciate that I was his victim and he was the cause of all of my problems, since arriving here. Now I am free to live my life, as I had already accepted that I had lost any feelings for Mary. Again, I realized how much Bev and I thought alike. There was no reason to cancel our dinner date, because of this crap.

I couldn't resist checking through the place again looking for traces that something else was missing. Stealing the medal seemed so ridiculous. It only had meaning to me, I thought and it was certainly not valuable. Suddenly, as I was getting dressed after my shower, a strange paranoia swept over me. The medallion would be valuable if someone wanted to try to frame me for leaving the scene of Mary's accident. If it were to be found on the scene of the crash, a detective might try to link it to me. At that particular time I certainly had a motive. Or so it would appear.

The knock on the door made me jump about a foot off the floor. I was about ready to stick out my hands for the cuffs when I realized that it was the maintenance guy there to replace the lock. He was an older Mexican guy that, strangely, didn't seem bothered to be out on a call on a weekend. I didn't recall ever seeing him before that but he obviously knew what he was doing. The only thing he said was a few reassuring words that he would be finished very quickly. He used metal to reinforce the splintered door frame and put metal plates on each side of the door around the doorknob. And like he said, he was done in less than a half hour. He handed me my new keys and slipped quietly out the door. As the door closed and latched, there was the sound of solid, like a bank vault ... or a jail cell.

A few minutes later, I was out the same door heading for a restaurant called Sergio's. I had never been there before but Bev had assured me that I would really like it.

It sounded expensive, so I had stuffed a couple of hundred dollars into my wallet. I still had a lot of cash left from Mike.

He told me to keep it after firing me. I didn't put it all in one place but I knew I would probably need that much cash, considering that I had no credit cards. I was determined to enjoy myself.

I enjoyed the last hour of light as I drove down the highway.

The air had a slight chill that invigorated me. I found Sergio's easily. It sat on an artificial looking bluff that offered a great view of the San Pablo Bay. I saw Bev's car on the parking lot as I drove in. If there was one thing you could say about Bev, it would be that she was never late. When I walked in, the maitre'd addressed me by name and led me to a partially secluded table surrounded by tall palms and short ferns. Bev had watched me cross the room. She looked lovely. I gave the headwaiter a ten.

She was smiling brightly like she was genuinely happy to see me. I sat at the side of the table next to her. Before we even started talking, a waiter brought me a bottle of my favorite imported beer and a chilled glass. I looked at Bev and whispered thank you. The waiter placed another glass of wine in front of Bev and removed her empty one. For a moment, I wondered how many had she had already.

We never mentioned Mike during that evening. And I don't think we were consciously avoiding the subject either. We were there that night to be with each other, and we had effectively blocked out any distractions. The conversation started out very light, remarking how crisp and beautiful the drive to the restaurant had been. We talked about the decor of the place and whether they had a fulltime gardener on staff to take care of the plants that filled every corner, creating natural partitions and a sense of intimacy. We laughed about it.

After we had ordered our dinner, the tone got more serious.

Bev began questioning me about what I was planning to do. She seemed very concerned that I might not be thinking clearly about it. She brought up the two choices that I had told her about, but rather than laughing at them as we had done the day before, she asked sharply if I had weighed the pros and cons of each. I told her that I was more concerned with enjoying our evening than worrying about something that would still be around the following day. I promised that I would spend my whole Monday evaluating my choices. I told her that I would report back to her on Monday evening with the results of the research and also could give her status reports as the day progressed. I hadn't realized how sarcastic I had become until I noticed that sad little girl look on her face. She looked like her feelings had been hurt. I stopped abruptly and backed out of the conversation.

I think we both realized at about the same time that we were not winning points with each other. We both slid back in our chairs and then smiled at each other. It was a smile that said, "Enough said."

Dinner was exquisite. It was the closest thing to a perfect meal that I had ever tasted. I don't think I have come close since then either. For the rest of the night we talked about each other. First during dinner and then as we walked along the beach. It was nearly three in the morning when I watched her drive away from the restaurant parking lot. Ours had been the only cars left. The night had felt like it was ours alone. The drive home was a long one.

By the time I reached my condo, I was beyond exhausted.

I laid across the bed without bothering to undress. But my sleep, even though deep, was filled with dreams. They took various forms and featured various characters but they were all about the same thing. They were trying to make me make up my mind about whether to stay or whether to go. I saw people from my past and present weaving in and out of situations in which I was the costar. But I had a strange perspective in that I was watching the whole scene from a vantage point off to the side. I could watch everyone's movements, including my own, and I could hear all the conversations.

In one scene I saw my mother and father arguing about what to do with "him." Should they let him stay longer or should they insist that he get out on his own. My father was not very sympathetic.

In another, Mike was seated at his desk at the yard reading through my personnel file. Although he wasn't talking, his face was saying, "He had such promise."

I saw Mary sitting by a window looking out. She was crying. I realized that she was in our old house in Florida and she was wearing the clothes she had on the day I left for California.

I suppose I was too tired to let any of the dreams wake me up but they unsettled me enough that I remembered them vividly after I woke up. When my eyes opened I saw the clock reading about ten fifteen. I had this crazy urge to call Dr. Goldman and ask him about the dreams and maybe get some impartial advice on what step to take next. I knew that our previous relationship had been rocky at best, but he knew me and I knew what to expect from him. If he would, in fact, see me, he might just be able to help me sort out a few things. I was calling him this time.

Goldman was definitely startled at my calling. He actually sounded happy that I called. We arranged a long appointment that afternoon. At that point I knew that I was committed.

I would not be able to escape his questions about what had happened to me since I had ceased our sessions. I decided that I would have to lead the interview and keep him on the track I wanted him to be on, although I had no idea how I was going to do that to one who was skilled 1n the art of controlling people. I resigned myself to just making the best of the situation and listening very closely to what the doctor said.

It seemed interesting when I reviewed the scenes in my mind that Bev did not appear in any of them. I figured that it was because I had spent that wonderful evening with her and I already knew what her feelings were about my future.

I treated myself to lunch at a nearby Chinese restaurant before heading downtown. I was feeling okay except the food was greasy and made me sick later.

It felt strange driving downtown to Goldman's office, especially since it was my own idea. I thought that maybe I was crazy. I began to wonder just how smart that visit was going to be. We had never really gotten along very well but, looking back, I think he did me some good. I may not have agreed with him but he could get to the truth. Suddenly I wondered if I wanted him to get to the truth.

I parked in the same garage and walked the same half block to the entrance of his building. Everything was exactly the same as before, although it hadn't been that long since the last time I was there and there was certainly no reason for anything to have changed. I felt remarkably like I had as a kid going into a doctor's office. This time, though, Goldman came out just seconds after I entered the waiting room. He was smiling and stretched out his hand to shake mine and welcomed me back. The guy looked like Dr. Goldman, but the behavior didn't fit somehow. I sat in the chair that faced his desk.

Our interview went smoothly. Since I had called the meeting, he let me set the pace and devoted his time to listening intently. His comments were basically questions of clarification. I talked for about a half hour and then it was his turn. He used the next half hour interpreting what I had said and tried to point out where I was allowing various psychological maladies steer my actions rather than logic and reason. He was obviously still convinced that I was a wacko but I have to say I think on this occasion he was being totally straight with me. I couldn't say that before ... or after.

His concluding suggestion was for me to return to Georgia and put my life back together on friendly turf. Whatever opposition I would get there, it would not match what I had been through in California. As I walked back to my car, I realized that I had never mentioned Bev and the way I was feeling about her. I wondered if that would have changed his counsel. It certainly questioned my likelihood of accepting it.

In my mind I developed a strange parallel with the past.

In Florida I had had a wife that I loved very much who wouldn't follow along the path that I needed to take. Now I needed to take another path and I needed someone to love who would accompany me. I cared deeply for Bev at that time, and although I had never said that I loved her, I was sure that I could be happy with her but I didn't know what the chances were of her going along. For some reason I couldn't see her leaving the west coast.

I knew that I would have to talk to her about it but I had to call my folks in Georgia first.

I rehearsed to myself just what I would say to my parents. I knew my mother would answer the phone. She always did, unless my father was the only one home. I knew she would ask what was wrong. I couldn't blame her since I hadn't called since I first arrived in Vallejo. Far be it for me to expect them to call. I would have to talk in vague generalities, so I wouldn't upset her. I didn't need something else for my father to hold against me. After a few moments, she would say that she shouldn't be running up my phone bill and will hand the phone to my father. He wouldn't ask me what was wrong but rather would ask what kind of trouble I was in. They both had a lot of faith in me.

I stopped and bought some beer on the way home. I usually needed something after calling or visiting my parents. Next door was a market and I picked up a few groceries. As I was checking out, I looked behind the cash register and saw the rack of cigarettes. I bought a pack of Salem. I had quit smoking just before I met Mary but for some reason I had an intense craving for a smoke just then. It was funny that I forgot to ask for a pack of matches. After getting in my car and trying in vain to get the lighter to work, I went back in for them. I felt a bit foolish. Mary had always hated being around smokers.

I wondered if being on my own again had anything to do with returning again to an old habit.

The first cigarette, in the car, tasted terrible and gave me a rush of lightheadedness. My first thought to follow that was why I had wasted my money on them. But my second thought reminded me that I had smoked for several years back east, so there must have been some lure. I lit a second cigarette. It felt smoother than the first and I felt a sense of pleasure. My third thought was whether Bev would approve.

After putting my groceries away, I searched the condo for an ashtray or something that could serve as one. I had always kept one around in case some smoking friends came over but since none of my friends in California smoked, I had packed it away somewhere. After about fifteen minutes of seeking, I took a small saucepan from under the sink and lit another. This time I sat back and tried to savor it. I inhaled slowly and watched the smoke as it circled to the ceiling. About half way up, it caught the gentle cross breeze from the slightly opened window and nearly vanished. I couldn't blow a smoke ring like my dad, but then, I never could before either.

I knew that I couldn't put off the call any longer so I smashed out my smoke and picked up the phone. I took a deep breath and dialed the number. When no one had answered on the fifth ring, I hung up.

CHAPTER XXVIII

A LITTLE SYMPATHY

Two hours later, on my third try, I heard the receiver being picked up and a deep voice with a southern drawl say, "Hullo." It was unmistakably my father. On his second "hullo" I knew I had to either answer or hang up.

I answered, "Hello, Dad."

I think he was totally shocked, because he kept stumbling over his words, as if he had lost all sense of order in his brain. My father was a man of few but carefully chosen words. He always preached that sort of efficiency of speech. He was a man that people listened to, because they knew that when he spoke, it would be something worth hearing. But not that night.

I took the lead by asking the obligatory questions about how they had been, etc. It gave him a chance to gather his composure with simple answers. He asked me similar questions and sounded like he was really interested, which was not like him. He sounded like he really cared. That caught me off guard.

After those first awkward minutes, we settled into a pleasant chat. He never asked me if I was in trouble and he never mentioned Mary. I finally asked if mom was around and he replied that she was out. Later in the conversation I found out that she had gone to the hospital two days earlier with chest pains. He assured me that she was okay. I spoke in vague generalities about my condition and the possibility of moving back. I suppose I needed to know what kind of reception I would get. I basically left it that streets in California were not paved in gold. He did squeeze in one "I told you so" but I let it slide. Maybe I should have listened.

When I finally hung up the phone, I realized that fifty-four minutes had passed. I didn't know if I had ever talked to my father for that long at one sitting. We were never talkers, just adversaries. I worried a bit about him. In the proud Southern tradition, he was not comfortable at home alone, without his wife. He was probably eating ham sandwiches every meal. I worried less about my mother, because she was also of the strong Georgia stock and was most likely enjoying a few days vacation from the house and him.

I called the hospital as soon as I hung up from my father.

They told me that she was in good condition and would probably be released soon. I accepted that as encouraging.

I did not sleep well that night, but it was not from worry but rather confusion. The conversation with my father had not gone as I had anticipated, but actually quite good. When I had narrowed my possibilities down to two choices, I had considered the move back to Georgia as the least desirable and the most degrading. That feeling had been altered. But I knew I couldn't make a decision without everything into consideration, particularly I needed to know if Bev would join me in Georgia. If she would go along; then, I am sure we would be able to afford to rent a nice place.

Bev was hard to get a hold of at work the next day. She called me back about mid-afternoon. She said she had been out in the shop areas all day. She said there was quite a stir about Mike, too. There was a lot of speculation and a few power plays brewing, but she said that my name had not been mentioned. Working out in the shop got her away from all the gossip and questions. She knew that I knew what she meant.

I told her that I would like to see her that night, but she said it was not a good night, she had made plans with a few of her friends. I said okay. I trusted her. And I knew that I really had no hold over her. I admit that I sometimes wished that I possessed her, but I also knew that I never would. If I was to spend any of my future with her, it would be on her terms or not at all. I guess I accepted that but I had a sense of urgency in knowing how she felt about me and Georgia. I was rapidly approaching a point in my life where I was going to have to make a decision, and when that time came, I would have to know which way I was going to go soon.

I didn't feel like going out by myself, so I decided to spend the night with just my beer, the stereo, and my cigarettes. The evening started off very peaceful. The whole neighborhood seemed restful, even for a Tuesday night. I opened the front window a bit and a soft breeze gently swayed the bottom of the blinds. I sat on the floor with my head resting on a sofa cushion. The sounds of an acoustic guitar massaged my ear drums. I didn't think anything could have ruined that moment.

But a banging on the door did just that. It startled me out of deep thought and I opened the door with a look that must have matched the feeling. It was Sunday's detective complete with stern face and badge in hand. I motioned for him to come in and then went to turn off the music. I had a strange feeling that I already knew why he was here. But I let him talk.

He said that a passerby had found my missing medallion on the side of the road, where the accident and injury had occurred. He asked me if I had any idea how it got there. I said no. He then started asking me questions about Mike's car. He asked if I ever drove it? I said yes, Mike let me drive it on occasion but I honestly knew little about it since the newer foreign cars were a lot more sophisticated mechanically than my old Austin Healey. He said, so you know more about American cars? I said well enough to change the oil and tune it up; then, his face became real stern looking.

Ropper said, "Mary Thomas was driving Mike Nobel's car at the time of her accident. It had been tampered with and a malfunction probably caused it to go out of control." I think he purposely didn't tell me too much about what kind of malfunction in the hopes that I would say something incriminating. I had nothing to say.

He made it clear that although the evidence was circumstantial, I was a suspect. He instructed me not to travel far from the area and to call if I had any information that I thought was pertinent. Again, he handed his business card to me, which I took without saying that I already had one.

Again I reviewed my situation. I was a suspect in the foul play accident. Mike and Mary were probably together in his car, as I figured they had been shacking up in the Vallejo Inn downtown. I had few friends and a criminal record, although no convictions. Also, Ropper or someone in the department was aware of my psychological condition, if they manage to get Dr. Goldman to hand over my records; then, they would find some interesting evaluations.

Given my firing, I doubted if Mike would continue my support. I figured I could probably go another month before I was broke. Bad luck was my middle name.

I decided to take a ride not really having any specific place in mind. That had become another common pastime amid my crumbling life. As I pulled away from the curb, I drove down the street at a moderate speed, so I wouldn't attract any attention. Again, this would have been just one more action that I would have to explain. There were no cars in the neighborhood driveways and all of the houses were dark.

Next, I decided to drive out to Bev's house. I thought there might be a chance that she had gotten home early. Looking back, I should have called. But I didn't. The lights were on in her house when I drove past and there were several cars parked out front. I supposed her friends had decided to go back to her place. I felt a little jealous. Actually, I felt a lot jealous. It irritated me that she was having a good time; while I was feeling so inauspicious. I drove away fast.

It had been quite seemingly a while since I had gone to a bar for a drink, excluding my surveillance work for Mike, that is. But that night I was in the mood for the music and the smoke and a few cold ones. Even if I would be at the bar without Bev, I always had a bartender willing to listen to my tale. Halfway back from Bev's, I spotted a polite looking establishment on the left side of the road. The sign said "Country Music on Tap" but I didn't care. I was thirsty.

The music came from a jukebox and the volume was adjusted down to a tolerable level. I figured that they must have live music on the weekends. But that night, it was the jukebox and about twenty or so patrons. One thing about country music bars, the beer is always real cold. I drank mine at the bar.

Just about everyone in the place was engaged in conversation.

There was this soft drone of words, too garbled to understand, competing with the jukebox. The music had become the backdrop. The place had its share of cowboy hats and boots, but also a few straighter looking couples. There was a college looking pair in jeans and cotton sweaters leaning over the table to each other, talking very softly. They looked like they were going to steal a kiss at any moment.

Two cowboys and their cowgirls were seated at a table near the wall to my left. They were louder, telling off-color jokes, which were answered by giggling laughter from the women. The cowboys were both big, brawny guys in their forties. The women were probably their wives of about the same age. Neither was very attractive but one of the women had huge breasts that pushed out of her tight plaid shirt. They heaved with every laugh.

There were two other drinkers at the bar. Three seats down from me was an old guy, dressed in western garb, and obviously not on his first beer. He looked like an old trail hand just in from the cattle drive like I saw in the old movies. A few seats down on the other side of him was a man dressed in a suit. He looked like maybe he was on his way home from work. Both guys were keeping to themselves, interested only in their drinks. I did the same. I lost myself in my own thoughts. That was why I didn't hear the guy coming up behind me.

It was one of the cowboys and he was saying that he didn't like the way I was looking at his wife's tits. I turned on the stool and stood up. It was not a situation for reasoning, because before I could say anything, his fist doubled me over as it slammed in just below my rib cage. Air exited my body at a feverish pace and stars twinkled around my head. At least I didn't fall on the floor.

The bar was suddenly quiet and every eye was trained on the cowboy and me. I wanted very much to look cool in that situation;

therefore, I must have said something else to set him off. This time his fist glanced off of my right jaw. I had jerked my head at just the right instant. Lucky me, again, because that hit had little impact but still added the planets to the display in my head. I felt that I would be ready for the next attack, but his friend pulled him away and the bartender told him to sit down or get out. I finished the last of my beer and left. I felt myself staggering out the door but not from the liquor. I grabbed a cigarette off the seat and lit it; while I leaned against my car. It tasted good in spite of the throbbing in my jaw and the sharp pain in my gut. Again, I thought how trouble seemed to follow me everywhere I went.

After a few minutes, the business man came out and said thanks for the show. He, too, remarked as to the size of the women's breasts and laughed. He said the cowboy was still pretty mad and running off at the mouth and suggested that I not go back inside. Then he got in his car and left. Discretion was the greater part of valor, so I flicked the cigarette away and got into my own.

My head was a combination of embarrassment and confusion.

Normally, I would have reacted faster and put him on the floor. Instead, I had taken two sucker punches and left the bar in shame. The more I drove, the madder I got. By the time I was ten miles away, I was ready to go back and finish that cowpoke off but I figured there was no point in it and kept driving. I conjured up some interesting images in my mind, like the woman's boobs bouncing all around; while she held her hands to her face and screamed "please don't hurt him." Meanwhile, I mashed him to a pulp, laughing the whole time. I was laughing so hard; while I was thinking about it that I just missed hitting a car that was stopped on the side of the road and protruding a foot or so into the highway. I heard my tires squealing but I regained control instantly and continued down the road. I knew how to handle my car.

The rest of the ride home went quickly. The car and my mind raced together. It wasn't until I was getting out of my car in front of our condo that I was reminded of that evening's activities. Once inside, I checked for bruises and then prepared two ice packs. Both areas showed the redness associated with that type of impact but no evidence of purple or blue. I laid across the couch in a position where I could prop both ice packs without holding them. I picked up the phone and called Bev.

CHAPTER XXIX

WHAT TO DO WITH HIM

I let the phone ring at least twenty times. I knew she was there but she wasn't answering the phone. It made me a little bit angry. I grabbed the last beer from the refrigerator and began sipping it. I didn't feel like going back out for more. I didn't feel like listening to music, so I clicked on the TV, something that I very rarely did.

I had never been much of a TV watcher although Mary had been known to spend hours in front of the tube watching a Redskins game. Once in a while I would watch Formula 1 or open wheel races on ABC Sports or some show that a friend recommended to me. Generally I had little use for it. I preferred FM radio in the car or listening to my records and tapes at home. With them, I had the freedom of choice.

I knelt on the floor in front of the TV and turned the dial to see what channels we got. It didn't have a remote control. Of the four stations that I picked up, none looked particularly interesting but I left it tuned to a variety show that, at that time, had a not-so-great magician performing. He might not have been very good but at least he was entertaining. I figured that entertainment was what I needed, so I got back on the couch and repositioned the ice packs.

I'm not sure when I dozed off, but I woke up at a little past one with a drenched shirt and sofa pillow with the water from the melted ice. I sat up, startled. I felt better but quite tired. The bottle of beer was still 2/3 full but now room temperature and that was my last bottle. I rolled my head from side to side, as I walked to my bedroom. I tossed my clothes on the floor and crawled between the covers. It would have been nice if Bev had been there with me.

I awoke the next morning feeling completely rested. I resisted the urge to call Bev until about two in the afternoon. She sounded as sweet as ever. I asked her how her evening had been and she said fine. She wasn't volunteering any information and I didn't think the time was right for me to start prying.

I told her that I really wanted to see her, and after a few moments hesitation, she said okay. We agreed to meet at a little Italian restaurant that was off the main drag. We had been there several times before. They had great food at a great price. We agreed on six o'clock. I got there at five forty-five.

I tipped the waiter a ten to get a good table with some privacy, not an easy thing in a small place. I ordered an iced tea and sat down to wait for her. She was right on time and spotted me almost immediately. She smiled and sat down looking me right in the face. I told her that I was glad to see her and that I had missed her the previous evening. She just said thank you but now she looked like she had something on her mind.

We both knew the menu, so ordering was quick. She always ordered the Alfredo Clams. She also ordered a glass of red wine. I knew that I had to talk to her about our future. There were some things I just had to know. But she was looking like she wanted to say something so I held back on the conversation.

On her second glass of wine, it began to come out. She said she felt I was trying to push her too quickly. I was a good friend and we had good times together, but she made it clear that she was still free to do as she pleased. She said that I had to understand that there was no mysterious bond holding us together. Then, she began talking about the previous night. She said that she spent her time with several people the previous night. There had been a party for a guy that she had been seeing for the last year. His job had just transferred him to Texas and Bev had given him a big send-off. I could imagine the kind of send-off she could give. She saw the look on my face.

She became the charmer again. She put her hand on mine and told me that she still felt strongly for me. I wasn't sure I knew what she meant by that. She stopped speaking as our dinner arrived. I suddenly wasn't hungry.

I suppose I didn't hide my disappointment very well. As she ate, she just looked at me with those eyes. She looked like she felt sorry for me. Sorry I didn't need. I excused myself, put the money for the check and tip on the table, and left. I drove right home. Bev had answered my question without my even asking it. By the time I reached our door, I had a pounding headache. I was a combination of anger, disappointment, and defeat. I had really lost everything.

I laid on the sofa and pounded the cushions. I hate to admit it, but I think I cried. The night passed slowly and quietly. At one point, I had the feeling that Bev would call me, but she didn't. Nobody called. At least, not until the next day. The ringing phone woke me at about nine in the morning. It was Dr. Goldman and he said he wanted to see me as soon as I could get down to his office. When I resisted, he replied sternly that he had gotten a call from Bev and we needed to talk. I said okay, reluctantly, and went off to take a shower. It really bugged me that Bev had called him. He had probably painted this warped picture of me as some kind a suicidal lunatic. I prepared myself for one of Goldman's sermons.

I had pegged Goldman pretty good. He would start off with the old father-son approach and ease into the sermon like a true professional. I arrived at his office building, opened the front door, walked down the main corridor, and noticed that his office door was propped open. I sat down on the couch in the waiting area. Shortly, he came out of his private office and said hello. We shook hands and I followed him into the office. He got behind his huge mahogany desk and sat down in the matching swivel leather chair. He pointed to the chair set directly in front of his desk and motioned for me to sit down in it as usual. Goldman began to tell me how I shouldn't try to possess other people's feelings, because that would only lead to pain and disappointment. In my head, I was thinking, tell me something I don't already know and I thought you were going to refer me to a Psychologist for talks.

He went on and on and I shut him out after about ten minutes. He probably knew it but he went on anyway. At the end of the session, he wrote me a prescription for a different psychotropic drug, which I was not comfortable with taking. He said it was just something to help me relax, so that I could think rationally about what my next step would be. He never said that I should come off of the other meds he had prescribed for me or that I should stop seeing Bev. He just cautioned me to know how much distance to keep.

I thanked him for his time but I thought about how he wasted an hour of mine and left.

I almost threw the prescription away but stopped short and slipped the paper in my pocket. On the way home, I stopped at the bank to withdraw some money. There was a pharmacy nearby and I took the paper out again and thought. I always hated the thought of drugs. With the exception of my aspirin, I really had no use for them and the side effects of Goldman's last regimen of pills had made me ill. I finally let out a deep sigh and went in to have it filled. When I got home, I put the little plastic bottle in the medicine cabinet. I looked at it again. The label said, Oxy something, which I couldn't pronounce and the words FOR RELAXATION. I took one.

Within an hour, I felt pretty good. I sat in a lawn chair on the balcony with my feet on the railing and watched the cars traveling up and down the street. Of the first ten cars I saw, seven of them were going up the street. And of the first five cars, three of them were silver. I tried to think about what I should do but my mind was racing from thought to thought too rapidly for me to focus. I did arrive at a few minor decisions. First of all, I wasn't going to call Bev.

She had betrayed me too. She had no right to call my doctor and say anything. It bothered me that she had done that. It seemed so out of character for her or maybe I was just seeing the true side of her for once. Whatever the truth was, I was not going to start anything more.

The second thing I decided was that I was not quite ready to go back to Georgia or Florida. I knew I would end up back in one of those states but not just yet.

I wasn't sure if that was the kind of clear thinking that Goldman had in mind, but it was the best I could do that day. I just watched the cars and ignored the ringing phone. I knew who it was and I didn't want to talk to her. I lit a cigarette from the pack on the table and, as I took a deep drag, thought about going out to get some beer. The smoke burned at my throat and chest. That lightheadedness swept me again and I liked it. Two blue Mercedes in a row went by, both convertibles. I thought about my old college buddy Jim aka Birdman and his wife Jennifer, who were living in Utah then. They were a really neat couple, who like Mary and me, had met on campus but they were still together. Birdman and Jennifer were living in a little house overlooking a beautiful valley that I had only heard about, one of those places that was beautiful all the time, they had said. I hadn't seen them in at least five years but they kept inviting me out when I had heard from them. I had their phone number, so it would be a simple matter to keep in touch but with Mary and me on again and off again, I just didn't do it. I thought that maybe I would give them a call and see if they felt like company. They would probably be very supportive, because that was the kind of people they were. I had never known them to judge anyone. They would probably give me some good advice and help me see the future a little more clearly. I thought, so maybe it was time to visit them and finally get to see their Shangri-La. My thoughts were broken again by the ringing of the phone. My head swam a bit as I got up from the chair. I held on to the door frame as I went inside. Picking it up, I heard Goldman's voice on the other end. At that moment I was feeling too good to listen to him preach. I must have told him something to that effect, but I don't remember. I know he got a little mad and threw a few mild insults my way. I remember laughing out loud and hearing the phone hanging up on the other end.

I laughed out loud again and realized that I felt great. I grabbed another of those pills and swallowed it with a glass of warm tap water. On the way back to the living room, I picked up my autographed Sandy Koufax baseball and fired a fastball that broke and lodged in the sheetrock at the other end of the living room. I yelled out, Strike!

I wanted to turn the stereo up real loud but I couldn't decide what I wanted to hear. I settled for something by Foreigner but put the volume at a respectable level.

I really wanted a beer but my head was swimming too much to go to the store. I settled back onto the sofa with a tall glass of OJ, Florida orange juice. The balcony door was open and a soft breeze was blowing in the sounds and smells of the street. I must have dozed off again shortly after that but I woke up to the sounds of someone banging on my door and calling my name. It was Bev.

Looking through my seemingly drunken eyes, I was glad to see her. She was looking sweet and attractive, the Bev that I wanted to remember. She came in and sat down beside me. She put her hand on my shoulder. She asked if I was okay and I told her that I had just taken some of the tranquilizers that Dr. Goldman had prescribed for me. I told her that I was having trouble getting to sleep. She told me it was okay and pulled my head gently to her bosom. It felt good and I relaxed for a few precious moments.

CHAPTER XXX

ROXANNE FLYNN

My head was still pretty foggy but I heard her voice, softly telling me what she wanted me to do. She told me that we were going to take a ride in her car.

She said, "We are going to have dinner with Roxanne Flynn at her townhouse in Richmond." I had never been to Roxanne's place in Richmond, California, so I thought that it would be good to see her again.

Bev said, "She lives in a unique part of that town situated in high country overlooking the valley and Mount Diablo in the distance." She told me that it would take the better part of two hours to get there, so I could sleep in her car, as she would do the driving.

I have no idea how I'm able to remember all this. I know

I was drugged so her words just kept echoing over and over. At least my symptoms fit the effects of a psychotropic, maybe the Haldol left in my system and the new drug were causing the bad effect in my brain.

It felt like something had been injected into me; then, I was out cold. Bev slowed the car down, as we pulled up next to a row of townhouses.

She said, "We're here Rob, so wake up." I got out slowly but the cold night air on my face was refreshing. I followed Bev, as we walked a short distance to a red front door. She knocked on it. Roxanne opened the door. She said, "Hey you guys, please come in."

As Bev and I followed Roxanne up a short flight of stairs and into her living room, I saw Mike Nobel sitting on her couch. Bev and I sat in two easy chairs opposite the couch, where Roxanne joined Mike. Mike smiled at me.

He said, "Rob, You just don't seem to get it. Would you like to tell us anything about your actions since you have been away from the shipyard?" When I said, "No," he stated that I had called the FBI and Naval Intelligence about security leaks at Mare Island.

I said, "Well, it is my right to call anybody I want to call, so what of it?"

Mike said, "Chuck Slater and I met with Naval Intelligence Agents to discuss your allegations. Chuck told me that the Marines at the gates have been notified that you are to be denied entrance to the shipyard. Mike told me that Chuck had instructed him to require me to see a Psychiatrist tonight for further evaluation. He told Mike that if I refused to voluntarily see the doctor; then, he would notify civilian authorities to escort me. With that said, I agreed to speak with the Psychiatrist. The four of us, got up and walked to our cars. Roxanne and Mike got in his car and Bev and I got back in her car. It was a short drive to what appeared to be a security gate. The uniformed rent-a-cop at the gate motioned for our two cars to pass through, so we headed down the road in front of us. Again, I became too groggy to ask questions but rather I continued to slip in and out, as Bev drove on. After what seemed like several miles, the road opened up into a small parking lot next to a one story white building, which was dimly lit from overhead lamps on high poles placed uniformly around the lot. These lamps were unlike the parking type that typically light up parking lots around the country. Bev pulled her car into a space directly under one of the overhanging lamps. As she got out of the car, I noticed that Roxanne and Mike were already standing next to Mike's Porsche. I continued to sit in the car, as Bev, Mike, and Roxanne spoke briefly out of earshot; then, they walked around to my side of Bev's car. Mike opened the door and said, "Hey Rob, we need to talk," as he offered his hand to help me get out.

Roxanne said, "Hello Rob," like we had just met. I thought how weird but I responded with a rather confused sounding "Hi Rocky." Bev and Roxanne acted like we just met there. Again, I thought weird, anyway, we stood there for a short time; then, Mike suggested that we go inside, as the weather had turned cold and damp. We walked down a concrete sidewalk toward double doors located on our side of the building. We approached the doors, as a very large guy dressed in scrubs greeted us, as he opened one door for us to enter. Needless to say, I was a bit surprised to see someone, who obviously worked in a medical facility. I said nothing at this point but simply walked with the group down a brightly lit corridor, which resembled a hospital corridor. The corridor opened into an even more brightly lit area, which appeared to be a Nurses Station. Our escort stopped us there and said to another large male dressed in the same fashion, "He's here."

As I was in a state of confusion, I said nothing, as the second man directed us into a room next to the station, which looked like a private room for an inpatient, as a hospital bed filled the middle of it. Roxanne spoke first, saying "Rob, please sit on the bed," which she pointed to, "and take off your shoes. Mike and I need to ask you a few questions, before we leave for the night." Now I was in a state of disbelief. The male escort left the room with the door open. Mike stood at the door and Roxanne sat in the chair next to the bed." I gazed at Mike and Roxanne with a questioning look that conveyed I am resolved to comply. Mike spoke, "I want you to explain your actions." Again, I said, "No" as I began to feel like I no longer knew my old friends in the room with me there. Mike said, "Rob, I say that you called the FBI and Naval Intelligence about security leaks at Mare Island." Mike continued to say, "Slater instructed me to require you to see a Psychiatrist here." I calmly said, " I am here to talk with this Psychiatrist tonight but what's with the bed." Roxanne and Mike looked at each other, as a man wearing a Nurse uniform with a name tag that read McDonald, RN entered the room carrying a clipboard of papers and stood next to me.

He said, "You are to be detained here for a court ordered medical evaluation. A Psychiatrist will see you tomorrow morning." Nurse McDonald handed me a piece of paper with the words Patient Record of Advisement printed at the top.

I said, "I want to call my attorney," but he denied my request. At that moment, the male orderly entered the room carrying two small paper cups and a somewhat larger clear plastic cup on a small metal tray. The plastic cup appeared to contain water.

Nurse McDonald took the cup of water from the tray and handed it to me; then, he handed the first paper cup to me, which contained a small amount of clear red liquid.

He said, "This will help you relax," which he instructed me to drink. It was bitter sweet, so I immediately followed it with a swallow of water; then, he handed me the second cup containing a small blue colored pill and a slightly larger white pill.

Nurse McDonald said, "The doctor's orders state that you are to be given medication, which will help you sleep." I swallowed the pills with more of the water and handed the empty cups to her. Roxanne stood up and joined Mike at the door.

Roxanne said, "I will call you tomorrow morning and good night Rob." Mike simply nodded toward me and smiled, as my "friends" left the room.

I awoke from a deep sleep lying on my back in a sweat soaked shirt and jockey shorts on what felt like a plastic covered mattress. I sensed that the mattress underneath me was elevated slightly, as I realized that I was in a hospital bed. My body was not covered with a blanket, so the evaporating sweat from my shirt left me cold and very uncomfortable. The room was dark but a bright light emanated from a small window in the door for the room. I attempted to move but it was very difficult, as my arms were bound across my chest in a "Straight Jacket" with additional leather cuffs around my wrists and ankles loosely joined together with a small metal chain attached to the same type of chain wrapped around my waist. I had an immediate need to urinate, so I shifted my weight toward the right side of the bed and slid off and onto my bare feet. My vision was blurry but I could slowly make my way to the light in the window. It was not possible for me to focus my eyes, so I could not see anything but light, which nearly blinded me by the brightness. I suspected that my blurry vision was a side effect of the meds given to me by Nurse McDonald. Only the need to use a toilet convinced me to call out for help but I could not hear the sound. I tried to speak again but my second attempt was no louder than a whisper. My throat was very dry and my attempts to speak only yielded pain. At that moment a person approached the door and looked through the window, as it opened. I stood there shaking from cold and fear, as I listened to a reassuring male voice say that I would be OK. I told this fellow that I needed to take a piss. He agreed to free my right arm from the restraint; then, turned a light on in the bathroom within the bedroom. I was greatly relieved to empty my bladder but my shackles were to remain, until I met with another Dr. Goldman later that morning. Dr. Goldman ordered the removal of my restraints and I was allowed to shower alone and given a hospital top and pants, a robe, and disposable slippers to wear until my own clothing could be brought to me.

Goldman said, "It is my opinion that you are not a danger to yourself or others; however, you will be staying with us for the time necessary to complete my evaluation of your mental health. Also, I may require you to take a regimen of medications, which will improve your ability to function in the outside world." Needless to say, I did not disagree with him but rather repeated the words "I understand doctor." Later that day, I was transferred to a double occupancy room at the far end of another corridor. My new roommate was a teenager named Buddy, who only gave vague answers to my questions of him.

NAME *Robert C. Thomas*   DATE *3 - 15 - 80*

CONDITIONS OF ADMISSION
TO
WALNUT CREEK INSTITUTE

I hereby apply for admission as _____ *Voluntary* patient in this Hospital, and agree to conform to the rules and regulations of patients in this hospital.

GENERAL DUTY NURSING: The Hospital provides only general duty nursing care. If the patient is in such condition as to need continuous or special duty nursing care, it is agreed that such must be arranged by the patient, or his legal representative or his physicians, and the Hospital shall in no way be responsible for failure to provide the same and is hereby released from any and all liability arising from the fact that said patient is not provided with such additional care.

MEDICAL AND SURGICAL CONSENT: The patient is under the control of his attending physicians and the Hospital is not liable for any act or omission when following the instructions of said physicians, and the undersigned consents to any X-Ray examination, laboratory procedures, anesthesia, medical or surgical treatment or hospital services rendered the patient under the general and special instructions of the physician. The undersigned recognizes that all doctors of medicine furnishing services to the patient, including the radiologist, pathologist, anesthetist and the like are independent contractors and are not employees or agents of the Hospital.

RELEASE OF INFORMATION: The Hospital may disclose all or any part of the patient's record to any person or corporation which is or may be liable under a contract to the Hospital or to the patient or to a family member or employer of the patient for all or part of the Hospital's charges, including, but not limited to, Hospital or medical service companies, insurance companies, workmen's compensation carriers, welfare funds or the patient's employer.

PERSONAL VALUABLES: It is understood and agreed that the Hospital maintains a safe for the safekeeping of money and valuables, and the Hospital shall not be liable for the loss or damage to any money, jewelry, documents, furs, fur coats and fur garments or other articles of unusual value and small compass, unless placed therein, and shall not be liable for loss or damage to any other personal property, unless deposited with the hospital for safekeeping. As a condition of admission no more than $20 will be retained by the hospital. Sums in excess of that must be deposited to the patient's account and handled in our regular banking method. The amounts thus deposited will be used to pay the patient's account and any credit due will be refunded after discharge.

FINANCIAL AGREEMENT AND ASSIGNMENT OF BENEFITS: The undersigned agrees, whether he signs as agent or as patient, that in consideration of the admission of patient in the hospital and of the services to be rendered to the patient, he hereby individually obligates himself to pay the account of this hospital in accordance with the regular rates and terms of this hospital. The undersigned hereby authorizes payment directly to this hospital of the hospital benefits otherwise payable to him for the hospitalization of the patient and understands that he is financially responsible to this hospital for all charges not covered by this assignment, and hereby assumes full responsibility for their payment. Should the account be referred to an attorney for collection, the undersigned shall pay reasonable attorney's fees and collection expense. All delinquent accounts shall bear interest at the legal rate.

DISCHARGE: We do not charge for the day of discharge if the patient leaves by 2 p.m. After 2 p.m. there will be a ½ day service charge and after 5 p.m. a full day's charge.

PROPERTY DAMAGE: Any damage to Hospital property, caused by patient, will be billed to patient's account at the cost of repair or replacement.

THE UNDERSIGNED CERTIFIED THAT HE HAS READ THE FOREGOING, RECEIVING A COPY HEREOF, AND IS THE PATIENT, OR IS DULY AUTHORIZED BY THE PATIENT AS PATIENT'S GENERAL AGENT TO EXECUTE THE ABOVE AND ACCEPT ITS TERMS

Patient *Robert C. Thomas*

Patient's Agent or Representative

Relationship to Patient *n/a*

a copy of this Document is to be delivered to the patient.

Date of signing *March 15, 1980*   Hour *11 AM*

Witness: *Michael Nobel*

As Dr. Goldman's prescriptions for me began to affect me, my tongue had begun to feel odd. I had some difficulty saying, "Hey, my name is Rob and why are you here?"

Buddy replied, "Dr. Goldman told my parents that I needed to stay here, so he could complete his evaluation of my mental health." I thought that that statement sounded familiar. Buddy moved out the next day after the doctors made their patient rounds. Thereafter, no one else occupied the room with me. Roxanne brought two grocery bags of my clothes to me that evening. She said that Mike would be joining her tomorrow evening, as he had to take care of a family matter tonight. Roxanne looked at me with sad eyes, saying that she only wanted to help me get better. She said, that Bev and Mike had told her that I had been acting odd, since I arrived from Florida.

"Rob," she said, "you and I have worked together for more than two years and during that time, I have never questioned your behavior. You and Mary are two of my closest friends, so I really do care about you. I trust that Chuck, Mike, and Bev did the right thing by you with only the best of intentions, so I hope that you understand and work on getting your health back, as soon as possible."

Unfortunately, my tongue had begun to swell, so it was difficult to express myself to her. I guess my attempt to speak made her uncomfortable, as she looked at her watch saying that she needed to take care of some things before it got too late but she would be back tomorrow evening. Shortly after her departure, the wall mounted speaker crackled with the message to report to the Nurse's Station for your medication. With every taking of the medicines prescribed by Dr. Goldman, it became more and more clear to me that the feeling of a swollen tongue was the result of his prescriptions. A dysfunctional tongue makes chewing and swallowing difficult. Initially, my seeming inability to control my tongue left me with the painful experience of periodically chomping down on it, which usually led to a bleeding tongue, which got very sore and physically swollen , as the day progressed. After going through the above process several times, I learned that I would bite my tongue less, if I limited my attempts to take in a minimum of food and chewed it very very slowly. Attempting to talk less was a relatively easy fix for me, as a swollen and dysfunctional tongue does not move naturally in your mouth, which results in undesirable sounds that resemble the voice of a person, who suffers with a speech impediment. During Dr. Goldman's morning visits to my room, he would ask, "Are there security leaks at Mare Island?" My father and mother taught me at an early age, that honesty was the best policy; therefore, I would emphatically blurt out the word "YES." Remembering that I had overheard Bev tell my coworkers Vicki Gilliam and Butch Rydell that she had slept with many officers assigned to our nuclear submarine fleet. I recall how Vicki covered her mouth with her hand to keep others from hearing her laughter; while Butch simply burst out laughing as those words left her mouth. The idea that Mike, Vicki, Butch, and Bev were all Operatives working for the KGB definitely crossed my mind. I thought about what Mike had said about Bev and the Walker family. I thought about how the radios for the boats were sole sourced from a questionable business where Mike was listed in their annual report. Mike was listed as Vice President under an assumed name. Oh sure, Mike had his own problem with the Marine Corps but that was, by his own admission, really about the anger he had for two of his former Marine Corps buddies, who called him a coward to his face, as he lay in a hospital bed in Camp Lejeune. Mike told me about breaking his leg just after his Brigade received orders for Southeast Asia. Reportedly, the Brigade left for "The Nam" without Hospital Corpsman Michael Nobel. I understood from Mike that his Marine buddies accused him of breaking his own leg at the ankle with the butt of an old Garand rifle rather than being deployed with them to Vietnam. Mike may have been a coward but I never saw it, anyway Mike's outspoken love for the USA was evidence enough for me to believe that he would not permit himself to work for the Soviets.

Vicki was simply too naive to participate in any spy scheme. She was her daddy's little girl, as she said, and daddy was a hardened WWII Marine fighter pilot, who saw action at the Battle of Midway and Guadalcanal. Vicki often spoke of her admiration for her father and he clearly served as a role model for her own life.

Butch Rydell was a different sort but not a traitor. I thought about how he and Vicki both laughed about his hippie days. Butch used to wear his hair in the counter culture fashion before he woke up one morning and said to himself that "I want a piece of the pie." On that day, he cut his shoulder length hair. As Butch told it, he graduated from Virginia Tech with a major in chemical engineering.

Butch said, "The year was 1969 and Vietnam was on fire." He had a II-S classification or Student Deferment from his local Draft Board but upon completion of his Master of Science in Industrial Hygiene there, the Board reclassified him to be 1-A or immediately available for the military draft. According to Butch, "I decided to marry Sonya and move to California and within nine months they were the proud parents of their twin boys. Fortune had found Butch, as he was married with children and therefore much less likely to be called up by the draft.

Vicki and Bev were both good looking women but that is where any similarity stopped. Bev was cut from a different mold. She never confided anything to me but Vicki seemed to know all about her best friend.

Just after Bev and Vicki graduated from college, Bev's father committed suicide.

Vicki said, "Bev found her father about five hours after his death when she came for a visit to his apartment.

She said, "Bev's personality seemed to change after the death of her father. Bev became more introverted, during the days following her father's death."

Vicki and Butch seemed to enjoy seeing the look of shock and dismay on my face after I had listened to their tale. Looking back at those events, I believe that Bev was somewhere nearby and probably wove her web around Vicki and Butch by unknowingly getting them to do her dirty work and participate in the "Blind Man's Bluff" game with me. I know that Bev and her "friends" designed their deadly game with the sole purpose of getting me upset enough to "Blow the whistle" to Naval Intelligence about a security leak at Mare Island, without any evidence, thus making me the incredible scape goat. Needless to say, I took the bait, hook, line, and sinker; while the "Lack of Naval Intelligence," as I came to call them latched onto me and allowed the Operatives to do their business with the Boats. Also, I did not help myself by being a horny young man, who had moved away from his usually not horny spouse.

Dr. Goldman would smile and leave my room only to return the next morning to ask the same question and I would repeat my allegation, as best I could with my swollen tongue. After several weeks of this routine, an Episcopal Minister by the name Peter Price arrived at the nurse's station to visit me one evening. Reverend Price was the local priest, who I once had a lengthy conversation with in his office following one of the services I had attended at the parish located in Vallejo. Dr. Price or Peter, as he liked his parishioners to call him, was a very charismatic and thoughtful priest. Although he was only thirty something years of age, he had the look of being a wise man and generally an impressive person. I guess that played into my decision to share my concern about security leaks at Mare Island with him one. We met in the corridor just outside of my room and had some rather strained conversation.

Peter whispered in my ear, "Rob, you know that you will never leave this place, unless you tell the doctor that there are no security leaks at the shipyard." I was stunned by his comment but at the same time relieved to hear these words, as I learned from Price about what I must do. I suppose that I had not permitted myself to think beyond the concept that the officials working for the U.S. Navy wanted me to speak the truth, as I understood it to be. After all, I had read several wall posters at the yard that stated "Report Loose Talk" or "Security is Your Business," signed Office of Naval Intelligence.

The next morning, Dr. Goldman arrived at my bedroom right on time. Again, he asked me the burning question; however, this time I would tell him what others told me he wanted to hear from me.

I said, "NO," which seemed to surprise him.

He asked, "So Rob, why have you changed your thinking about security leaks at the shipyard?"

I said, "Dr. Goldman, you have given me the time I needed to clear my thinking and I realize that I had acted without justification but rather on emotion." Dr. Goldman smiled at me.

He said, "I am very pleased with your progress. I will write the order to change your medication, which will gradually ease the sensation of a swollen tongue."

SUPERIOR COURT OF THE STATE OF CALIFORNIA

FOR THE COUNTY OF _____ Contra Costa _____

The People of the State of California Concerning

_____ Thomas, Robert C. _____

Respondent

NO. _____

NOTICE OF
CERTIFICATION

The authorized agency providing evaluation services In the County of _____ Contra Costa _____ has evaluated the condition of:

Name _____ Robert Chandler Thomas _____ Date of birth _____ 9-19-47 _____ Sex _____ Male

Address _____ 1333 Camino Alto #306, Vallejo, Ca. _____

Marital status _Married_ _____ Religious affiliation _____ NA

We, the undersigned, allege that the above-named person is, as a result of a mental disorder or impairment by chronic alcoholism:

* (1) A danger to others.
* ~~(2) A danger to himself.~~
* (3) Gravely disabled as defined in subdivision (h) of Section 5008 of the Welfare and Institutions Code.

* Strike out all inapplicable classifications.

The above-named person has been informed of this evaluation, and has been advised of, but has not been able or willing to accept referral to, the following services: _____

_____ Continued Psychiatric Care at Walnut Creek Institute _____

_____

_____

We, therefore, certify the above-named person to receive intensive treatment for no more than 14 days beginning this _10_ day of _____ March _____ , 19 _80_ , in the intensive treatment facility herein named _____ Walnut Creek Institute _____

We hereby state that a copy of this notice has been delivered this day to the above-named person and that he has been informed of his legal right to a judicial review by Habeas Corpus, and this term has been explained to him, and that he has been informed of his right to counsel, including court appointed counsel pursuant to Section 5276 of the Welfare and Institutions Code.

We hereby state that a copy of this notice has been delivered by _____ James Macdonald, RN _____ and that the patient when advised of his rights to a judicial review, (~~requested such review~~) (did not request such review).

(Cross out one)

March 10, 1980

Date

Signature _____ _James P. Knightly, MD_

Countersignature _____ _Robert C. Jensen, MD_

CONFIDENTIAL PATIENT INFORMATION
See California. W & I Code Sec. 5328

Original: SuperiorCourt
Copies: Person Certified - Personally delivered
Person's Attorney/public Defender
District Attorney
Intensive Treatment Facility
Department of Mental Health

STATE OF CALIFORNIA DEPARTMENT OF MENTAL HEALTH
FORM MH 1536A (7/78)
REF. SEC. 5250 W&I CODE

NOTICE OF CERTIFICATION

FILED

MAR 2 1 1980

County Clerk
CONTRA COSTA COUNTY

By_____ Deputy

G. TOANA

IN THE SUPERIOR COURT OF THE STATE OF CALIFORNIA
IN AND FOR THE COUNTY OF CONTRA COSTA

IN RE HABEAS CORPUS OF   )   No. 468955
)
        ROBERT CHANDLER THOMAS ,   )   ORDER
)
_____)

To: Kevin Dyuse , Administrator, Walnut Creek Institute ,
2000 La Santa Ana Parkway, Walnut Creek, California or his
        representative.

        FOR GOOD CAUSE SHOWN, you are hereby ordered to release

ROBERT CHANDLER THOMAS from Walnut Creek Institute forthwith.

Dated: March 21, 1980

                              RICHARD L. CARLSON
                         _____
                         Judge of the Superior Court

CHAPTER XXXI

TELL THE TRUTH

DEPARTMENT OF THE NAVY
MARE ISLAND SHIPYARD
VALLEJO, CALIFORNIA 94592

IN REPLY REFER TO:
100X
11 May 1980

S. A. Goldman, M.D.
Walnut Creek Institute
2000 La Santa Ana Parkway
Walnut Creek, CA 94595

Dear Dr. Goldman:

I am writing you to express my concern with the therapeutic regime you
have initiated for Rob Thomas. It appears to me that the dose of
Haldol being prescribed by you exceeds the required maintenance level
recommended by D.M. Schnell.
I can't help questioning the need for such a high dosage of
haloperidol. If Rob was still in an acute care setting, it might be
wise to prescribe a high dose to ensure management of his condition
and control of his agitation by keeping him in a state of stupor.
However, once Rob or any other patient is released from the institute
and returned to society, he must be able to function without the
support of the medical staff. The tremors and stupor caused by such a
high dose of Haldol only makes this readjustment more difficult.

Rob has returned to work but his activities have been limited to tasks
just within the office. He is having some difficulty with this
transition, because of the side effects he has been experiencing from
the Haldol. Rob cannot afford to take anymore sick leave. He has used
up all the advance leave that the Navy can give him. It is therefore
recommended that you begin reducing the dosage of haloperidol so that Rob
can control his tremors and remain alert enough at his job and in
society. The only other alternative is to take full responsibility
for any adverse consequences, which may result from his current
condition.

I find it difficult to understand the need for Rob to take Artane and
Cogetin since they both have similar therapeutic effects. It might
even be possible to eliminate both of these drugs if you reduced the
dosage of Haldol. It appears to me that the best therapy would be one
that would gradually reduce the dosage of haloperidol once a
therapeutic response has been reached at the lowest level as possible,
which will control Rob's mental illness.

The PDR states that the "occurrence and severity of extra pyramidal
symptoms are dose related, since they occur at relatively high doses
and have been shown to disappear or become less severe when the dose

S.A. Goldman, M.D.   11 May 1980
                              -2-

I would recommend that you and Rob seek a second medical opinion, perhaps the
U.C. Medical School in San Francisco and/or the Pharmacy School there. It
appears to me that at a minimum a consultation with another physician outside
your group would be the least you could do for Rob. The overall pharmaceutical
goal should be to reach a control of the psychosis, using only one or at the
most two drugs with the lowest dose possible.

I believe that you have a responsibility to Rob, both legally and ethically to
prescribe a treatment regime that does not produce the severe side effects,
such as the stupor and tremors he has been experiencing.

                         Sincerely,

                         M. Nobel

                         M. Nobel, Supervisor
                         Certified Industrial Hygienist

I could walk the half mile to the Vallejo General Hospital Emergency Room and get some other doctor to tell me what was wrong with me, as I simply did not trust Dr. Goldman anymore. I got up off the bed and began my walk to the hospital. I could see the sidewalk and I knew that I needed to walk three blocks; then, take a left at that intersection. When I arrived there, I found the crosswalk button and pressed it. I waited for the word "WALK" to appear on the sign next to me and as I did not hear any traffic, I carefully stepped off the curb and gingerly walked across the street to the opposite curb. It was four more blocks to hospital from there. I walked the last steps to the Emergency Room Entrance ONLY sign above a sliding glass door, which opened in front of me. Going through the door, I walked down a hallway to a glass window with a speaker in it. I could not see behind the glass but a female voice came through the speaker.

The woman said, "May I help you."

I said, "My vision is blurred, so I can barely see."

The woman said, "Sit in one of the seats behind you and a nurse will be with you soon." Approximately ten minutes passed when I noticed that someone was standing in front of me.

A woman said, "I am Nurse Miller. Are you able to fill out the form on this clipboard, which she handed to me.

I said, "I cannot see it very clearly. Would you fill it out for me?" as I held the clipboard up for her to take from me.

She said, "OK but you will need to answer the questions on it, before the doctor will see you. What is your name? She asked, "What is your home address and telephone number. Next of kin, employer, and insurance company name and address?" and so on. I signed at the bottom with a very shaky hand.

Then, she said, "Do you have a family physician?

I reluctantly said, "I see a Dr. Goldman at the Walnut Creek Institute."

She asked, "Are you taking any medications?"

I said, "Yes, Haldolite, Artane, and Cogetin."

She asked, "All at the same time?"

I said, "Yes Mam." I heard her take a deep breath and let it out slowly; then, she told me to wait here and she would come back shortly with the doctor. Another 10 minutes passed when I heard a door open and I could see the nurse walking toward me with another person, who I assumed was the doctor.

A man in a white coat introduced himself to me saying he was Dr. Freedman. He told me to walk with them back to an Exam Room. As we walked into the room, Nurse Miller told me to sit in the chair next to the wall.

She said, "I will need to take your temperature and blood pressure, OK?"

I said, "Please and took the thermometer from her with my mouth. She wrapped a blood pressure cuff around my right arm and pumped it full of air; then, gradually let the air out." After about 5 minutes, she took the thermometer from me.

She said, "Everything is normal, so I will show your results to Dr. Freedman," as she walked quickly out of the room. A few minutes later, Dr. Freedman entered the room.

Dr. Freedman said, "Mr. Thomas, as you are under the care of Dr. Goldman, I am reluctant to give you any medication but I think that 5 milligrams of Benadryl will help you relax and reduce the side effect of the blurred vision that you are experiencing today. Nurse Miller will give you the injection and I want you to wait here to determine if it helps your body to relax." After the shot, I began to feel better and remarkably my vision became clear again.

Dr. Freedman said, "Good; then do you feel that you can walk home from here?"

I said, "Yes, thank you doctor," as I shook hands with him and I walked out the door into the hall; then, I stopped at the glass window. The woman behind the glass had my paperwork.

She said, "Do you have an insurance card with you?" I passed the card through an opening in the bottom of the window, which she returned to me in short order. The woman behind the glass told me that the hospital will bill your insurance but you will have to pay your co-pay when you receive the bill for it in the mail.

I said, "OK and thank you," as I turned to begin my walk home. Upon my return to my condo, I was exhausted and crawled into bed without undressing. The next thing I recall was walking up with the sun in my eyes. I looked at the clock on my bedside table and I was startled to read 6:30 AM. Apparently, I had slept through the night, as I was dressed in my street clothes. Immediately, I noticed that my legs moved in an unsure and rigid manner. Also, my arms behaved in the same way. I felt like I was a machine that had not been properly oiled.

I gingerly prepared a bowl of Raisin Bran cereal and managed to pour milk from a jug into it. I found that eating the cereal was a different matter. I could barely hold the spoon, which I could not stop from shaking in my hand. Also, I spilled my cup of coffee onto the table, as I held it to drink. At 9 AM, I called Dr. Goldman's office. Surprisingly, he answered the phone. I told him about my condition but he did not sound concerned.

Goldman said, "Rob, the rigidity and tremor you describe is to be expected. I prescribed three medications for you to take daily, which can cause the symptoms you describe. As time passes, the tremors should cease and the rigidity of your leg and arm muscles will become less pronounced." I thanked him for his advice and care for me.

DEPARTMENT OF THE NAVY
MARE ISLAND SHIPYARD
VALLEJO, CALIFORNIA 94592

IN REPLY REFER TO:
106-Ser 295
5100
7 October 1980

MEMORANDUM

From: Head, Occupational Health Technical Division (Code 106.1)
To: R. C. Thomas, Industrial Hygienist (Code 106.5)

Subj: Advance Notice of Proposed Removal

Ref: (a) 5 CFR Part 752

1. In accordance with the provisions of reference (a), you are hereby notified that I propose to remove you from employment at Mare Island Shipyard for the reason of excessive unauthorized absence from 22 September through 3 October 1980. The proposed removal, if found warranted, would be effected no earlier than thirty (30) calendar days from the date that you receive this notice. During the notice period, if you present yourself for work you will be carried in an active status.

2. The specific reasons for this proposed removal are:

   a. On September 1980 you did not report for work. You notified me by telephone that you were ill, and that you had returned to Jacksonville, Florida. On 23 September 1980 your spouse called me and said that you would be hospitalized for one to three months and re- quested that leave be approved for you.

   b. In as much as you had exhausted your accumulated leave, including advance sick leave, earlier in the year, your request for leave on 22 September was accepted as a request for leave without pay (LWOP). Shipyard regulations require that the Department Head be the approving official for LWOP requests exceeding thirty calendar days. Your request was presented to Mr. Charles H. Slater, and after consideration of your attendance record during employment with the Shipyard, your request for LWOP was disapproved.

   c. You were hired at the Shipyard on 3 February 1980, as an Industrial Hygienist, GS-11. Since your appointment you have used 182 hours of annual leave, 246 hours of sick leave, and 119 hours of nonpay status. You were issued a letter of caution about your leave usage on 8 September 1980, and a letter of medical certification requirement on 17 September 1980. While I am aware that you have medical problems over which you have no control, I must weigh your need for absence against the mission of this office, and the needs of the Shipyard. Your extended absence places an unfair burden on the other employees of the Division and materially impedes the accomplishment of our mission. Therefore, I propose your removal from the employment rolls of Mare Island Shipyard for your excessive unauthorized absence from 22 September through 3 October 1980 to promote the efficiency of the service.

3. You have the right to reply to this proposed removal personally, in writing, or both, and to furnish affidavits in support of your reply. You may be represented by an attorney or other representative. Any replies must be submitted to me no later than fifteen (15) calendar days from the date of this letter. Full consideration will be given to any reply you make. The material relied upon to support the charge of excessive unauthorized absence may be reviewed in the Employee Relations Division, Code 160, Building 698, extension (707)647-3487. If you return to duty you will be allowed a reasonable amount of official time to review the material.

4. As soon as possible after your reply, or after expiration of the period allowed for your reply, you will be notified in writing by the Director, Occupational Safety and Health Office of the final decision on this matter.

M. T. Nobel

Copy to:
106
160

DEPARTMENT OF THE NAVY
MARE ISLAND SHIPYARD
VALLEJO, CALIFORNIA 94592

IN REPLY REFER TO:
106-Ser 294
5100
24 October 1980

From: Director, Occupational Safety and Health

To: R.C. Thomas, Employee No.1049306, Industrial Hygienist
(Code 106.15)

Subj: Proposed Removal; decision on

Ref: (a) 5 CFR Part 752
(b) Your ltr dated 11 October 1980
(c) Physician's Statement dated 13 October 1980

Encl: (1) Copy of Advance Notice of Proposed Removal
dated 7 Oct.1980 (2) Copy of MSPB Regulations
and Appeal Form

1. In accordance with the provision of reference (a), you were
advised of the proposal by Mr. M. T. Nobel, Head, Occupational
Health Technical Division, that you were to be removed from
employment with Mare Island Shipyard for the reason of excessive
unauthorized absence from 22 September through 3 October 1980. The
specific reasons for the proposed removal are hereby restated by
attachment of enclosure (1). During the notice period, since you
have not returned to duty, you have been carried in an
unauthorized absence status. By enclosure (1) you were advised of
your right to reply orally, in writing, or both, and to have an
attorney or other representative. You replied by writing,
reference (b), and a statement from your physician was received,
reference (c). References (b) and (c) were considered in reaching
the decision stated below.

2. I have carefully reviewed all of the material presented to

me, pertaining to your adverse action case, including your written reply. It is my finding that the charge of excessive unauthorized absence from 22 September through 3 October 1980 is fully supported by the evidence and warrants your removal. Therefore, it is my decision that you be removed from the employment rolls of Mare Island Naval Shipyard, effective 12 November 1980, for such cause as will promote the effectiveness of the service. A Standard Form 50 confirming this decision will be sent to you under separate cover.

3. You have the right to appeal this removal to the Merit Systems Protection Board Petition for appeal must be filed not later than twenty (20) calendar days after the effective date of this action. Your appeal must be in writing, and submitted to:

106-Ser 294
5100

Subj: Proposed Removal; decision on

Chief Appeals Officer
Merit Systems
Protection Board
525 Market Street
San Francisco, California 94105

Additional details concerning the appeals procedure are contained in enclosure (2) You have the right to request a hearing, or you may choose to have the determination based on the record. You may be represented in any matter relating to the appeal.

If you have any questions concerning your appeal rights you may contact Miss Roberta Smith, Employee Relations Specialist, Code 106, Mare Island Shipyard, Vallejo, California 94592, telephone (707) 646-8787.

4. A self addressed envelope is enclosed. Please return your Shipyard ID and vehicle decal.

C. J. SLATER

The following Sunday, I picked–up a copy of the San Francisco Times newspaper at the local 7–11 convenience store. I was mainly interested in the Sunday comics section but as I flipped through the other sections, I was suddenly looking at the words:

"Psychiatrist and Businessman Killed Near Yosemite National Park"

The article did not provide many details but Officer Brumley, spokesman for the California Highway Patrol, stated that officers responding to a 911 call found a Dr. Samuel A. Goldman and a Mr. Charles J. Slater in the remains of an automobile at the bottom of a gorge located below State Highway 120 and west of Tioga Pass. It appeared that the car containing the deceased plunged more than 2000 feet off the highway. An investigation will be conducted to determine how the driver of the vehicle managed to go over the guardrail at the location of the accident, as it was not disturbed. The California License Plate on the vehicle was registered to Samuel A Goldman of West Nile Drive, Walnut Creek, California. The Bridgeport Coroner's Office report is pending. Later I would learn about the findings of the Coroner. According to the Coroner, both men had broken necks, prior to leaving the highway. Each man had a missing fifth digit on his left hand. I immediately called Bev about the article.

Bev answered the phone and said, "Hello"

I said, "Bev, this is Rob, how are you doing today?"

Bev said, "OK I guess, how are you doing Rob."

I said, "I am in a state of shock. I just read an article in the Sunday Times stating the Dr. Goldman and Chuck were killed in a highway accident near Yosemite National Park."

Bev said, "OH MY GOD!"

I said, "I will call Mike.

Bev said, "Well he is in Sacramento visiting his mom this weekend."

I said, "Oh, he didn't say anything about it."

Bev said, "Rob, I will call you this evening." She hung up the phone. News travels fast, so after returning to the condo, I got a call from Mike.

Mike said, "Are you OK? Bev called me at my moms and told me about the article you read, so I picked up a copy of the Times at the local drugstore here. I don't know if I can believe the words. I will call the Highway Patrol and get more information. Bye for now." Mike hung up the phone. It was all true. Later that evening, Mike called again to tell me about the telephone conversation he had with an Officer Brumley, who told Mike that the 911 call came from a woman, who did not want to give her name to the 911 Operator. Reportedly, the Operator told the police that the unknown woman caller spoke in broken English. The 911 call was recorded, so it would be made available to the public. It seems that they skidded out of control on a curve in the mountains. They didn't have a chance. It did seem odd to me, though. In spite of his flashy car, Dr. Goldman was not one to speed or drive carelessly. He was always afraid of drawing attention to himself. Bev told me that Chuck used to have a fit any time he rode with her and she exceeded the speed limit. In my mind it seems peculiar that they went skidding off the road in such an out of the way place and so far from Vallejo. What were they doing in the Yosemite area that night? Where were they going? Who were they going to see or who had they met before the accident?

Apparently, the police were asking the same questions? They were sifting through the wreckage and interviewing friends and workers. It seems that the detective in charge had his questions about the relationship between Dr. Goldman and Chuck, and particularly how Mike, Bev, and I, fit into the whole picture.

Mike spoke first. He said, "Chuck was a great guy and I will miss him. As you know Chuck and I go way back together. I worked for Chuck for more than 15 years, so it will be a long time before I am over this." We all nodded in agreement; although, given my troubled relationship with Chuck and his decision to remove me from employment at the yard, I would not have that problem. As no one contacted me about continuing Dr. Goldman's treatment with a different Psychiatrist, I decided to gradually reduce the amount of the three meds, which Dr. Goldman originally prescribed for me. The process of getting off the meds took three weeks. I felt like a new man and ready for anything. I decided to accept my dismissal and temporarily move back to the house in Florida.

The trip was uneventful but it took me four days to drive across the country. I arrived to an empty house. The power was on, so I guessed that Mary had paid Florida Power through the end of the month. Also, the water had not been turned off, so I guessed she paid that one too.

With the help of my neighbor Tom Brown, we unpacked the UHaul trailer. After we finished the job, I took Tom to the local LUMS Restaurant for dinner. LUMS served only draft beer from the tap in a frosted mug. It tasted heavenly! Their hot dogs were good too, so we both had two with all the fixings. I drove us back to the house and Tom walked home to his house down the street. I went inside and took a hot shower. It felt great. I finished putting my jeans and a clean T-Shirt on when at approximately 8 PM, I heard someone pulling into the driveway. I looked out the living room window and saw police officers sitting in a marked car and van. I watched three Jacksonville police officers exit their vehicles and walk to the front door. One of them knocked hard on it. I opened the door with considerable apprehension.

The officer said, "Are you Rob Thomas?"

I said, "Yes"

He said, "Your wife has filed papers with the District Court to have you committed to a psychiatric hospital. Do you have a history of mental problems?

I said, "No, as I did not want to muddy the water."

He said, "You are required by court order to be taken to Saint John's Hospital at 1022 Riverside Drive, Jacksonville, Florida where you will be evaluated by a Psychiatrist." He told me to turn around and put my hands behind my back. I was handcuffed by the officer and forcibly removed from my home and placed in a police van. We traveled across the St. John's River and back again, as if they were lost and finally arrived at the hospital. I read the words Samuel Wells Complex, East Wing on the glass entrance door. Someone on the inside opened the door, so an officer escorted me down a long corridor to what appeared to be a behind bullet proof glass nurse's station. There a person dressed in a white pants and smock entered the corridor from a side door and directed us into a small room. As we waited for him to open the door, I noticed that Mary and her friend Brenda, who lived across the street from us, standing inside the entrance doors that we had walked through earlier. We walked into the room equipped with a chair and a shiny metal push cart laden with various glass jars with chrome colored metal lids. One jar contained 4X4 pads and the other contained cotton balls. There were various sized Vacutainer tubes with different colored rubber stoppers, and a thin rubber hose was coiled on the cart tabletop. The person dressed in white held a clipboard with a green colored piece of paper clipped to it. The person, a man wore a name tag with the words Jim Tolliver, LPN printed on it. Jim handed the clipboard to me and said, "Will you sign this form?" which states that you wish to be voluntarily admitted to this hospital. If you refuse to sign the form; then, you will be involuntarily admitted." With no real choice in the matter, I signed the form. At that point, the officer removed the handcuffs from my wrists and left the room with the nurse. Shortly thereafter, the nurse opened the door holding a small paper cup, which he handed to me. The cup contained a small yellow colored pill and a larger white pill. The nurse said, "These pills will make you sleepy. Dr. Dr. Snead prescribed these pills for you, which you must take, so I suggest that you do not refuse. Having experienced forced medication at Walnut Creek Institute, I agreed and took the cup and emptied the pills into my mouth. He handed me another larger cup.

He said, "Drink this water, it will help you swallow the pills. Dr. Snead told me to tell you that you should sleep until morning. A breakfast tray will be brought to your room around 9 AM and Dr. Snead will see you, during his morning walk around the ward between 10 and 10:30." I began to feel very tired, so we walked down the corridor to Room 15A where the door was open and a large florescent ceiling light filled the room with a bright white light.

I asked, "Do you know if my wife and her friend are still in the hospital?"

The nurse said, "I saw your wife talking with Dr. Snead about an hour ago. She was standing there with Dr. Snead and another woman. I believe that they left the hospital at the same time."

What appeared to be a pair of white with blue striped pajamas were laid out on a hospital style bed in the room. The bed linens were white sheets and a light blue knit blanket. It actually looked good to me, as I took off my street clothes and put on the pajamas. The nurse put a pair of Slippers in front of me but I simply climbed under the bed covers and passed out. The next thing I was being shaken by someone standing next to the bed. I opened my eyes but everything was blurred. I was feeling very groggy and my stomach was a little upset but I did not feel like I would vomit.

I asked, "Where am I?"

A woman said, "You are a patient in Saint John's Hospital." She helped me sit up in the bed. My vision improved, so I could see more clearly. The woman next to me came into focus. She was a kind looking woman in her late twenties. Her brunette hair was cut short and above her ears. She was dressed in pajamas like my own and wore a pink colored robe that was not tied with the cloth belt that hung from the robe loops. I asked, "Where is the nurse and have you seen Dr. Snead?"

She said, "I haven't seen anybody but you this morning."

I asked, "What is your name and why are you here?"

She said, "My name is Bernadine and I was taken from my home by two people that I do not know. They kidnapped me and took me here. My doctor Quinn said, "Bernadine, you were lying on the ground in your front yard and screaming at the top of your lungs for no apparent reason. One of your neighbors called the police, who called Psychiatric Services of Duvall County. The two people with you are counselors employed by the county."

Bernadine said, "That is not true Dr. Quinn. The man put his hand on my shoulder and told me not to argue with the staff but that I should voluntarily admit myself to the hospital."

I said, "That sounds familiar." Listening to her talk helped to clear my head, so I got out of bed and put on the slippers and robe at the foot of it. Bernadine continued to tell me her story, as we walked into the corridor and stood at the doorway to my room.

She said, "I am gravely concerned about the safety of my fifteen year old son, Christopher. No one seemed concerned that he was left alone in our house when they kidnapped me. Dr. Sanchez here told me that if I attempted to leave the hospital, I would be stopped by the police and returned here. Also, I could be sent to the state psychiatric hospital in McClenny." I thought to myself WOW what a story! At that moment, a nurse arrived carrying a tray of food.

He said, "According to the forms you filled out, during your admission last night, you did not indicate any food allergies. Is that correct Mr. Thomas?"

I said, "Yes, I am not allergic to any foods that I am aware of but I do not recall that I filled out any forms. I do recall signing myself into the hospital but nothing else."

The nurse said, "That is OK, so enjoy your meal."

Bernadine said, "I better go back to my room to eat. I will talk with you later today." I did not see Bernadine again. I asked about her at the Nurse's Station window. The nurse there told me that they did not have a record of a patient named Bernadine.

I said, "Well a person with that name visited me this morning!"

The nurse said, "I am sorry but I cannot help you." I was stunned to hear her reply but rather than risk a confrontation with anyone, I turned away and walked back to my room. As I was about to enter the room, a young man holding a safety razor ran toward me. He stopped within a foot of me.

He said, "I am going to cut you!"

I said, "Nooooo!," as I grabbed the arm holding the razor.

I yelled, "HEEELLLPPPP, as loud as I could and struggled with my attacker in the corridor. Two very tall and muscular looking men appeared from behind me. One man reached around the young man twisting his knife holding arm behind his back, which caused a cracking sound. The man yelled something and dropped the razor, which skidded across the polished tile floor; then, suddenly I felt an arm coming from behind me and around my neck. Someone was trying to strangle me by putting me in a Half-Nelson hold around my neck. I passed out. I awoke lying on my back in what appeared to be a padded cell. I sat up on a padded floor and tried to understand what had happened to me. My neck was sore, which caused me to remember the arm around my neck and two men running toward me. Also, I thought about the unknown man holding a razor in a threatening way. Someone was opening the door, as I stood up on the mat. A rather short stocky man in his late forties and wearing an orange colored polo shirt and green pleated slacks entered the room in his stocking feet and reached out toward me with his right hand saying I am Dr. Phillip Snead, M.D.

Dr. Snead said, "Rob, I understand that you became violent yesterday for no apparent reason."

I said, "Dr. Snead, someone attacked me with a razor; then, someone else strangled me and caused me to pass out. Now I am in here," as I gestured to the walls with my raised hands. Dr. Snead looked puzzled.

Dr. Snead said, "OooooK, we can talk about all of that later. You appear to be coherent to me, so I will escort you back to your room." He handed me a pair of slippers, which I carried with me, as I followed him through the doorway and stood in the corridor, where I put on the slippers and he slipped on a pair of penny loafer style shoes. When he finished, I walked with him back to my room. It was there that he asked me if I knew why I had been admitted to the hospital? I told him that I remembered the police cars arriving at my home; then, there was a knock on my front door but that was all.

Dr. Snead said, "Rob your wife and her friend Brenda filed a complaint with Psychiatric Services of Duvall County stating that you threatened your spouse with bodily harm. The complaint states that you returned from your job at the 7Eleven Store on Beach Boulevard and confronted your spouse and her friend Brenda Caldwell on the front porch of your home yelling something about being held up by people from California. You said that there were eight men, who entered the store at 2 AM and began to shout at you to get behind the register. According to the complaint, you told your wife that there are security leaks at Mare Island Shipyard, which will be the cause of a nuclear war with the Soviet Union. You told your wife that you knew that the men, who entered the 7Eleven at 2 AM on Sunday, September 22, 1980 were there to silence you."

I said, "Dr. Snead, I was held up at the store but I never thought that someone was going to murder me!"

Dr. Snead said, "Well, we will need to talk later, so I will prescribe something that will help you relax.

I said, "Please do not prescribe Haldolite, because I became sensitized to it about a year ago. At that time, I was living in California where I was under the care of a Psychiatrist, who had me take that drug over a period of three months.

Dr. Snead said, "I will prescribe Librium and Diamex, which you will need to take every morning. I will order blood work for you each morning before breakfast, as I need to monitor the level of Librium in your blood. Is that OK with you?" As I was not familiar with either drug, I decided to go along with him but the idea of taking any drug bothered me given my experience in California. Dr. Snead said goodbye and told me that he would see me in the morning. Later that day, a Dr. Cheveski came to my room. He was a man, whose skin complexion was light brown, which he covered with a full beard. His height was about six feet tall. His hair was black, which he obviously oiled and it was pulled back into a short ponytail.

Dr. Cheveski said, "Rob, Dr. Snead ordered a consult with me, as part of your evaluation. "Would you follow me?" I was beginning to feel a bit lethargic but I agreed to go with him. We walked toward the Nurse's Station and through the door where the Med Tech came through upon my arrival last night. Two corridors converged at the doorway. We walked down the down the corridor directly in front of us and stopped at Room 126, which I noticed painted above the door. The doctor opened the door and held it open, as he gestured for me to come in. I walked into the room and Dr. Cheveski closed it behind me. I was standing in a rather small office with no windows. A small gray metal desk with a chair behind it and a lighted brass looking lamp with a white shade set on the desk. The florescent light on the ceiling was off. "Please sit down in the chair behind you. I had not noticed the chair but I acknowledged him and turned to sit in it.

He asked, "Are you familiar with the Baker Act?"

I said, "No."

He said, "The Baker Act was made Florida law in 1969. The law permits two people to file a mental health complaint with a Magistrate, who decides if there is merit to the complaint. If the Magistrate finds that there is merit; then, he or she will order that the subject of the complaint be picked up by the local police and taken to a psychiatric hospital for a 72-hour detention. The hospital administrator assigns a Psychiatrist to determine a diagnosis for the detained subject person. If the assigned doctor finds that the person in question is mentally ill; then, that person can be held against their will for a period not to exceed eight days. At the end of the eight day period, the detainee must be released from the hospital or ordered by the doctor to be sent to the state hospital in McClenny, Florida for further detention and evaluation there. Dr. Snead ordered an eight day stay for you. Do you understand what I have said?"

I said, "Yes, I understand you."

He said, "Good; then, I will see you again later in the week." At that moment, I realized that whatever the circumstances of my case, I would need to agree, agree, and agree with whomever needs me to agree with them or I will be sent to McClenny. Dr. Cheveski opened his door and escorted me back to the door to the main corridor, where I smiled at him and held out my hand for him to shake but he only smiled back at me. I opened the door and walked into the corridor. By Friday of that week, I was moved to an open ward. I was assigned a room, which I called home for what would amount to eight more days. On the afternoon of my second day there, I was standing at a six drawer dresser putting away some of my things that Mary had left for me at the Nurse's Station. Surprisingly one of the items was my wide leather belt, which had a chrome metal buckle. Apparently, the staff realized that I was not a danger to myself or others. As I stood there, a voice next to me spoke my name. Startled, I turned toward the sound with caution. There stood Mary. She smiled broadly at me and put her hand on my shoulder.

Mary said, "How are you doing Rob?"

I said, "I am fine" but needless to say, a lot had happened to me that was not fine.

Mary said, "Rob I am sorry that I felt the need to have you removed from our home but I believed that you intended to harm me."

I said, "I am sorry darling that you felt that way, as I love you more than I love myself."

Mary said, "Dr. Snead told me that you will be leaving here soon, so I wanted you to know that I moved out yesterday. I rented an apartment on the other side of town. I took all of my things and one of the guest beds. Also, I took the Dining Room table and chairs, as that furniture was given to me by my friend Brenda, who lives across the street from the house, during the time you were in California."

I said, "OK but I am sorry for causing you to not trust me and feel the need to move out of our home.

Mary said, "Please do not be angry with me but I filed for divorce today. I no longer believe in our marriage and to be perfectly honest Rob, I was raised in the Catholic Church, which does not recognize marriages in the Episcopal Church." I looked at her with tears in my eyes.

She continued, "Rob I never felt married to you." I was shocked to hear her words but I did not attempt to discourage her from her decision. Somehow, I knew that it was over between us. Given how she felt about me and understanding that her father sexually abused her, I knew that she may never fully recover from it. Today, I truly regret my selfish decision to go to California without her. Mary had pleaded for me to wait until she graduated from Nursing School. On the morning after the 7Eleven robbery, my harsh words to her, she took to be a threat against her life. I guessed that the anger and fear that I expressed to her over the phone from the 7Eleven and upon my return home were enough reasons for her to file for a divorce. The state of Florida allows either party in a marriage to file for divorce without a waiting period. I received a certified letter from Thomas Tygart, Attorney at Law directing me to the enclosed copy of a pending FINAL JUDGEMENT filed in the district court for Duvall County. In his cover letter, Mr. Tygart informed me that if I had no objection to the wording of the proposed decree; then, I needed to sign the decree at the courthouse. Until that moment, I did not fully understand that Mary could no longer love me or any other man. She was too damaged from her father's abuse; while she lived under his roof and until our marriage and her moving to Georgia in 1974.

Life goes on and for me that meant the life of a single man.

The decree stated that should I sell our marital property; then Mary would be awarded any equity realized at the time of sale. Within a month of our divorce, I noticed an ad for employment, as a Technical Sales Representative in the Classified Section of the Sunday newspaper. The ad was placed by Hareleco Diagnostics, Inc., Wilmington, Delaware. The company manufactured medical laboratory stains and dyes. I had decided to seek employment in the private sector, so I mailed my resume to the indicated address. Shortly after mailing my resume, I received a telephone call from a Mr. Brian Prell, Regional Sales Manager for Hareleco. He said, "Mr. Thomas, I have your application in front of me and I would like to interview you for the position. Are you available to meet with me at the Jacksonville Airport next Thursday at 1 PM?" Naturally, I agreed to meet him, so we arranged a meeting at the airport restaurant adjacent to the main lobby there. Brian and I had a lot in common. He had served in the Mobile Army Surgical Hospital Corp., (MASH), as a Medivac helicopter pilot, so my service in the Navy Hospital Corp. hit a chord with him. Later, I learned from Brian's wife, Nancy, that Brian drove a logging truck for a year after returning from serving in Vietnam. According to Nancy, he was deeply distraught over a decision to transport Vice President Agnew instead of wounded soldiers, during his visit at the MASH unit from where Brian flew missions.

Brian said, "A lot of soldiers died in the field hospital that day." He resigned his commission in the Army and immersed himself in the driving of trucks for a year, because, "I was too angry of a person to tolerate much contact with other people." Anyway, only a week had passed following the job interview when the phone rang and Brian offered me the job. My territory would be the eight Atlantic coast states from Delaware through South Carolina and Kentucky. I immediately secured a Realtor to handle the sale of the marital property and flew to New Jersey to begin my all expenses paid training. I completed the training on the same day that I received a phone call from Pat, my Realtor in Florida. She told me that a young couple had made an offer on my house, so I caught the next flight into Jacksonville. My car was untouched where I had parked it in the long term lot. I drove to the Realty office, where I met with Pat and the couple and signed the sales agreement. I flew back to New Jersey, where I searched for an apartment to my liking and signed the one year lease. Again, I flew back to Jacksonville and met the moving van at my former home, which my new employer had arranged for me. My belongings filled twenty-five numbered boxes. In addition, Mary had left me a couch, two end tables, two lamps, and our bedroom set. All of the above items were packed and loaded onto the van for transport to my new apartment in Wayne, New Jersey.

I spent my last night in Jacksonville at the Ramada Inn on Atlantic Boulevard. I slept well, which I attributed to exhaustion; then, awoke at sunrise, shaved, showered, and _ _ _ _, checked out, got a large cup of coffee and two Egg McMuffins at the Mickey Ds Drive Thru, and headed for my new life in New Jersey. Once settled into my apartment, I began a year of more training, sales meetings, and "cold calls" or appointments with existing hospital laboratory customers or prospective ones. Periodically, Brian would work with me, as I called upon our customers. My life was filled with routine and my sales numbers continued to climb steadily.

EPILOGUE

CAMDEN

As usual, Brian asked me to attend a Regional Sales Meeting in Camden, New Jersey on August 15, 1983. Prior to that meeting, I was sitting at a table in the hotel lounge awaiting the arrival of fellow salesmen. As I had entered the lounge, I noticed two young men seated at the bar and the only other customers. I was sitting at a table enjoying a glass of Miller Highlife beer that the waitress had set in front of me. I looked up from admiring the head on the beer, as the two men at the bar got up from their bar stools and walked toward me. I immediately noticed that these men very muscular individuals, who appeared to be in their mid-20s'. Both men wore very tight fitting colored T-shirts and dress slacks. One of the two men looked directly at me and said, "May we join you?" Their apparent desire to sit at my table felt odd, as there were many other unoccupied tables in the lounge. I acknowledged him by saying sure, as they sat down at my table. One man sat next to me on my right and the other man sat directly across from me. The man next to me extended his hand and introduced himself, as John. We shook hands, as the other fellow leaned across the table and extended his right hand to shake mine.

He said, "My name is also John and chuckled to himself. We sat awkwardly looking at each other, as the John across from me stated that they worked for Bectech Corporation." John, who sat next to me, leaned over toward me and whispered in my ear "There are no security leaks at Mare Island." He looked across the table at his friend

John, who acknowledged his glance with a wink and a slight node. Needless to say, his words set off alarms in my head but I tried to show no emotion. A minute passed, so I commented that I did not have any more interest in the security of Mare Island Shipyard but rather I was interested in making money. John seated across from me commented that he too was interested in making money and we all laughed out loud.

John sitting next to me said, "Did you know that TVs have been dropped out of a ninth floor window of this motel and it was understood to be just an accident." We chuckled about his comment, as they got up from the table. He continued to speak in closing with the statement that he really enjoyed our conversation but they had other business to take care of that night. Each man shook hands with me for the second time. The two men said goodbye and left the lounge. The band began to play, so I left too.

CPSIA information can be obtained at www.ICGtesting.com
Printed in the USA
LVOW08s0649200414

382327LV00002B/4/P